INHERITANCE

Also by David Pryce-Jones

INHERITANCE

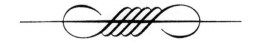

DAVID
PRYCE-JONES

Weidenfeld & Nicolson
London

First published in Great Britain in 1992 by
George Weidenfeld & Nicolson
91 Clapham High Street
London SW4 7TA

A catalogue record for this book is available from
the British Library.

ISBN 0 297 84057 6

Typeset at The Spartan Press Ltd
Lymington, Hants

Printed in Great Britain by
Butler & Tanner Ltd
Frome and London

ONE

'Elderly people want birthday treats too. It's next Tuesday,' Dina said, 'and I'd like to do something special, we might think of an outing?'

'You know Assisi? When were you last there?' asked Sandra. 'The frescoes are deteriorating badly, on account of the visitors; it's all a matter of their breathing and sweating in that enclosed atmosphere. Too much moisture. Professor Ricciarelli tells me that the only solution is to shut the place down, like Lascaux or the tombs at Luxor. Aren't we disgusting? Like cattle in a shed.'

'If we stick to the back road, there'll be fruit trees in flower at this time of year. So pretty. Those white almonds. But it'll be a long day. Let's go in my car, I'll drive. Then there's only the one place to have lunch, that hotel with the restaurant. I'm inviting you, *please*.'

When Sandra tells the story of what happened that day, she insists that there had been no warning, that Dina had been her usual self in every way. The world at large, it is true, had been particularly troubling. Stock markets had not recovered from the collapse of the previous year. The price of oil had doubled, then doubled again. The conquest of South Vietnam by the North was gathering pace, and catastrophe loomed in neighbouring Laos and Cambodia. Those who lived on fixed incomes like Una Macleod or the Whitakers were panicky. Don't sell under any circumstances, Dina advised, better to run up an overdraft than to toss out sound stock. There must have been a lot of stress for her, really.

Extraordinarily, Sandra says of her, she's more like a man, with that brain, no wonder Andrew gave her her

1

head, and he was no fool either. On the afternoon when we'd arranged the Assisi trip, we were at Mugniomaggio, sitting out for the first time that spring. Ask Anna Karcz, she was there too, poor darling Anna who refused to come with us in case she had to pay for her lunch. I remember Anna saying that it was like the Thirties all over again, with one little country after another disappearing off the map. Don't you love the accent, and that hair, like an eighteenth-century peruke, so distinguished. And Dina told us that what with one thing and another in Asia, she didn't trust Japan even, and certainly not Hong Kong, which was sure soon to be sold down the river. Pippo often mentions that, as proof of her far-sightedness. Well, we walked along the path to the basilica through a horde of the usual dreadful Germans, women in heavy woollens and lace-up boots lining up behind a leader with a differently coloured flag for each group, and barking like walruses at one another. Dina went ahead of me. She must have turned to the right, into the transept. On the wall above there's a scene depicting the Virgin with accompanying angels. I sensed something must be wrong when people began hurrying over. Dina lay on the ground, on the stone flags, face down and arms out, as if she'd dived head first. It was terrifying, I was sure she had dropped dead. Then I heard her saying, Why isn't he speaking? Why doesn't he tell me what he wants?

At the time everyone agreed that Sandra had saved Dina's life. It was wonderful how she had coped in the crisis, ordering two vergers to lift Dina back into the car, organising the hospital and the transfer by ambulance to Rome, summoning Professor Vierchowod who had been about to leave to attend a conference of heart specialists at Forth Worth. Just the opportunity I'd been hoping for to cancel, the professor said, those Americans want only to investigate how we do things over here. It's of far greater importance to have given this lady her pacemaker.

I sent for the children, Sandra says, but by the time Alexander and Ursie had arrived, the operation was over, and that was that. Nothing else was possible, not with a man of the calibre of Professor Vierchowod. *Madonna*, how angry she was, she treated us as if it had all been our fault.

Nuns at Ogni Santi still wore coifs which had a prickly silhouette when against the light. The rooms were high and vaulted, and whole families came and went in them, noisy with their own dramas, encamped like gypsies, their settlements defined with parcels and bundles and food. Alexander and Ursie stayed in a hotel a short walk down the street. Its rooms were dusty and wretched with the woes of those living there solely in order to be within reach of their relations in hospital. On each landing there was a communal bathroom, and basins from which the plugs had been carefully removed. The owner and his wife smoked ceaselessly, bored with the sufferings or privations of others.

'This is what we've feared for years,' Alexander said. 'Mother in the villa, and incapacitated. Not that she ever had the least physical capacity, that's one mercy. But there's so little one can do, and I've got responsibilities.'

Ursie said, 'So I hear, though quite what they might be, not even you can tell me. And I've got a job, I can't come out except for a holiday, or a weekend at a pinch.'

I could see that she was going to be all right, Sandra says, old birds like us aren't killed off so easily. It was the children I was most worried about, they've known this country for most of their lives but seem to have learned next to nothing about Italians. For a start they didn't like the ward. And you should have seen their faces when Dina gave them her version of why she was face-down on the church floor. I can see those delicate hands of hers wrinkling up the sheets. What had happened, she said, was that Andrew had emerged through the frescoes, past the angels in a brilliant aura of light, not rising from the dead but among the living. Naturally she prostrated herself before the apparition. Oh, their faces were a picture! Luckily there's nobody better than Carlo Vierchowod, he took those hands away from the crumpled sheets and stroked them and said that of course it must

3

have been just like that. Everyone who's had this experience confirms it. We really don't know anything like enough about the relation between blood supply and the colours that the eye registers. In some cases he'd known patients who think they're in a red glow which they take to be some general conflagration, or perfect peace and the end of time. Or golden patterns. Even royal blue.

That's where we made our mistake, right at the beginning, Alexander is to argue, we should have had the courage to come right out with it and tell her what nonsense she was spouting. Father had been dead for years, she should never have been indulged like that. Yes, I know she was in hospital, but still, it was a case of being cruel to be kind. Afterwards, it was too late to tackle her.

What would you know about cruelty? Ursie asks him. Had anybody ever spoken the truth to him, and what was truth anyhow? And why would it do the faintest good in the circumstances? Pretty cheeky too, when he himself was a world specialist in being indulged. The reason they didn't have everything out with Dina had already been settled in the long-ago past, in the difficulties of Dina's character and in their own responses to her. A lifetime's acquired skills of self-protection; a lifetime of learning how to steer past her moods and angers.

We can't break through, Ursie likes to explain, because in the last resort she doesn't want us to. She's someone private. She prefers us to acknowledge her world and her ideas, like the good children we are. So we nod our heads, and agree to whatever she says. Love is the word for that. Love puts people in the position of not knowing what to do.

A nurse would have to be found, and Sandra took it on herself to place the advertisements in the newspapers. In that hotel sitting-room, vacuum-dry with nicotine, they interviewed the three best-sounding applicants, and engaged Chantal Hérault from Liège. Until the previous month, she had been looking after an ageing theatrical impresario in Antibes: 'Ah, *monsieur*, he died one two three, *hop-là*. Like someone who's got a taxi waiting at the door, and had to hurry away.'

4

My mother is rather resentful, Alexander explains, she doesn't believe that her life was in danger. She thinks she had a vision of truth and the afterworld, and that the operation was unnecessary, that Professor Vierchowod and the rest of us have taken advantage of her. When blood doesn't circulate properly, you can have hallucinations, but that's too mundane and materialistic for her.

'I did my training in Montpelier,' said Chantal. She has the straight back and shoulders of someone lithe and athletic, with good deportment. According to Alexander, she's definitely got a message for the gentlemen. What he likes about her is that she doesn't shave her legs. That's French women for you. Silly boy, Sandra says, we've had quite enough of that sort of thing from you. But evidently she doesn't really mean it, taking pleasure in what she seems to be criticising.

Dina likes Chantal's squashy little nose, all innocence. For some reason she thinks it is Belgian. There's an air of natural enjoyment about that nurse, she says, we can hit it off, she's got high spirits and that's half the battle. Also they will be able to speak in French and the nurse hasn't got enough Italian to be always making trouble with the others in the villa.

'I saw him as plain as I'm seeing you,' Dina told Chantal, 'about twenty feet up, that special smile on his face. I call it his Donatello look.' That was the revelation of his secret self.

'It must have been very frightening for you, *madame,*' Chantal pulled her lips thinly together at the thought of it. She never wore make-up.

'Not a bit. Uplifting. Now I know he's communicating with me. Could I have had a better birthday present? A perfect treat.'

Regularly Sandra came from Mugniomaggio. Leonora Pigri despatched red carnations in the shape of a gigantic heart. But the one person above all others whom Dina wanted to see was Anna Karcz. It had been she who had arranged for Golovin to paint the portrait of Andrew at the villa; and Golovin had captured, well, not the whole

5

Donatello look, that would have been impossible, but something of it, a twist, a suggestion. More: Andrew in Assisi had been wearing the suit and bow tie in which he had once sat for Golovin. We are an artistic family, Dina repeats to her visitors, and I was brought up to retain details like that, I'm never wrong when it comes to visual memory. How had Golovin come to conceptualise Andrew as he had, and what had he to say about that expression of inner mystery? Anna Karcz wrote to excuse herself from the journey, too proud to mention that she could not afford the expenses. Unfortunately Golovin had not lived up to his promise, she thought that he had even stopped painting. When last she had heard of him, Golovin had joined the gold-mining rush in Brazil, but that might have been rumour.

If anyone is going to have a vision, in the opinion of Nini and Roberto Canavese, it would be Dina. Jacques Lemasle, the Debussy expert, found her a book by a Jesuit on apparitions and other inexplicable phenomena of the Middle Ages, analysing a number of instances when individuals and even whole congregations had observed movement in statues and paintings, and how saints had levitated and the righteous had witnessed such manifestations. It's a defiant message from the enemy camp, he said. Rationalism must win.

These things take time, Professor Vierchowod explained, the system has had a thorough jolting. Sometimes quite a different personality seems to emerge, though I'm sure she really believes in what she saw. You and I might do the same. It must have looked completely realistic. One can convince oneself, as in a dream. It'll calm down, these modern pacemakers do their work most efficiently. We may have to change the battery after a number of years, but that's nothing to worry about.

'I saw my husband, I saw Andrew plain,' Dina never changed tack, 'just as Golovin painted him. All of you say it's heart failure, it seems to me more like heart success.'

TWO

After the election of the Attlee government, Andrew Lumel had lost confidence in England. 'We are the masters now,' some socialist bigwig had crowed, and the phrase hit hard. The Soviets were acquiring their hold on Europe, Andrew explained, and this government of boobies was doing nothing to hinder them, on the contrary was tacitly encouraging a red takeover. Hindus and Muslims would kill each other off in India, then the Jews and Arabs in Palestine, and then it would be our turn. The factory had done well in the war, admittedly, but there was practically no point in going there now, nothing to be done except to read official bumf announcing the myriad regulations and taxes which were bringing business to a standstill. He was damned if he was going to invest in such a climate. Now was the moment to sell. They might keep Maydeswell, the house from which he commuted to work, but a bolt-hole abroad was needed. Who could imagine bringing up two small children in a country where tuppenny-ha'penny politicians with no experience of anything practical claimed to be masters? Besides, in the eyes of the British, no matter how long they lived here nor what they contributed, he and Dina would always be bloody foreigners. Away, away.

The heat in that summer of 1948 had a pre-war sensuality. Through the factory, Andrew had arranged to take possession of the new model Armstrong-Siddeley, with a chrome strip down its inclined bonnet, the dark blue sheen as deep as a mirror. High off the ground, solid as a tank, this looked an accident-proof car. In order to travel abroad, special permission had to be obtained from the Bank of England for currency. Business, he wrote on the

7

form in the space asking the purpose of his journey. The allocation might have lasted three or four days, if they were careful, something which he had never been, and did not intend to be now. From the back of the driver's seat, a walnut-wood tray could be lowered, and he folded up five-pound notes into this hiding place. Think of being able to eat properly again, he said to Dina. Before they left Maydeswell, they handed their ration books to Mrs Ackroyd with instructions that she was to make sure to fatten up the children on their meat and eggs and butter.

Crossing the Channel, Andrew had held on to the rail running round the deck of the ferry, gazing at the coastline thinning to a grey smudge. On holiday, he knotted a silk scarf round his neck rather than a tie. Ostentatious in his clothes, he was wearing a pair of blue linen trousers. People used to have a second look at someone so obviously pleased with his own appearance. 'A little man on the Lido made me these trousers. Ages ago,' and he pulled the waistband out to show how he had kept his figure, had actually grown thinner, though his hair had gone white since first those trousers had been cut.

Nowhere in England was it possible to drive so fast as down the straight stretches of the N6 under the diagonal shadows of plane trees. On either side the fields disappeared to a horizon. Nowhere in England was it possible to sit out of doors at a table with a chequered cloth, and to eat what you liked when you liked. A small crowd would gather round the parked car to admire its outline and bodywork.

Varendy is near Grasse. The closer they came to it, the rustier the colour of the Provençal earth, and the more Dina insisted that this was a part of the world where she couldn't live. That page had been turned. It's no use, she said, if you're thinking of returning here. I simply couldn't. Besides I've never really liked the French, and especially not now.

Until 1940, Dina had lived at Varendy, her parents' dutiful daughter. After the collapse at the end of May, she escaped without a second thought. At their age, the parents would be all right, but she risked being interned, she had heard the radio announcer saying so. What to others might be occupation was liberation to her. She had kissed them goodbye, caught a train to Marseilles, walked with her suitcase to the docks, to find herself on board a boat next to Somerset Maugham. Not that long before, he had stayed with her father while his portrait was being done. Recognising her, he had suggested that they stick together, and in that painful stammer of his had predicted that they would all be ruined but England would win the war. The boat's most recent cargo had been some black substance – manganese, Maugham said, evidently romanticising the word – and they were soon grimy with its dust. When he had described these events in a book afterwards, she had been pleased to read how he had found her a stoic travelling companion who could look after herself.

When last she had seen her father, he had been wearing his black felt hat with a broad curved brim, a properly bohemian hat, as worn by his peers from the turn of the century, Helleu, Jacques-Emile Blanche, Oswald Birley. During a tour in Morocco at the invitation of Marshal Lyautey, he and Lavery, his closest friend and the chief influence on him, had painted portraits of one another in just such a hat. Returning in 1945, Dina had minded more than anything else that this shabby but stylish hat was still hanging on its hook in the studio. Superstitiously, life had been maintained in it. Somehow it had proved stronger than the looters.

Varendy is built of irregular stone, vividly coloured in a range between brown and orange, with all manner of mineral streaks in it. Unable to get about in the last years, John Napier had painted the field rising behind the house towards another farm, belonging to the Lavagnacs, a family with many sons. They paid to pasture sheep on the coarse grass. Finally he had sat in the front of the house, within an irregular courtyard whose tall gates shut as though for a fortress. There, in his black hat against the sun, he had made careful studies of the stonework. A departure for him: closely observed abstractions, the only work he had ever done without a figurative subject.

The looters were interested in china, linen, glasses, household things which they could use. They had wrenched off some of the shutters. The watercolours were still where John Napier had left them, on top of folders of a lifetime's sketches. Canvases stood in stacks. Almost as soon as Dina was back in the house, people began to arrive unannounced, to whisper who had stolen what, and where she could recover her property, and for what price.

On that first post-war visit, Dina had walked uphill to the cemetery outside the huddle of the hill town. Side by side, the twin bumps in the ground consisted of a heaped and stony spoil not yet settled. There would have to be a surround, and some sort of upright stone, for John Napier and his wife Marguerite, née Dalhem. She had been a model who had entered his life, never to leave it, dedicated to making sure that he had whatever it was he wanted. She had protected him by sacrificing everyone else, first and foremost herself. He's working, she would say, he can't be disturbed. A great man's wife, but no sort of a mother.

Apparently it had taken the German army to release Dina from her parents' grip. Strange that resentment should be felt only now that nothing could be done about it. Those two bumps were like weights in a balance forever fixed against her, without a chance to appeal. It was lucky that Lionel and Minou were offering to take the house off her hands, to dissipate the numinous force of that black hat.

Lionel Frampton. He was Andrew's ideal of an Englishman, with that healthy bullish manner, and a public-school confidence in himself and what he stood for. as a young man, his cheeks had been smooth and pink. It wasn't the Home Office that naturalised me, Andrew used to say, it was Lionel, he taught me the p's and q's. In early days, the factory nearly came to grief more than once, I needed his services. There was a period when the customers weren't paying their bills. Lionel gets what he wants, I have to hand him that. You mightn't need him delicate negotiations, but he crashes his way through the thickets. Don't forget he played rugger to a pretty high standard. And his contacts are the best.

Younger than Andrew, Lionel was already a partner in a London law firm specialising in international business. We can be grateful to him, Andrew said, but that doesn't mean he ought to be handed Varendy on a plate.

Dina answered, I'd pay him to take it off my hands.

Lionel greatly enjoys telling the story of his war. Seconded from his law firm as a special advisor to the embassy in Berne, he had dealt with long-drawn issues of bringing home escaped British prisoners, airmen who had been shot down, the select few who made their way across the difficult neutral frontier only to be interned. Others had been agents, their missions important, and the Swiss authorities had to be cajoled into turning a blind eye. I could tell you a few things, Lionel says, leaving the implications up in the air. One of his throwaway lines is that he is the only resident of Berne with the CBE. Andrew talks a lot about that factory, but he hasn't got decorations to sport at a white-tie affair, has he?

That difficult neutral frontier had impeded him from acting when he heard from Andrew about the poor old boy's death. And then the former model of a wife had just turned her face to the wall, she didn't have what it takes to live alone. But he himself had just married Minou, and she could come and go on a Swiss passport. She was game – she always is.

An epic has formed in his mind around Minou and her heroism, how she herself chose to live at Varendy through the crucial months of July and August 1944 when Marguerite had nobody to look after her, and the Americans had landed down at Fréjus. The whole country was in such a state of lawlessness that anything might have happened.

Minou says, I couldn't leave her. I mean, she wasn't able to feed herself or anything.

Hotly Lionel says, If it hadn't been for her, there'd have been nothing left. The minute she turned her back, up they'd swarm to steal. You owe the contents of the studio entirely to her.

Minou presents herself as someone whose purpose is to encourage Lionel, to feed him the right cue for his interminable stories and jokes. She stoops as if under the load of wifely devotion, the way Marguerite had done.

There wasn't anything brave about it, she says modestly, Micky was a baby in arms, I used him to protect myself. They weren't going to harm us. We stood in the road watching the Germans pulling back from Toulon, and they waved on their way through, so everyone waved back.

The locals aren't wicked, Minou says, but like everyone else they weren't going to turn up such a wonderful opportunity to enrich themselves. Everyone's the same the whole world over. We love living here.

At that time, Minou curled her hair in the style of Paulette Goddard, and it was only later that she bought the clothes which Lionel expected his wife to be wearing.

You're a hard man when it comes to striking a bargain, Lionel liked to say to Andrew. I did you a good turn taking this dump on when nobody else would. Minou fell in love with the countryside. It's a bloody nuisance, I can tell you, to make your way here from Berne.

In his forties, Lionel carried himself like someone younger, shoulders back, chest in. Look at me, the stance proclaimed, and you will discover someone a cut above others, a man of the world, who knows what's what. At some point, he must have been impressed by some matinee idol or perhaps a film about corsairs: a Douglas Fairbanks at second-hand. He had become lean accordingly, the colour drying out of his cheeks. His suits were in charcoal shades, dramatic at the waist and shoulders. On his shirts were his embroidered initials. His shoes were also handmade. Expensive things tumbled out of his pockets, a gold clip for folded banknotes, a gold keyring, the newest lighter for the cigarettes which he affected rather than smoked. At that time he hardly drank during the day. To speak was to raise his voice so that everybody had to listen. The point of those set-piece stories and suggestive jokes was that he starred in them. The wit was all his. Nobody was going to have the edge on him. Nobody was more popular, and nobody could compare to him in the use of smut to create the atmosphere he relished. Any business or social contact was as good as a friend. Already names like Axel Heydt the Ruhr steel king, Soubeyran the chairman of the largest Swiss insurance company, Gutierrez of the World Bank, had begun to feature in his talk as though no explanations were necessary. He let it be known that he kept company with the rich and successful, with playboys as with power-brokers: Palm Springs and Long Island, Biarritz and country houses at weekends. Laughing, he stretched back his lips to reveal a full bite of the jaw and frighteningly pale gums.

The Armstrong-Siddeley was a car to delight Lionel. Immediately he set his heart on driving it, to test whether it could reach the hundred and forty miles an hour registered on the speedometer. It could. As for himself, he had ordered a station-wagon, then a novelty from America; its bodywork was in imitation wood intended to be indistinguishable from the real thing.

'In a few years, they won't be able to make stuff as good as this,' he told Andrew. 'I saw quite enough of those people in the war. Minds of the finest type, perfectly closed, unable to imagine that the world isn't going to run on their doctrines. It's only a wise precaution, old man, to pull out while you can. Next thing they'll be withdrawing our passports.'

Old man, old chap, old sport. Take her out for a spin. Bowling along. Lionel has become stuck in dated slang appropriate to his appearance. He mistakes the words for intimacy. One of his affectations is to stake a claim by gripping or squeezing the arm of whomever he is talking to. Always promoting something, always more sure than you are of what's in your own best interest. He's never been a good host. What with having to humour him as the moods alter like clouds driven by the wind, a day in his company is exhausting.

He means well, Andrew assures Dina, just make allowance for the manner, that's all. That's a friend. If ever we were in trouble, Lionel's our man, he'd know how to handle whatever comes along.

Close to Varendy is Sanary, where in old days the Huxleys had been neighbours, joining together in picnics on hills scented with thyme and lavender. The John Napier portrait is reproduced in books and many of the articles about Aldous; it injects into his intense bespectacled expression an air of surprise, almost alarm, as if discovering some huge new field of human endeavour not yet surveyed. Their house now belonged to a couple who were never there, and Lionel proposed that Dina and Andrew make an offer for it. It will be awfully jolly, he said.

Dina was adamant that she was never coming back here: too many memories.

Memories of what? Oh, of childhood, and growing up, and speaking foreign languages, and rich food, and speeding in the Huxleys' smart red Bugatti and swimming off beaches still unexplored, or waiting to be introduced to exiles from Hitler's Germany describing with tears in their eyes what it had felt like to watch their work burnt by men without the capacity to understand it.

A load of cobblers, Lionel answered, your trouble is that you won't forgive yourself for walking out on the parents. But their day was done, they were strangling you. It was the best thing that ever happened to you. If you'd stayed, you'd never have met Andrew, you'd have become a sour old spinster. Creeping out at the back in search of one of the Lavagnac sons – they service everyone around here, as far as I can tell.

'Will you really be all right in Italy?' Lionel persisted doubtfully. 'A little of that art goes a long way. The religious stuff gives me the creeps. Saints being flogged, arrows through the belly, you know what I mean. What will you find to do all day?'

They would garden, and learn Italian, and read, and take up music and make friends, and do all the things there never was time for. Andrew might invent something else, and start another factory, you never could tell.

What about Dina? What about the children? Were they really to become little Italians? Surely a France which was remaking itself after such a calamity was better, or come to that, Switzerland.

You aren't a lawyer for nothing, Andrew said. And when he was alone with Lionel, he added, 'If you must know, there's Iris Warren.' An amusing woman, he explained. She hits a golf ball like a man. An incredible swing. She might turn up in any kind of weird clothes, dungarees, a turban, and she said whatever came into her head. Quite a character. A friend of his by the name of Lewis Grindley had introduced them, and somehow they'd fallen in with a whole set. These things happen. Iris had come between them. Italy might be a new start.

How Lionel loves something like that, with real confession in it. Iris Warren! Built generously, is she? Something you can get a grip on? There's more to that good and strong type than ever there is with the itty-bitty French, all high heels and headaches. There's this *mannequin* in Paris, and she has a friend, and the four of them could make a party of it one evening, the next time he happens to be in Paris. The girl's mother lays on private entertainments for everyone who's anyone, she lives with a nightclub king. Guess what, she told me herself how she's brought up her daughter never to go out to work in the morning until she's had something hot inside her.

At the end of that visit, Minou took a photograph of the others, standing in the courtyard, with behind them the Armstrong-Siddeley already packed for Italy. Evidently Lionel had edged himself into the picture at the last moment, possessively pleased with this great friendship. Dina is at the centre. After the birth of her two children, she had never quite recovered her figure, and never would. The way she stands, four-square and legs apart, shows someone who makes no concession to exercise and being out-of-doors. Even in that holiday snapshot, she is in city clothes as usual, a skirt and matching jacket, a shirt with a tie as part of its collar. A clever rather than a pretty face, one to look at twice, to try to interpret the contradictions visible in it. The mouth is wide, but then the lips are level, mobile, suggesting something restless and dissatisfied. Dark eyes are set deep in their sockets, and below them swell pouches, which might be watery and reddening, either from fatigue or from a rage almost too stormy to be retained.

In that photograph Andrew has an arm round her waist, and they look determined to enjoy themselves, in spite of Iris Warren or the spatter of Lionel's smut. A glaze of sunshine holds the scene. Andrew is jaunty in an alpaca cardigan, and a silk scarf carefully at his neck. In the background is the car, as expensive-looking as a yacht, its front door invitingly open. The spokes of the wheels are racy. That was a moment when there were neither possessors nor possessed, but only a journey ahead.

THREE

One of John Napier's portraits was of the young Iris Origo, which is now in the National Portrait Gallery. Andrew and Dina began by calling on her at La Foce. A house somewhere between Rome and Florence would suit them, they explained, in Tuscany or Umbria, in the Lazio, not a kingdom of its own like hers, but a retreat with character. Somewhere which meant that they never regretted England.

At that point Iris Origo was in the closing stages of a book about Byron and his affair with Teresa Guiccioli, and she spent her time away in the loft where she used to work. Out of self-protection, she introduced them instead to Sandra Piccolomini, who asked for nothing better than to go house-hunting for other people. Sandra was then – and still remains – someone who makes things happen. Vivacious, interested with equal intensity in whoever and whatever comes to her attention, she should have been an agent or a publicist rather than the wife of a shy landowner who preferred to leave Mugniomaggio as little as possible, unless it was to study lepidopterae. Pippo's life work has been the reclassification of Mediterranean butterflies and moths. As Sandra's enthusiasms have burst upon him, he has cultivated a way of retiring to remote parts of the castle, and to science, more like a father to her than a husband. In the family, they spoke an Edwardian English, sometimes too perfect to be correct, which they were passing on to their son Niccolo by means of the same English nanny who had taught it years ago to Sandra. If you get on the right side of Pippo and Sandra, Iris Origo assured them, you'll be in safe hands, they have a firm belief that they and their friends ought to obtain whatever they want. Unlike us, Iris added, they didn't have the Germans crashing about all over the place, I think they must have taken one look at Sandra and thought better of it.

In fact the only German who had come to Mugniomaggio during the war was a general who one day drove up frightening everybody, only to reveal that he was a Solms and his grandmother had been a Piccolomini and he wanted to see this historic house he'd often heard about. They drank a bottle of their *riserva* with this general and gave him another, and sent him happily away. Prudently the contents of the house had been stored, and when Andrew and Dina first arrived there, some of the rooms were virtually deserted and others under dust-sheets – Niccolo was to be a grown man before everything settled down and a programme of restoration was undertaken.

Said to have foundations going back to the eleventh century, Mugniomaggio imposes, especially at night when the electric lighting is too antique and dim to reveal how much of the house is a Walter Scott pastiche. Mysterious archways lead to unlikely doors or steps winding up to turrets, and in unsuspected quarters live unsuspected relations, dependants, pensioners of one sort or another, who have a way of appearing when obligations have to be met, in particular at mealtimes. Naturally you'll stay with us, Sandra said to Andrew and Dina, you'll merge in with everyone, we're never quite sure how many people there are around the place. Canasta was coming into vogue as a card game, and Sandra liked to rope them into marathon sessions lasting far too late. Even in summer the huge room in which they played had a chill. The ceiling was vaulted, and the walls depicted a series of battle scenes, done by a local pre-Raphaelite with a taste for armour and horses with rolling eyes. Every time you put down a card, Andrew used to say, you see another head up there being sliced off.

Among the places they might have bought was Monte-tremaldi. An astonishing road wound to this hilltop, snaking up until it petered out in a straight and steep dirt track. There Andrew left the Armstrong-Siddeley and they walked the few hundred yards uphill. On the path lay a porcupine quill and Andrew picked it up, afterwards experimenting to see whether it could be used as a pen (it couldn't). From the top, the view was dramatic, over the entire range of the hills of the Valle Tremaldi. The group of buildings included a church, a simple but wide rectangle in form. Its once green door was chained, but so loosely that it could be pulled open enough to peer in at the plaster pilasters which alone remained of the furnishings. Soaring above it was the bell-tower, a landmark, a shaft as elegant and daring as when it had first been built, its dwarf windows increasing in number with each floor, each one incorporating exquisite miniature pillars in marble. Round the back of the church had been built a shapeless lean-to of a *casa canonica*. The man who lived and farmed there invited them in, to meet his wife and rowdy ragged children who wore no shoes. He showed them the barns, and what he harvested, and had no inhibition about discussing his budget down to the last lire. On the hardened earth floor of one of the barns was a seed-drill collapsing on a single bent wheel. In years to come, Andrew and Dina would return here, to walk in these woods, to present shoes to those barefoot children, and then eat Sunday lunches in the Badia, a restaurant two hilltops away in what had been a monastery. Think of what we could have made of it, Andrew would muse, that pencil of a tower, and converting the church into a big room the way it is, ideal for a party. Sandra Piccolomini made enquiries from the bishop, but the Church wasn't considering selling the property – perhaps just as well, since they soon found La Grecchiata.

It happened to be night when first they had seen the villa. Sandra had taken them to dine with Leonora Pigri, the woman who looks so sultry in publicity photographs about her and her gallery. That's a beautiful house, Leonora had said, but haunted, it has a jinx on it, and the owner's a brute, he doesn't want to sell as far as anyone knows. Still, they had turned off the road, through trees which blocked a view until the moment when they drove up to the gravel circle in front of a flight of steps. The façade looked pristine, bone-white, lifted from the set of an opera. No light was visible. Through the shadows they walked round the closed villa. At its rear was a terrace, and beyond that four rose beds had been laid out around an ancient well-head. An iron seat surrounded this well-head, and they lingered there under a cloudy moon which threw gleams over stone and leaf. Over the top of this well was fitted an iron grille, the bars in interwoven diagonals. Andrew dropped a pebble down, and it vanished without a sound. When he called, 'What's down there?' the echo boomed and choked in the depth.

In daylight they could see that much of their first impression had been romantic illusion. A cypress avenue leads up to La Grecchiata. Almost top-heavy, here and there the tips creasing under their own weight, these trees form a dark streak on the landscape. Between them, the drive is a cindery strip, off which in summer a car raises a powder which lingers like mist and stains the trees a fine grey until the next rain. At first glimpse, to be sure, the visitor supposes the house to be monumental, but closer up, this becomes evidently a matter of setting and clever architectural design. The steps are spacious, the front door is high and varnished to a shine, while jutting straight above it on an iron stanchion are the arms of the cardinal who built this country retreat for himself. But a buddleia has rooted itself somewhere behind that stanchion, and is pushing up over the arms like the weed it is. Nor is the house pristine and white; several chunks of soft and aged yellowing plaster have fallen away from the rendered surface, to expose underlying brick. As a finish at the corners and around the windows is massive rustication, and for this the cardinal had brought the hard bright stone from quarries which are on the other side of the Valle Tremaldi, visible like a distant scar. Under the guttering, in patches below the roof, are greenish discolourations of rain and damp.

That first day, Luciana and Ubaldo were waiting for them, evidently nervous at the prospect of showing strangers round. Tweedledum and Tweedledee, mur-

20

mured Andrew. Husband and wife, the two have always looked more like twins, so obese that they waddle rather than walk, their features pudgily obscured with years of good living.

A staircase occupies the centre of the villa, a space like an inbuilt refrigerator, cooling in summer but freezing in winter. At the far end of this space is the door on to the garden, a glass door, and if the shutters are open the view of the garden and the well-head is fresh and inviting. To one side is the *salone* which has retained a number of original fittings, including bookcases and an elaborate fireplace. The ceiling shows an allegory of the triumph of Love over War, attributed to Quarretti, best known for designs in the houses of the Veneto. Satisfied with himself and his handiwork, the cardinal himself is represented on a throne in one corner, and the artist has given him a highly contemporary double chin, a superb match to Luciana's and Ubaldo's. In her book about Italian villas of the period, Georgina Masson argues against this attribution to Quarretti, on the grounds of its inferior quality, and she also laments the poor preservation of the painting. True: water has seeped indoors as well, leaving blotches even on the ceiling, little tidal encroachments with each flooding. Luciana remembers being told by her parents that when the original family here had finally exhausted its fortune, the villa had been virtually derelict, and that at one point these downstairs rooms had been used to rear rabbits – there had been hutches everywhere, and an acrid fug. To the other side of the staircase is the dining-room, and then a library. A passage leads to the kitchen, a cavern of a room in height, and in its way a museum preserving associated ranges and boilers and tanks, ovens long defunct, a coke-fired heater around which the floor is blackened, shelving with pots and pans too high up the walls to be reached without a step-ladder.

Luciana and Ubaldo shrugged, as much as to say, you see how things are here, how we're expected to live.

'My friend is a famous industrialist,' Sandra explained to them, so ennobling Andrew and Dina once and for all into *signore barone* and *signora baronessa*, 'he is an aircraft manufacturer, and has a factory in England. It would be the villa's salvation if he were to buy it.'

The cardinal may have had trouble with his legs because the stone treads are so shallow, leading to wide turns all the way to the top. The upper floor has a corridor running the length of the house, and that too is always cool and cloistered, lit only by leaving open doors which lead into bedrooms. Closed, as they usually are, the shutters allow past the windows at best a submerged light. 'You this end, me the other, and the children in-between,' Andrew said. 'Room for guests too, but not too many, thank God. What a place, what a view.' That is what visitors were usually to exclaim, unconsciously quoting him.

When the family in its decay had finally sold La Grecchiata, the new owner was someone doing well in the Mussolini era, a *squadrista* with a sideline as a supplier to the army. Moving out the rabbits, he had used the hutches as firewood. His plans had come to nothing. The day had arrived when the *squadrista* had driven up with a lorry to pack his possessions, and then disappear. Nothing was known of him or his whereabouts except that once a month an emissary appeared to pay Luciana and Ubaldo.

The *barone* and *baronessa* were so imposing, Luciana and Ubaldo were to say in the future, they were so English, like people from another world. We were all so poor then. And Ubaldo was longing to drive that beautiful blue car, he was thrilled at the idea of being the chauffeur. It was embarrassing to show the *barone* and *baronessa* where they themselves lived, in the *podere* behind the villa, and at right angles to it. A laurel hedge runs between the rose-garden and the *podere*, hiding much of it except the three tall brick arches of its front. To reach their quarters, Luciana and Ubaldo have only to walk along a short path from the kitchen.

Behind the arches are storerooms and granaries, all now abandoned. Old implements such as hoes, cracked wheelbarrows, even a lathe and a workbench, clutter the corners. Everywhere the timbers are worm-eaten. One door opens into what used long ago to be a night-watchman's room. Towards the end of the war, a German deserter had been sheltered here for months and so it has come to be known as the *camera del Tedesco*. Luciana had been nineteen at the time, and she used to bring this man his food. She and Giulia provided him with civilian clothes and burnt his uniform in the incinerator. On the morning after they had sent him on his way, the Germans came in a search party, a major and a sergeant, and a detachment with loaded weapons. Luciana likes to describe how she screamed. There were so many of them – she rolls her eyes at the drama of it – they threatened they'd rape me if I went on screaming but I couldn't help myself, I really couldn't. One of them put his hand over my face. I was saved because the men arrived from Sant' Ambrogio. My voice must have carried that far, or they'd heard the soldiers. We never had trouble after that.

The bed the deserter slept on is still there, an iron truckle frame with sacking tied over its springs and a mattress stiff as a plank on top of that. The room also has a chest of drawers and a washbasin. Across the window the shutter has long since jammed at a slight angle, leaving a ray to penetrate like a searchlight in miniature through the gloom.

After hearing that story, they walked through the garden, and on round into the olive orchard, at the bottom of which is the *contadino*'s house where Giulia lives with her husband Armando. Luciana and Ubaldo are fat and welcoming; Giulia and Armando in contrast not so much thin as eroded, with unspoken tension in the air around them. They too have always worked for the owner of the villa; she cleans, and he is the gardener, he grows vegetables, and because he must, grudgingly, roses, and he is responsible for the olives. They sit and they eat in a front room in which polished wood and metal shine and blink, especially in the evenings under an overhead light-bulb with no shade.

No, there's not much land, Armando said, with a hopeful twist in his voice that these prospective owners might be rich enough to buy more. And there are problems. Prowlers. The strangest people feel free to drive in at night, and stroll around as if they owned the place. And dogs squeeze through the wire netting, there are holes everywhere, it needs replacing. He thinks dogs from Sant' Ambrogio must have some way of passing on a memory that once rabbit used to be on offer here. Children too. How much better it would be if the villa was inhabited. A sack of gold would have to be spent on it, though.

Sandra pushed them to buy. We want neighbours like you, she said, you'll love it here. And it's a chance in a lifetime. A bargain. Look at its character, so typical. Think of the incredible luck in finding not one but two couples of the best salt-of-the-earth kind already installed. She'll make it her business to telephone Dr Grazioso, her lawyer. Meanwhile they must find the *parocco* of Sant' Ambrogio, he'll be a key to the deal.

The netting round the property was indeed in bad repair. There was little point sticking to the path leading to a gate in the direction of the village. Sant' Ambrogio is a cluster, all walls and angled rooftops of red tiles and chimneys, no straight lines anywhere, an anthill of irregular lanes, with a couple of shops and a bar. Don Alvise was already the *parocco*. In those days he left the door of his house unlocked although he was out. We'll have to come back, Sandra said, we need him on our side, but you'll see, the *squadrista* will be only too thankful.

The result of their visit was that a hammer and sickle was painted on the front door of the villa, spoiling its varnish. Luciana wept. How had anyone known about the *barone* and *baronessa*, who anyhow mightn't have made their minds up yet? None of them had whispered a thing, they could swear to it. Who were they, these Communists? She'd lived all her life in Sant' Ambrogio, and harmed nobody. The emblem was squiggly. Slapped on in a hurry, some of the red paint had run and dripped.

Pippo Piccolomini said, in his too perfect English, 'It's enough to give you chicken-flesh,' and the phrase became a standing joke between Andrew and Dina.

24

'Our Communists will turn out to be someone's cousins, we can arrange things,' Sandra said, 'not like with your Stafford Cripps.'

The day when Dr Grazioso reported that the villa was for sale at six thousand dollars (and the pound at that time was seven dollars eighty) was also the day on which the Soviets blocked access to the western zones of Berlin and cut off the supply of electricity. It had to do with the quarrel with Tito, Andrew thought. If there had been a common frontier between the Soviet Union and Yugoslavia, another war might have broken out. Perhaps after all aircraft might be needed again, and the factory would have a future. Sandra and Pippo remember him saying that really it had been easier to survive the war against the Germans than to persuade Cripps and the Bank of England that he was on to a good thing.

FOUR

Maydeswell remained in the hands of Mrs Ackroyd, cleaner
and cook, and specialist in the art of silent complaint. Of
uncertain age, she never refers to Mr Ackroyd, and doubt
exists whether there has ever been any such person.
Whenever pressed by the children with this question, she
would retreat. 'What I know, what I've seen in my time,
you could fill whole books with.' Then, after a meaningful
pause, 'But I'm not telling, my lips is sealed.'

Without Mrs Ackroyd, the English end of their lives
would have collapsed. In the absence of Dina, she ran the
house. She was the one to remind Andrew to ensure that
special deliveries of coal were made from the factory. As
rationing persisted, she wheedled unobtainable food out
of the butcher and grocer; she may have created the
demand-side of the black market in that otherwise virtu-
ous stretch of the Home Counties. 'It's a crying shame that
these growing children can't get what they need,' was her
unanswerable argument. 'I ask you,' she would snort, 'this
lot feeds the Germans but not us, oh no, we're not good
enough for them to look after.' Mrs Ackroyd used to tie her
hair up in a scarf, wartime style. In her eyes, Andrew
could do no wrong. 'You don't like Mummy, do you?' Ursie
and Alexander would try cross-questioning. 'Don't be so
daft,' was the reply. 'You've got good parents and don't
you forget it.'

Italy, it was understood, was to blame. They were
foreigners there, and no good came of associating with the
likes of them. They jabbered, you couldn't trust them, and
daren't eat their food. All that oil and grease, Mrs Ackroyd
would say, wrinkling her nose with distaste at the thought
of it. As for their plumbing.

But it's a beautiful house, the children said, you'd love it, it's huge and all falling down, with a much bigger garden than here, and everybody's so friendly.

'I dare say they are. They would be, wouldn't they? Your parents are much too kind-hearted.'

The Cold War gave the factory a reprieve. A new generation of military aircraft required more complex instrumentation. As costs of research and development increased, Andrew sought a manufacturing company with which to merge. In the end he did the deal with Vickers, and it was their condition that he remain an executive director. Then there were protracted journeys to Australia and America, journeys which the children could track by means of postcards with stamps of exotic plants or animals, a gaudy whiff of those foreigners who aroused Mrs Ackroyd's suspicions. If it happened to be the holidays, Mrs Ackroyd took care of everything, more indulgent than Dina would ever have been. Spoiling them came naturally to her. She picked up their clothes, brought them breakfast in bed if they slept late, and the expression on her face alone gave away what she might be thinking. Otherwise, Andrew drove off in the morning to work, as he had always done, returning to Mrs Ackroyd's suppers in a house from which his wife and children had seemingly just fallen away.

Gyroscopes, X-ray crystallography, isotopes, radar, particles, solenoids, molecules: if ever there was a foreign language, it was Andrew's conversation with the men he sometimes brought home. 'Right, you two,' he said one day to the children, 'we're going to begin to teach you physics.' Copper-knickers was all very well, but then did the sun go round the earth, or the earth round the sun, and in which direction, and who started it off, and why? Galileo, Torricelli, the names span daydreams of the villa. Let something equal x, he'd begin. But that something was itself, and it was a silly game to pretend that it might equal something else. What was the point of creating confusion? Andrew hadn't time, or patience. If everyone was as slow as you two, he'd say, the human race would still be heathens living in caves, and by the sound of it that's where we're heading.

To the children, their father was the man who arranged to fetch them from boarding school, and then put them into the sleeper at Victoria Station. Too busy and too important to be approached, he was a stranger under some obligation to be particularly kind. Since they couldn't be serious with such a person, they tried teasing, quite successfully, discovering for instance that it was a clever trick to tug at the ends of his bow tie, disintegrating the dapper effect, with the bonus of observing how he then had to loop and pull and insert strong fingers into a strip of material as elusive as a fish.

'I want you to be specially kind to Mummy,' he would tell them, as though he were not on the platform saying goodbye as they leaned out of the carriage, but far away in some quite other place. 'She's so looking forward to having you. Be considerate. Think of her feelings.'

As they grew older, even this stopped. A car and chauffeur from the factory would pick them up, to drive straight to the station without even a stopover at Maydeswell. The ritual of the envelope never failed. Either in person, or through the chauffeur, Andrew ensured that Alexander was to receive it – always buff and thick – with 'Travelling expenses' pencilled on it in his hand. Some secret place had to be found for this, where thieves and customs men wouldn't possibly think of looking. It's illegal, old chap, Andrew would laugh, and it'll be a spell of prison if they catch you. Sorry about that. Should things get hot, the last recourse will be for Ursie to burst into uncontrollable sobbing, that'll embarrass them and maybe touch their stony hearts. Look as pretty as you can too, my darling, with plenty of tears on those pink cheeks.

In the sleeper, they fought for the top bunk. Alexander used to win. Then he'd count out the French francs and Italian lire, and they'd decide how to hide them between the brown scratchy *wagon-lit* blankets or in their underclothes. This game led to another, of disguises, and in the dining-car they played at being Lord and Lady Maydeswell or Conte and Contessa di Sant' Ambrogio, devising conversations which were supposed to allow eavesdroppers at other tables to guess who they were. No customs man so much as questioned them, and the attendants in their blue high-collared uniforms never showed surprise at the notes extracted by Alexander from the envelope.

During the night, the train would shudder to a simmering halt at the frontier, with a crescendo of hissings and screechings, followed by a hammering somewhere along the undercarriages which resonated and broke into sleep. And when at last the journey restarted, the train lurched and clanked to a new rhythm. The morning brought with it quite another sky. In the expanse of Rome station, under its glass covering, Ubaldo was waiting, like an overweight boxer, to fling his arms around them, embracing and hugging, in a rush with the latest news. Only the final lap of the journey, and then there would be the cypresses, and beyond them the familiar yellow front and heavy windows of the villa, and the stairs to race up, to knock at Dina's door, for the gruff voice to say, 'Oh is that you at last? I was expecting you an hour ago,' as though this were the school round on a day like any other.

Their rooms were off the corridor. The very first glance down on the terrace and the garden signified that the holidays had begun, that there was no need to get up early, and that there were now quite other dimensions and possibilities. Jekyll and Hyde: in these rooms accumulated evidence of their other selves, Italian magazines and posters, and photographs curling at the edges, clothes that couldn't be considered suitable in their stuffy England. Soon they would gravitate to the vital centre of the house, Luciana's kitchen with its receding vaulted ceiling and installations which nobody could be bothered to modernise.

Luciana has a way of showing affection with small rapid touches on other people's arms or shoulders, she welcomes noise and untidiness, she takes it for granted that everyone likes to be eating most of the time, and that the best of life happens round a table with plates on it. Cooking for her is a campaign, requiring strategies. Considering her size, and that her bosom seems to roll forward into other comfortable folds which might be waist or might be stomach, she is agile and energetic. She wears unexpected flowery skirts which she makes herself, and below them brown stockings which never quite fill out but wrinkle round the calves, and she waddles in slippers looking like cardboard. Her hair, a pepper-and-salt mix of black edging to grey, is evidently going to change no more. In her smile is a gold tooth. On the side of her face, a mole, like a sultana, has curly, worrisome hairs growing out of it.

Under the window, and bulking against the length of the kitchen wall, is a leather sofa, its frame long since collapsed, so that Ubaldo seems to slouch down into it. There he likes to spend the time of day, keeping his wife company, reading through football magazines and filling in crosswords in the local papers. An effort is required to haul his bulk out of the depths of that sofa and its cushions, and he rises unsteadily on his legs, resenting disturbance. Energy on his part is confined to mealtimes, when he tells stories and laughs and eats as though swallowing much and fast was akin to a conjuring trick. The polite and podgy face gives little away otherwise, but he doesn't hide a mocking sort of antagonism towards Giulia and Armando. That Red Indian, he calls Giulia, referring to her dark pinched looks and high cheeks. As for Armando, he brings vegetables and fruit into the kitchen, and Ubaldo rebukes him, always too little for the household, unripe, not what we could have had at the season. Behind Armando's back, he likes to throw out wild accusations that the best produce is being sold secretly and that fiddles on an unimaginable scale are going on, and it's time for the *barone* or *baronessa* to put a foot down.

Tullio is the son of Luciana and Ubaldo. Four years older than Alexander, seven years older than Ursie, he sets the example, he shows them what's what in Sant' Ambrogio. From him they picked up idiomatic Italian, first of all rude words and swearing. In the early days, there was still the local cinema, a real fleapit, where the film changed once a week, and he would arrange for them to come along with his crowd of friends. Whatever it was – shaving, exploring the body of a girl, drinking a bottle of *sambuca* – he seemed to have done it before anyone else of his age. Not his parents' child for nothing, he was all puppy fat, and then a somewhat glandular teenager. For a time so protracted that it seemed to last for years, he did little except roar about on a motorcycle, revving up and down the drive and weaving away as fast as he dared through the twists and curves of the village. If ever he could galvanise his father, it was to experiment with the sparking-plug and carburettor.

Why is Daddy away all the time? the children used to ask. Why doesn't he come out on the train with us? Doesn't he like it here, like Mrs Ackroyd says?

Because he is so important, because of his responsibilities, because as the breadwinner he has to be looking after the family, because it is none of your business.

And if they still pestered Dina, she turned angry. The first warning appeared in the pouches under her eyes: they swelled, and darkened to a damson-red. 'Can you spit from your eyes?' Ursie once asked at the sight. The next step was a real rage, issuing as on a rising wind to a gale of tears and crying, to withdrawal into her room, to locked doors and seclusion and ostracism. Then the children would seek refuge almost continuously in the kitchen, where Luciana would imply that she knew much more than she could possibly tell about the poor *baronessa*, who missed her husband and was so sad and lonely without him. Like someone surrendering under a white flag, she would carry up a tray with camomile tea and vanilla biscuits.

Besides, Andrew was sometimes there, the criticism wasn't fair. For instance he insisted that he should be the one to supervise the packing of the contents of the studio at Varendy, and their transportation to the villa. More than one journey was necessary, and Alexander and Ursie have the most vivid memory of him driving up to the front door, and unloading cases out of the car. It was highly unusual to see him in his shirt-sleeves engaged in work of lifting and carrying like that. Everyone, even Dina, had to be roped in because pictures were to be distributed in this or that room, and some of the stuff had to be stored up in the attic. I drove straight across the border, and damn the French customs, the children heard him say.

The best of these pictures were hung, Andrew giving instructions to Ubaldo and Armando. Portraits in the *salone*, and eventually the landscapes in the dining-room. Dina placed the picture of her mother over the writing desk between the windows of her bedroom. That's the only thing I really wanted, she said. The children sensed, as children do, that something wasn't quite right, that feelings were involved here too important to be questioned openly.

A comparable memory centres upon the piano which was bought when they were installing themselves: a nineteenth-century instrument with a marquetry top, overblown on swollen carved legs, a bastion of an object. Andrew played by ear, he strummed pre-war Cole Porter and Noël Coward songs. Whenever he was there, the children developed a ritual of begging him to play before dinner; it put him into a good mood, and Dina would stand at his shoulder looking pleased for once, as familiar with the words as he was. There was a period when a teacher used to arrive, a distracted and elderly lady who gave the impression of extreme incompetence in everything she did, whether dressing, eating, combing her hair. The house echoed with scales and arpeggios and Scarlatti and Diavelli exercises. Andrew even practised, and the children watched him unbelievingly, this adult doing his homework in the *salone* against a background of the bookcases filled with technical books shipped from England, on aerodynamics and engineering, subjects they knew they would never understand any more than they could play the piano. The person I'd most have liked to have been, Andrew said one day, was Dinu Lipatti. And where did he come in, the children wondered, who ever was he? The name became an unfathomable part of the mystery that was their father.

Friendship with Anna Karcz dated from that early time. On one of her first visits to the villa, she had asked, unprompted, 'Who collected those beautiful Napiers?' and then couldn't get over the answer. To her, he was one of the most underrated of English artists. With a father like that, she would say to Dina, no wonder you're so special. That portrait of Marguerite Dalhem, she adds, I first saw that at the Beaux-Arts in 1932, when I was a student. Who'd have imagined that it would turn up here like a long-lost treasure?

Anna Karcz's house is one of the minuscule buildings within the walls of Sant' Ambrogio, more of a hideaway than a home, with neven stairs leading to a single studio room in which she lives and cooks and eats and works, and where the divan converts into a bed for the infrequent guests, chief of whom is her nephew Julian. More rickety steps lead up to the large loft, its thick beams and tiles exposed, very characteristic of the region's rustic type of building. She earns a living painting furniture, and has used available walls and doors to show what she is capable of: pretty floral designs, *trompe l'oeil* scenes and perspectives.

I've never seen such distinguished hands and ankles as hers, Andrew said, but she's a good deal tougher than she looks.

Very good skin; hair as though she had stepped out of the hairdresser; the same small wardrobe of well-made clothes: Anna Karcz seems fit to be a lady-in-waiting at court. And what of her past? Nobody knows. Nothing has survived of it except Eastern European stresses and intonations when she speaks. Once I asked her outright where she spent the war, Sandra Piccolomini says, and she told me that she has relegated all such memories to her dreams, and it's bad enough to have to live with them at night so she refuses to think about anything like that during the day. Who could blame her? I've started a life here, Anna herself says of Sant' Ambrogio, I'm very fortunate. She gravitates towards people as cosmopolitan as herself. Anna Mahler is her friend, and Gian-Carlo

Menotti, who used to employ her on the stage sets for the Spoleto Festival, and every summer William Walton invited her down to Ischia.

To Dina, she spoke in an exact drawing-room French. *Chère amie*, the one called the other, exchanging compliments. It was only natural to want to do a favour to Anna Karcz, and so to be on the best of terms with this congenial neighbour who lived within walking distance. Nor would it be anything but a good investment if Nikita Golovin were to paint Andrew's portrait. Golovin was a protégé of hers, a White Russian apparently on the verge of making an international reputation. The portrait would be likely to double in value every few years; he was the new Lucian Freud.

Taciturn to the point of rudeness, Golovin failed to please as a person. He didn't wash much, he wore grubby clothes. Savaging the drinks tray, he would find his tongue, only to boast in rather an affected way about his art. At least he was prepared to come to the villa, and he proved a quick worker. In this portrait, Andrew is depicted conventionally enough in a suit and one of his polka-dot bow ties. Skilfully captured in those regular features is 'the Donatello look' – as Dina called it – a smile with the charm of mystery about it, suggesting complicity, and the self-regard of someone who has made a success of life and is not to be judged superficially. With a less sure touch, Golovin chose to place his sitter amid rocks and waves on an incongruous seashore which owes a lot to de Chirico and Dali. Exposed as too conventional, Andrew also seems to be in the hopeless, even slightly ridiculous, posture of trying to impose order where this can't be done. It hardly helps that the portrait is almost life-sized.

Because Golvin had no agent or gallery to represent him, Anna Karcz in the end sent the bill, and Andrew paid her directly.

Quite right, Sandra Piccolomini said, very generous of you too. Of course it's more money than they first mentioned. She needs all the help she can get. Every commission counts.

At opposite ends of the villa, Andrew's room and Dina's were symmetrical. Both originally ran from front to back of the house, but had been divided for the sake of bathrooms. Andrew's had a view over the olives out towards the Valle Tremaldi, while Dina's gave onto Sant' Ambrogio and its rooftops. I've got the better of the deal, he used to say, my poor Dina has to suffer those bloody awful church bells. Two bells do indeed resonate at her end of the house, a deeper one with a satisfying toll, and a shrill one, usually rung with insistence to sound like a child's whine. The morning crowing of the cocks in nearby farms is another disturbance for her.

Not much decoration was done when they moved in. The floors upstairs were tiled, and Andrew said that they had two hundred years of lustre in them, he much preferred them to any old masterpiece, and took an interest in the kind of wax Giulia used on them. Some of this wax has rubbed off on the pale yellowish curtains which Dina installed, slightly discolouring them at the hem.

Between the two main windows in Andrew's room stands a chest of drawers, with on it the photograph of him taken with Churchill in December 1943, on the occasion of an official visit to the factory. Addressing the workforce, the prime minister had congratulated them on the precision instruments they were making. Brilliant inventors had designed these navigation aids and bomb-sights, he had said, but they were the technicians and skilled men who were turning blueprints into practical tools, thereby establishing supremacy over the Luftwaffe. The harder they worked, the sooner the victory. Afterwards Churchill and Andrew had almost been mobbed as they emerged at the main entrance and posed for the photographer. Whenever he told the story of that visit, Andrew liked to emphasise the extraordinary boost in morale and productivity that resulted from the speech. In the photograph Churchill looks exhausted but stubborn, with his face slightly turned towards Andrew, and his hand held up in the celebrated victory sign. Across the right-hand bottom corner runs Churchill's signature in black ink.

To begin with, the Golovin portrait was propped in the *salone*, but it loomed too large even in that space, oppressive, a presence like a ghost's. So it was moved up to Andrew's room, parked there out of harm's way. Held with clamps on an upright easel, it served much like a screen to the bathroom; and of course a pendant to the Churchill photograph.

'Why do Mummy and Daddy sleep so far apart?' the children asked. 'Are they divorced?'

In those days, much of their time was spent with Tullio. With him they explored the *camera del Tedesco* and other premises, and climbed onto the roof of the villa, to examine how the cardinal's arms were fixed. A single shop in Sant' Ambrogio sold what were then the first model cars in metal, together with lead soldiers. Chewing-gum was the currency Tullio wanted. To reward him, the children would beseech Andrew to have some sent from America, or to bring it back from one of his transatlantic journeys: the stuff came in slabs, in shiny packets, as valuable as bullion when it came to bartering in Sant' Ambrogio among Tullio and his friends.

Don Alvise, the *parocco*, had programmes for Tullio and these boys, consisting of lessons and classes and organised hikes or scouting parties. Not only the children but Andrew and Dina were in touch with him from the moment the villa was bought. What you'll have to do is give the community something, Sandra Piccolomini advised, a token of goodwill to show you understand the part he played in getting the previous owner to sell.

Even when young, Don Alvise had the elongated masochistic air of an El Greco figure, no flesh on him, and all awkward bones and uncoordinated movements. Tilting his head to one side, as he does, he seems to be apologising for himself, with some relish at his inferiority to whomever he happens to be speaking to. Unhealthy and vitamin-starved, the face has always had a perpetual hue of ivory, with a hatching of blue-grey where he scrapes as he must with his cut-throat razor. The nose is sharp, the chin sunken, rodent-like. Teeth in chaotic disarray will trouble him all his life. Disconcertingly, he can lose himself in his thoughts; more than daydreaming, he seems to float away from reality into some unearthly sphere familiar only to him. Then he hardly listens. In mid-sentence of some humdrum conversation, his voice can brake and dry. However when he talks about what interests him, the brown eyes are intense and highly expressive, and he flutters long and sensitively shaped fingers.

'How do you do?' is about the limit of his English, and 'please' and 'thank you' (pronounced as 'tank-u') with some strangulation in the throat, sending a prominent bump of an Adam's apple bobbing up and down.

When first Don Alvise had been invited to lunch at the villa, he had brought with him a twelve-year-old, without explanation or advance warning. Put out, but overtly grinning to make his feelings known, Ubaldo laid an extra place. This boy was one of Tullio's circle, and already known to the children as a hoarder of chewing-gum. Scarcely speaking during the meal, this boy shovelled food into his mouth with his knife, as with his fork, first one implement then the other, and he expertly bunched bread and even salad with the fingers of one hand, to stuff it in.

That priest is a good old shirtlifter of the best kind, Andrew said, no harm in that, the boy's at least getting a square meal.

The church of Sant' Ambrogio is Romanesque, severe and geometric in outline, the sole monument of any note in the district. Its interior used to be much disfigured by plaster statues of saints, and in particular, of the Madonna with a halo illuminated by small light-bulbs in five glaring tints. A number of flags and devices woven or embroidered by the pious also obscured the rough-hewn walls. In time, Don Alvise was able to clear the lot out, and return the body of the church to its primitive simplicity.

Below the church are uneven steps spiralling down to what had been a southern gateway, today the far end of the restricted one-way circuit which cars must negotiate. Close by the wall is a cramped space, hardly a field, more gravel than grass. Until now, the previous owner of the villa had paid an annual rent for it on behalf of local children. Andrew grasped the point, and volunteered to do whatever Don Alvise thought fit in the circumstances.

Duly this patch of a sports ground acquired the name of its benefactors, as the Campo Barone e Baronessa Lumel, shortened and Italianised in speech to the Campo Luna. No sooner had Andrew paid the purchase price than Don Alvise came with bad news. His face almost in spasm with the pain of what he had to import, he explained that he had just discovered that there was also a cousin to be bought out. This man wanted at least as much again. Why didn't you tell me? Andrew wanted to know, it's not that I mind doing this for the village, but I'd thought we were friends.

Sandra Piccolomini pointed out that there was always a concealed cousin or relation waiting to be sprung on you – that was Italian law, children had to inherit in equal shares from their parents. What with the Golovin picture, and now the Campo, she promised, nobody would think badly of them, there'd be no burglars in the villa, and no Communists either.

These priests, Armando said, they're all the same, black crows feeding on whatever they can. Why hadn't they come to him before finalising the Campo purchase? He'd have told them about the cousin, he knew a set-up like that for what it was worth. As for wasting time with Tullio – he shrugged. A good-for-nothing, greedy like his parents.

Armando of course listened to what Dina and Andrew told him but didn't pay great attention. He has never believed in growing what cannot be eaten. Resenting the rose beds, he plants winter cabbages in them, or artichokes or cauliflowers, and shrugs as if the vegetables had grown of their own accord. He stares at Dina in a way which means that a man like him can hardly be expected to indulge a woman like her. Weatherbeaten, he has no identifiable age. In summer, his singlet reveals arms of scrawny sinew, highly anatomical in detail. His everyday trousers are a rough blue faded by Giulia's hand-washing, and bunched in round the waist by a strap of a belt whose end he tucks back beneath a brass buckle. Indoors, though, he manages to have on a shirt, and it is always clean, nobody knows quite how this is contrived, where he rustles it up from. His special joy is the olive orchard; his special implement there is a long-handled hoe with a right-angled blade like a spade's, an object straight out of the Middle Ages. A grim pruner of those gnarled and twisted trees, he piles branches beehive fashion, to be used one day as fuel. Whoever drives up or down between the cypresses is likely to catch sight of him, moving into their field of vision in order to glare, shading his eyes with a hand if he has to, watchman of everybody's business.

At the sight of Ubaldo driving away, or Tullio racing and bucking on the motorcycle, Armando is likely to spit, not exactly in reference to them, but to one side, in a way which would enable him to claim that he meant nothing malicious but had something to clear from his mouth. The whispering campaign is conducted ably on both sides.

There's the Fat One off to buy a week's food at the *baronessa*'s expense, says Armando. Also, he syphons petrol out of that car. Sometimes his lips are blistered.

Luciana and Ubaldo ask, who do you think painted the hammer and sickle to ruin the front door? Why, everybody knows that Armando's a Communist. Look at the way he treats Don Alvise. All our olives, and never enough oil for us, what more do you want.

Couldn't we stay here? the children pleaded, and go to school with Tullio and everyone, and see you when we come home, lessons stop at lunchtime. Just because the holidays are over, do we have to catch the train?

FIVE

At an English boarding school in the Fifties, you feared the worst if they sent for you in mid-morning. You knew you must have infringed some rule, and were due for serious punishment, almost surely physical assault. When Alexander was summoned out of his classroom one February day, he endured several minutes of stomach-tightening anticipation outside the headmaster's study. On account of a wizened head at an angle like a vulture's on his shoulders, the man was known as Rubberneck. His room had a reek to it of leather chairs, pipe tobacco, the jacket and gown into which sweat had dried year after year. Like someone coughing, he cleared his throat. There must be some misunderstanding, Alexander realised as he scrutinised Rubberneck's expression and the unusual way he was groping for appropriate words of kindness. The news, as it sank in, was almost a relief: there would be no physical assault after all. His father had been ill; bronchitis had turned to pleurisy. You'll be going home, Rubberneck was telling him, your mother's come over from Italy and is waiting for you.

The headmistress herself drove me home, Ursie re-members, she told me I was to cry as much as possible, it's called a relief mechanism. She studied medicine, and she knows.

Things ought to have changed at Maydeswell, but they hadn't. Winter light on the trees and bricks patterned on the path up to the front door, Mrs Ackroyd and her preparation of tea, a fire lit in the drawing-room. How is one to behave in grief, what are the right manners for it? Many times they had hidden away from Dina's outbursts of rage and those fierce tears, but now her normality was

40

hardly less terrifying. She sat upright on the sofa and sipped the tea poured out for her. Her face was dead white, with the consistency of dough, and eyes like prunes.

'I didn't tell you,' she said, 'because there didn't seem much point. You'd only have worried and couldn't have done anything about it. Either he was going to get better or he wasn't.'

Dead. The word had a metallic ring, it clanged between them. You could think about something else, you could talk brightly, but the echo of that hard short word lingered in the head. 'He didn't suffer,' Dina said, 'he lived right to the end just as he would have wanted.'

Couldn't we see him one last time? Ursie tried to ask as though this were a request like any other. Otherwise, she said, I'm not going to believe it.

Apparently this wasn't the done thing, children had to be protected from such a sight. Pretences were right and proper.

On the sofa, with that day's newspapers in disorder about her, Dina looked pouchy and irritable, as if her thoughts were still at La Grecchiata and she had come home for a slightly unwelcome half-term break, none too sure how to entertain the children. The light soon faded. There seemed to be nothing to do, except sit and watch Mrs Ackroyd trying to help.

Unpretentious, Maydeswell was a large farmhouse, red brick; a sloping and irregular tiled roof with squat chimneys. Prosperity had encouraged previous owners to enlarge, to lay the crazy pavement path that led up to the white-painted front porch, to enclose the kitchen garden at the back. In the run-up to the war, Andrew had bought it from the Crane-Dyttons, of Dytton Abbey, a mile or so away on the far side of a handsome wood. The house remained much as he had done it up. A desk in the drawing-room was reserved for his use. The dining-room, bare except for its table and set of chairs, was almost regimental. As in the villa, Dina had liked to treat her bedroom as somewhere to read and write, more a study than anything else. I have no taste, she used to say, and no colour sense, and besides domestic things bore me stiff, I can't bear women who go trotting round designers.

Upstairs are poky and unpredictable corridors. Floorboards creak under even the most careful and measured step. Going to each other's rooms, Ursie and Alexander have always given themselves away, no matter how hard they tried to scout out a silent path over these floorboards. When together, they had a habit of whispering. It was conspiracy. Alexander had collected lead soldiers, and Ursie had dozens of furry animals as well as the novels of E. Nesbit and Louisa May Alcott: each had filled available space with these props, and there was nowhere to retreat except to the floor or to sink into the eiderdown on the beds. One of Alexander's earliest fantasies had been that the house was haunted, and their parents were not their parents at all, but ghostly impersonators. They hover around us, he used to say, making up their minds what they're going to do to us, they haven't quite decided yet. He could shift Ursie swiftly from crying with fear to laughter, and back to fear again.

Neither of them were ever to forget those first hours when their father seemed to have shaded into that ghostly fantasy and they were by themselves, and Dina sat immobile with newspapers around her, and Mrs Ackroyd came and went helplessly.

Into that void Lionel burst, with Minou and Micky trailing behind him. At the airport he had arranged to be met, and there was an owlish chauffeur who had to be packed off to the Fox and Goose for the night. Lionel's presence carried, he made enough noise for all of them, everywhere at once, the supervisor of the normality he was imposing. Old boy, he said, and old girl, and he clapped them on the shoulder or round the back of the head, and added, Never mind, it can't be helped, you'll see you'll be all right. A wonderful life, he said, and a wonderful death too. You're only feeling sorry for yourselves, and there's nothing to be gained from that.

Leave it all to me, he said to Dina. We've been partners in crime since first I was in chambers, not to worry.

The financial side of things is properly sewn up, we've seen to that.

Vingt-et-un, Lionel proposed in order to make the evening pass. He scoured up as many matches as he could, including the box Mrs Ackroyd was using for the kitchen stove. A halfpenny a point, he said, jolly fair stakes too. His luck was in. Once all the matches were heaped in front of him, he counted them and distributed them once more. For the second time he scooped every match. On a sheet of writing paper, he calculated what the children owed him; far more than their weekly pocket money. Then he thrust this sheet at them without comment as though he really expected them to pay up.

Throughout dinner, he was the one to do the speaking, teasing Mrs Ackroyd on her roast chicken – 'This drumstick's quite purple, I wouldn't care to have been kicked by that bird when it was alive.' Afterwards he handed out sleeping pills to everyone, as though a family doctor, with glasses of water too. A good night's rest is the thing, he told them. Slipping it under her tongue, where the taste spread a little bitterly, Ursie refused to swallow hers but spat it out into the lavatory. Alexander managed to hide his in the palm of his hand. Confiding in each other, they felt that they would be all right after all, and conspiracy might succeed.

The cremation was to be at Brookwood, with its artificial backdrop of conifers and beds for potted plants. Lionel spent his time making the arrangements, which meant giving orders to everyone. From time to time, the chauffeur and the hired car fetched him away, so that there was a reprieve from the sound of that barking voice downstairs. No detail was too trivial for him. It was then the fad for the girls in Ursie's school to grow their hair long, so that they could toss it about in what was thought to be a grown-up manner. It wouldn't be respectful like that, Lionel said, it looks precocious, too silly for words. Her hair would have to be tidied away, put up, plaited in a pigtail, anything except all over her shoulders. Then I'm not coming, Ursie said.

You'll do what you're told, Lionel warned, or I'll lay you across my knee the way your father should have.

On the day, busy with inspecting how everyone in the family was dressed, he seemed to have forgotten this matter of the hair, and focussed instead on how badly Alexander's grey flannel suit fitted. There was a cold drizzle; the car's windscreen wipers imposed a hypnotic silence all the way to the crematorium. Those who gathered there to wait under umbrellas included all sorts of one-time guests at Maydeswell, from the factory, the Vickers and Air Ministry people, politicians, a stiff frieze of figures. Greeting these people, escorting them to their seats, Lionel was the centre of the occasion. He was the one to read the lesson, his voice was the loudest bass to the hymns.

What happened afterwards is something which Alexander prefers not to deal with. As he recalls, he went after the service to have a look at wreaths and flowers placed on a lawn. There was one which bore his name, and a message purporting to be from him. I felt awful about this, Alexander says, and I expect I wasn't in control of myself either. The next thing I felt was someone grabbing me from behind and it was Lionel. His eyes were an animal red, I realised I was going to be hit, it was just like being in the presence of the headmaster at school. You stop snivelling, those were his words, and then he hit me. You know what I still remember? How I put my hands up to ward that slap off, and my school suit was too tight, I'd outgrown it, so some of the stitches somewhere in the lining burst. I worried I'd be laughed at. And I've retained this impression of lots of strangers in black staring at the two of us and doing nothing about it, all those boring respectable people Andrew seemed to have spent his life with. Minou was the one exception. She held on to me, and I can repeat exactly what she said, Everybody's terribly upset, at moments like these they can't really help themselves. He's only trying his best.

Years have passed since then, and Alexander has never been able to tell his mother about the impact of this incident. At times, he has wondered whether he might have made it up, somehow fantasising the shock of death

44

into an assault against himself. One way forward would be to confront Lionel with the memory, but this he cannot bring himself to do. Minou's apology is vivid. And Ursie confirms that the punch was real. No wonder you've always had such complicated emotions about him, she says, he wanted me to put up my hair and he knocked you to the ground, that's the way the man is. People were so embarrassed that they didn't know what to do. We'd driven over there in a ghastly silence, and that was how we drove home too. Is it possible for imagination to become reality, perhaps more real even than reality?

Back at school, everything was as it had been. There they didn't register events outside the grounds. At the start of a foggy week in February one played games and sat through a Latin or a maths class, and at the end of the very same week the classes and games resumed, there was still fog, and one's father was dead and buried, trundled away out of sight in a coffin on runners like a model railway, through a tunnel. Friends behaved as they had done previously, they took no account, they didn't like to know.

In the course of another morning that term, Alexander was again summoned to the headmaster. This time it was to receive a registered packet from Switzerland, and to sign for it. Twelve pounds were owing as duty, and the sum would be put on the school bill. Lionel had sent him a watch, clearly an expensive one, perhaps not real gold, but convincing enough to be able to claim it as such. The second hand leaped with satisfactory jerkiness round the dial, and the winder was sharply ribbed. Confusingly, in spite of himself, he was grateful. No other boy had a possession to match it.

The watch lasted until the summer. Going in to bat in an afternoon's game of cricket, Alexander realised that he still had it on his wrist. So he strapped it to one of the slats at the back of a bench, and asked someone to keep an eye on it. The game was over before he remembered about his watch, and raced for it from the school down to the pitch. Sorry, his friend said, it completely slipped my mind that the thing was there. It was never discovered who had stolen it.

In those years after Andrew's death, there was a groundswell of talk about selling La Grecchiata. Excitement had ebbed from the overnight train journey; the villa had become almost a chore, a place which had to be visited because its problems needed sorting out. Money ought to be spent modernising the central heating; the roof might not hold in a severe winter; more and more of the plaster was peeling off the front. I can't take much more of Luciana's and Giulia's quarrelling, Dina used to say, I haven't the energy to cope, nor the inclination either. Hadn't Andrew been proved wrong? Conservatives followed the Socialists in office, the country had survived.

'Maydeswell is for you,' she told Alexander. 'That's what your father wanted. I'm staying here only till I can hand it over. And where shall I go then?' The answer to this rhetorical question was the villa. Nothing was to be changed in that Italian limbo. His clothes remained in the chest of drawers and his suits in the cupboards. His hairbrush and a comb, wide-toothed; an early example of plastic as transparent as if it were glass. Also several books, including bestselling novels from before the war. His slippers. And by the bedside, on a wall shelf, his last pocket diary, the blue marker ribbon placed by Dina on the day of his death, 17 February 1953.

Now she spent her time as she liked, in her room, reading. She opened an account at Galignani's, the Paris shop, and new books would arrive regularly, the pristine paper-bound slabs of French publishing. Court memoirs, for the most part, and histories of kings and queens and their ministers, Richelieu, Lafayette, Boulanger. From the moment that he learned the word and its meaning, Alexander called her a bluestocking.

Another consequence of Andrew's death was interference in the children's upbringing on the part of Lionel. I'm the executor of the will, he would say, *in loco parentis*. Send them to us for the holidays. Minou and I will keep an eye on them. They already speak fluent Italian, they should learn French now, for School Certificate and all that.

You're packing us off, the children pleaded with Dina. Don't. We'd rather stay at home or be in the villa.

What nonsense, Dina said briskly. It's good for you to get to know Micky and his friends. You're better off enjoying yourselves there than moping around here. You're extremely lucky. Spoiled, I'd say. Lionel is incredibly generous, just be grateful.

Train journeys to Varendy, via Lyons and Toulon, were of quite another sort, unglamorous, full of foreboding. From the minute that they arrived at the station and were met by Minou and Micky, there seemed to be nothing to say but much that had prudently to remain unsaid. Every day was an open minefield. Years were to pass before they were able to acquire any perspective: to ask themselves what kind of a mother Dina had been to push them away in that manner, why she so preferred solitude to company, and repulsed physical contact, immersing herself in those parcels of books from Paris.

It was possible to sense, as though by animal instinct, whether Lionel was in the house, out of doors, or mercifully away in his office, at that time in Geneva. Even when he had shut himself into his room in order to telephone his secretary or to catch up with his work, his presence could be felt far and wide beyond it, as colourless and deadly a radiation as a First World War gas. The door to that room of his was only the most fragile of retaining dams. The same animal instinct dictated whether it was safe to talk in a normal voice, to clatter about and play some game with Micky, or on the contrary to be as invisible as possible and shrink into a corner, the hairs on the forearms rising from fright of what was to come, the spine tingling like an alarm bell.

Hitler, the children called him behind his back, and Tiglath Pileser, a nickname Alexander brought from school lessons and whose happy arrangement of syllables summoned up an unjust ruler and human sacrifice, with a comforting element of mockery in it. He couldn't quite be taken seriously, not with the male-model assurance of his looks and the squaring of the shoulders and that ivory flash of a smile.

Meals were the worst of it. It was hard to get through without a crisis in which he would swear at them, and they would run out of the room before he ordered them to go. Or he would tell lengthy stories about clients in his world in which the stakes were sex and money, and he was obtaining more than his fair share of both. When he rambled about nightclubs or the ins and outs of recent scandalous divorces, Minou stared at her plate. And what about you lot? he would growl in a tone of rising menace. Got any girlfriends? Who's been kissing you, Ursie? From that point on, the steps led inexorably to being shouted at to leave the room like the babies they were and not to come back till they had better manners and something to say for themselves. Tiglath Pileser would finish the meal flushed with success, opposite a silent Minou.

The generous side of him was every bit as confusing, a switch of mood as flashy as a rainbow in a storm. Out would come the gold clip from his trouser pocket, with in it a folded roll of the banknotes of ten thousand French francs then in circulation. These were in light blues and yellows, and so unwieldy and floppy that they rustled. The impressive noughts indicated unlimited spending power, though they were later to be simply chopped off in a currency reform. The moment Alexander and Ursie entered the house and were still travellers rather than his guests, Lionel peeled off a number of these notes, one by one, exaggerating, so that his wife and son were witnesses to this act as a careless exercise of power. Legs apart and shoulders more braced than usual, he struck a heroic pose which refuted any idea that he might be doing something kind for its own sake, or even something as conventional as leaving a tip in a restaurant.

One Easter he took them to a hotel at Pontresina, close to St Moritz. In the highest of spirits, he led them on the first morning to a Sporthaus to open an account in his name for the boots and skis they were to hire. Neither

Alexander nor Ursie had skied before; he was full of advice, about how to bend the knees, where to distribute one's weight, the safest position on a T-bar. On the nursery slopes, he was expecting to be obeyed. 'Bend!' he began to shout, 'Go on, lower still, not like that, you bloody drips. How wet can you be?' People around them stopped to listen and watch. Crossing the tips of his skis, Alexander fell heavily, and Lionel came for him with one ski pole raised in the air like a cudgel. Apparently catching himself at the last moment, he swore instead that he was damned if he was going to do anything more for them, skiing stiffly away. That was the end of his coaching.

That hotel had been selected because it was a convenient distance from the villa of the Shah of Iran. Quite what business Lionel had, or hoped to have, with the Shah was not clear. He hinted at high finance, diplomacy, the ins and outs of international law. 'You'll be invited, and I want you to look your best,' he told the children, 'the Shah's very sensitive to that kind of thing.' He grumbled that Alexander's shoes were too down-at-heel, and Ursie's dress too middle-class for words.

The car that fetched them had a row of bucket seats in the back. Next to the driver sat an unsmiling aide in a formal suit. A barrier marked the start of the private road to the Shah's villa. Snowbound fir trees loomed darkly. The house itself was in the style of an old-fashioned chalet, but overblown and gloomy. About a minute passed while the Shah looked them over, proffered a languid hand, and dismissed them. You have to be with people who count for something, Lionel said, pleased with himself. 'Never miss a trick, that's the motto.'

I'm never ever going back to Varendy, Alexander told his mother, but she forced him there until his final year at school. A specialist in the classics, in Latin and Greek, he was due to sit the Oxford scholarship examination. This boy has a feeling for the languages and their literature, his report said, and the only obstacle to the scholarship is his character. To be awarded it, he had to want it. The Varendy schoolmaster, Monsieur Patin, had coached

Micky in the past. Weedy and monkish, he was among the last Frenchmen still to wear a beret, flat but puffed like the top of a toadstool on hair which deposited dandruff on his collar. His spectacles had lenses as thick as bottle-ends, and he drifted in the street as though always unsure where he was heading. An authority on Horace, he had published learned articles. When Alexander asked if he could have daily lessons, Monsieur Patin answered, '*Sic me servavit Apollo.*'

That man's a laughingstock, Lionel cried out. The whole village knows he can't keep order in class. And his house, it stinks like a badger's earth.

To counteract this influence, he set up a shooting range behind the house. The field there was stony, on a rising slope towards another farmhouse, almost a mile away on a ridge of its own. At a distance of a hundred yards or so was a natural bank of earth, and Lionel propped the target against it. This consisted of a thin wooden frame, with clips to hold replaceable sheets of cardboard, the bull's eye and rings in bright colours. First they practised with an air-rifle, then with a .303. A good shot, Lionel was in his element, demonstrating bolt-action, use of sights, grip, and enjoying himself afterwards with the pull-through and oil to clean the barrel. The boys were at best erratic. A shot on the target punched a hole with a satisfying serration around it.

In order to practise one evening when they thought Lionel was away, the boys removed the rifle from the cupboard in which it was stood. Then they placed the target a couple of hundred yards higher, beyond the bank of earth which stopped the bullets. The ground still sloped upwards; the farm was far to the left of the field of fire. Micky fired first, and they went to inspect the target. Then it was Alexander's turn. He was lying down and aiming when he heard Lionel behind him, saying, 'Put that gun down.' Slightly out of breath, he had evidently been hurrying.

What Alexander noticed as he stood up was the monogram L.F. on Lionel's shirt, and cufflinks like little gold dumbbells. Where was his jacket?

'Who gave you permission to move the target?' he was asking. 'Have you telephoned Lavagnac? You might have killed any of them. And what about their sheep?'

Dangerously controlled, the voice was warning enough of what was about to happen. He was beyond making any attempt to control himself. Yet neither Alexander nor Micky took any step to protect themselves. The blow, when it landed, caught Alexander on the side of his face, and knocked him to the ground. Yet surprise still counted for more than pain, which was inconsequential: the scene had a quality of slow-motion about it, and Alexander heard himself saying, 'I lost my balance.'

'You'll have to hit me too,' Micky said, 'we did it together. It's as much my fault as his.'

And Lionel swung again, this time landing his signet ring on the socket of Micky's eye. The bruise was immediate, swelling as though blood were pumping into it. Holding the rifle as if he were a soldier advancing on the enemy, erect and self-conscious, Lionel stalked indoors.

Such is the natural order, they were expected to conclude. This was education. Authority of his kind was a sort of storm, which blew itself out. That evening there was another spoilt meal, when Minou and Lionel dined alone. It seemed a revenge to catch sight of him in the kitchen with his hand in a bowl of water and ice cubes; Minou said it hurt him to bend his fingers, especially around his signet ring. She wetted cotton wool with something medicinal, the colour of methylated spirits, and bathed Micky's face. For her too, this was the natural order.

Micky's bruise was still black when Lionel organised the evening that was evidently to make amends. They're doing *Andromaque* in Toulouse, he explained, Racine and all that, just the thing for young swots like you two. A taxi would drive them there and back.

For this treat, they put on suits. Along the road out of Varendy, the setting sun slanted through plane trees. The taxi-driver offered them Gauloise cigarettes. The rue Gambetta where he finally drew up had no theatre in it.

51

Instead he rang the bell of a house with a carriageway entrance. A concierge arrived. He'd be back at eleven, the taxi-driver said, and wouldn't mind waiting so long as they were having a good time.

It must be Madame Virginie's, Micky whispered. My father's often spoken about her and about this place, she gets girls for everyone who's anyone. In Paris too, but she likes to live here.

The room in which they sat had a pair of wide-armed sofas, and heaps of cushions in assorted colours and sizes. On shelves round the walls was a collection of glass animals, mostly miniatures, some with pink and blue streaks in them, and statuettes, copies in plastic or metal of the Eiffel Tower, the Leaning Tower of Pisa, Big Ben and the Empire State Building.

Madame Virginie had a husky Mediterranean accent. She wore an evening dress to the floor, with a sea-swirl of *diamanté* sequins down one side. *Ce cher Lionel, ton papa,* she said, *comme il est amusant. Et généreux comme personne d'autre.* The black hair had henna highlights in it.

'Relax,' she laughed, 'enjoy yourselves, everything's been put on his account, he does it in style.'

In a room upstairs were Leila and Zaynab, who claimed to be sisters, and Lebanese from Beirut. Both were full in the face, and almost masked with face powder and lipstick; they talked about themselves and their home city with much grimacing and gesturing. First, champagne; then dinner. Do you like dancing? they asked, putting a record onto the turntable of an old-fashioned gramophone. It was after ten when the boys found themselves being led to other rooms.

'Your first time?' Zaynab asked Alexander, '*ça c'est bien sérieux*, especially when we have on our hands a young Englishman like you. They don't like it in your country, do they, where it's too cold to take your clothes off. *Au travail.*'

Rationally, Alexander has never known what to make of these incidents. Had Lionel really been frightened that they might have had a shooting accident, and lashed out with some muddled notion that he was doing it for their own good? Had he felt remorse, and so decided to give them the treat he would have wanted for himself, with two plump Lebanese tarts?

Alexander has a memory of driving home from the rue Gambetta that night under a barrage of questions from the taxi-driver, who wanted the juicy bits. The window was wound down, the night had scents and warm air blew into their faces. *Elles baisent bien, ces filles.* But could it really have happened, as he also recalls, that Lionel had waited up for them, and was impatiently standing in the little hallway at Varendy, to come out and ask, Well? How was Racine? Hot stuff. And could he truly have put a hand on Alexander's shoulder, with words to the effect that since he had to be a father to him, his duty was to make a man of him. 'There's one gun I hope you'll be firing all over the place.'

A nightmare formed at that period of Alexander's life; a recurrent nightmare. With murder in his heart, Lionel was stalking him through a dark room, and he knew he had to run for his life. Escaping he found himself cornered in the entrance at Varendy. On the wall there is a rack with in it a collection of whips and sticks, and his heart almost bursts with fear as he grabs one, his last resort, to slash at the bloodless inhuman face whose lips are drawn back to show that cruel bite. The whip cuts into flesh as into some pulpy vegetable like a turnip or a swede, and Alexander wakes up sweating, and the momentary relief to be safe and alone is submerged by what becomes a lasting frozen shame at the man's power over him.

SIX

On a scholarship, Alexander went up to Oxford. He was to read Greats. At first glance, the college seemed crumbling, its brick dulled to black and the stone paths underfoot eroded by the generations of undergraduates who had passed through, seasonal migrants in the building with its sunless inner cloister. From the medieval hall, a reek of fried food permeated; from the chapel, a funereal draught.

Stocky, Alexander appeared to have an athletic body, but on slightly too large a scale for the legs actually carrying it. This made him look as though he was always walking in a hurry, sweeping round the corners of that cloister in his scholar's gown with some special and rather overbearing intent. Conventionally cut, his hair was already rather thin, revealing the dome of the skull. As people did then, he dressed to look inconspicuous and even poor, in flannel trousers which had long outworn any hint of a crease, a brown sweater in danger of unravelling at the elbows, his familiar tweed coat.

It's been twenty years and more since Alexander was there, but certain impressions remain as vivid as ever: the porter's lodge, and the search for one's name on type-written lists, just as at school, and the confrontation with so many strangers who might prove friends or competitors, or both. In the other room on the landing of his staircase was Simon Smith-Dawson, a small and slippery fellow who affected a red waistcoat. To him, Oxford was the station where the passengers jostled to obtain first-class seats on the train to higher success. Look at that man with greased hair, he would say, he already sees himself in the Cabinet (and the prophecy has indeed proved accurate, much to Simon's ironic pleasure). Look at all the embryo television producers and presenters and pundits strutting about, this university is where the media high priests are taught their sacraments. Simon himself was sending articles to London newspapers, and had already clinched a job on the *Birmingham Post*. It was his speciality to know everything and everyone, introducing a supposed Habsburg descendant, and someone who was the only Westerner ever to have spent two years in Maoist Sinkiang (on a forestry programme, according to him, but certainly a spy, Simon said); also a Soviet diplomat seconded to St Antony's; and the son of an international trader based in Singapore who had rented a manor out at Hanborough for his three years; American Rhodes scholars, a Greek, several Italians due to inherit family businesses and impressed by Alexander's familiarity with the Piccolominis at Mugniomaggio, a Nigerian reputed to be a paramount chief. 'And me,' Alexander used to say, 'descendant of orphans and expatriates, as my father liked to rub in, born a bloody foreigner.' It wasn't Brideshead, but a coterie of sorts all the same.

His tutor was an elderly man with a crabbed expression slipping sideways, as though after a stroke, so that his speech came grinding through clenched lips. 'The ideas on Horace in that essay you wrote, whose were they? Yours, really? I never encountered better in a young man your age. It's not a first you should be after here, but a chair, if you want it.'

Professor Sir Alexander Lumel, OM, FRS, Simon used to tease him, that's how you'll turn out. You ought to make it your duty to read Cyril Connolly's article every Sunday, and learn the pitfalls.

Alexander's first piece of writing was commissioned by Simon, who had a contract to edit a collection of essays intended to be by and about their contemporaries, 'What the young are really thinking,' in Simon's words. It was to be another Gollancz book, typically angry and slender. It was harder than it had seemed to put together a composite portrait of the undergraduate as careerist, spiking the fellow with the slicked-down hair whom for no special reason he regarded as an enemy, and trying to get the measure of the television grandees-to-be with their know-ingness and mutual back-scratching. When the proofs arrived, he flinched at prose that seemed muscle-bound in expression, shallow in concept. Professor Zaehner, to whom he went for special tuition, said about this essay, 'What you ask about a writer is, does he have a moral position? It's the equivalent of asking whether a country has the rule of law. Nothing else matters.'

At the beginning of his third year, when he and Simon were moving into digs, Ursie came up too. From the outset, she had an inseparable friend, Val, properly Valerie Russell, blonde, and more robust than her waif-like looks might suggest: they were to hunt as a pair. They fitted into the circle of friends around Alexander and Simon, and perhaps on that account delighted to take their distance from others, especially from the cat-loving principal of their own college and her squad of frowsty and broad-hipped dons. The women in this place, Val said, make you think of cracked linoleum. One quick route to unpopu-larity was to remove bicycles from the racks provided, and ride off. Their main achievement was to oblige the law-abiding to buy and use padlocks for their property.

Ursie read modern languages, specifically Italian and French, in both of which she was already fluent. Otherwise I expect I'd have been sent down, she now thinks, I was pretty intolerable. Dame Helen Gardner saved my life. I don't remember quite why I had to go to her rooms, but I did, immediately spotting what was on the wall. A Napier drawing of her, in charcoal, very flamboyant, it couldn't have been by anyone else. How do you know, she asked me. It turned out that she'd been to Varendy, taken there by the Huxleys before the war. I think it tickled her to hear someone like me talking about all that sort of thing, we were not supposed to have heard about Iris Origo or people like that. She took Val and I under her wing. One time Dame Helen came out to the villa, and pretended to recognise Dina from years ago, but I don't think she did.

In the summer vacation, the two of them would go to La Grecchiata, as in old days. They lugged out suitcases of books, but a good number of these somehow remained unread, what with the arrival of Simon and Val and others to stay, or the daily skirmishings between Luciana and Giulia, and the need to attend to Dina. Julian would be staying with his aunt Anna Karcz in Sant' Ambrogio; Sally might be at Corubbio with her mother, Lady Una Macleod.

Swimming pools were then a rare luxury, part of a way of life imported from America and not quite native yet. The one installed at Mugniomaggio was hidden behind high clipped laurel hedges, it had a ceramic surround and gleamed the brightest blue. Behind it was a wooden pavilion in which to change, and where lunch could be carried out on dog days, with everyone too lazy to walk back to the house. Come whenever you like, Sandra Piccolomini invited them. And they did. The social life of La Grecchiata was often transposed there.

Nico Piccolomini had his mother's skinny physique and the same intent expression, as if it was always worth making the effort to listen to what other people were saying. Nothing seemed to have come to him from his father, except perhaps the confident sense of who he was. In his red Ferrari he made the roads dangerous, teaching himself to corner at high speed, even into the approach to Mugniomaggio, yelling *Cretino* at whoever might be in the way. Nominally a law student, he did little except drive huge distances to parties or in pursuit of a girl. He set himself targets that couldn't be met, sixty minutes to Rome, one hundred and twenty minutes to the sea, three hours to Naples; four girls every month throughout the winter, but only two between May and September, the serious months for love. On a pile of damp towels in the pavilion by the swimming pool, he seduced Ursie.

This means we're engaged, he told her, you should leave Oxford, your degree hasn't the slightest significance to you or anyone.

If she stayed with him, he let it be implied, then he

would certainly be faithful, they would marry and have children and Mugniomaggio would eventually be theirs. But if she were to abandon him on his own, then it would be hard; he knew himself, he would chase other girls, and who knows, they didn't all have scruples like hers.

You don't go staying out all night, Luciana said to her, nor spending all your time with Nico unless you're in love. I wasn't born yesterday. I can tell how things are.

Marry him, Luciana urged. You'll be riding on the pig's back. A *marchesa*. They're millionaires, the Piccolominis, billionaires probably, you'll be able to snap your fingers and have everything you want. It's a paradise.

If he can't wait for me, she answered, then he himself isn't worth waiting for.

Luciana spoke about love as though it were an inconvenient obstacle to clear thinking. Don't waste a moment, she used to repeat, and what does it matter if he runs off afterwards? All of them do, it's in their nature, men can't help themselves.

That was the year when Ursie understood that she wouldn't marry Nico and wouldn't get a good degree either. One couldn't concentrate, one had to muddle through, there weren't solutions to the problems of wanting more than one thing at once. What made it worse was that it was also the year of Alexander's twenty-first birthday, and Maydeswell was made over to him. Nothing was said about treating her on an equal basis.

'I shan't myself ever live here again,' Dina said, 'My life is in the villa from now on. Your father's reasons for going abroad were sound.' But she reserved a right to return, imposing upon herself a condition that she would in that case pay the expenses. She said to Alexander, 'I wouldn't ever want to be in your way.'

He asked, 'How could you be?'

A meeting took place, in London, in lawyers' offices at Lincoln's Inn. It was another occasion for Lionel to take command as though by right. He introduced a colleague of his, Dr Albert Golaz, from Geneva. Lionel unpacked from a briefcase a number of files.

'Oh didn't you realise?' he said. 'Your father made me his executor, I've been putting the whole estate into shape. Here we are.'

Maydeswell, it appeared, was now the property of a Swiss company, of which Dr Golaz was a director. You're the beneficiary, Lionel assured him, all you have to do is send him bills. Also he'll send you your allowance, you're a very fortunate young man. Separate arrangements existed for the villa.

Now when Dina repeated that she wouldn't want to stand in his way, she seemed to him almost too emphatic, he wasn't sure how to handle the remark. And there was Lionel explaining what had happened to Andrew's holding of Vickers shares; unfortunately nothing could be done about them, a sale was not advisable, the tax liabilities would be most unfortunate.

Outside it was an early spring day, and in the centre of Lincoln's Inn cherry trees were in flower, like pink cotton wool. Dina patted Alexander's face, fingers extended, tap-tap-tap. 'You're independent, the whole of life's before you,' she said, 'that's what we always wanted for you.' Over her shoulder, Lionel loomed, as stiff as if he had been buckled into his blue coat with a velvet collar. Off to a lunch to celebrate the morning's work with his mother and Lionel, Alexander experienced a contrary feeling, of being manipulated by means of the fat files in that briefcase. You signed on the dotted line, and you heard that you had become financially independent; everything had changed, yet nothing had. Once before he had felt this hollowness, when going down to the football pitch at school, to play a game as though he had not just witnessed his father's cremation.

Lionel brought Minou to Maydeswell for a birthday dinner. Mrs Ackroyd would never do for such an occasion; he engaged caterers and chose the food and wine. No doubt he must have forgotten that he had ever given him a watch, because now he presented him with an expensive one, like his own, on an expanding gold strap. By the time that he came to make a speech, he had drunk too much.

Afterwards he backed Alexander into a corner. I like these friends of yours, he said, good chaps they look to me, you ought to visit the one in Singapore and that Nigerian and the Greek, those are the kind of contacts that come in useful whatever work you're doing.

'He's not as bad as I'd imagined, not like Alexander makes out,' Simon said to Ursie. 'Vulgarity and champagne are no crimes.' Had this much-discussed lawyer ever hit her? She shook her head.

In the course of his last year, Alexander holed up often at Maydeswell. Days would pass when he was by himself, filling notebooks with jottings from what he was reading, sometimes breaking off to walk through the wood at the back of the house, in the direction of the abbey. It's not healthy, Mrs Ackroyd would complain, you'll do yourself an injury, you'll be stale, and don't you have any ideas of your own that you've always got to be poring over those books? Now and again, he missed something from the house, for instance Dina's writing table, and some of the chairs. The packers came for that, Mrs Ackroyd said, your mother wants those things over with her, and you can't stop her, how can you, it's her right.

After his finals, he was called in to an interview with the examiners. The one with the cadaverous head was Professor J. L. Austin. 'It was a pleasure to read your papers,' he said, and he stood up to shake hands with a series of shy disjointed movements. 'And what will you do now?'

On the spur of the moment Alexander answered, 'I shall write about perfectibility. The perfectibility of man.'

'An admirable but incompatible junction of words.'

Appreciation of Professor Austin's paradox was the purpose of this education.

Because there was no other obvious alternative, because he had become accustomed to the rut of studying and proved his aptitude in it, he stayed on to prepare a doctorate. And because, and because, he told himself – do I need to justify what I do? Self-discovery is justification enough for all the professors of the world.

Of all people, it was Professor Zaehner who jolted him out of it. He himself had been in intelligence during the war, in the Middle East. Such a timid man to have had such adventures. The cradle of civilisation, Zaehner said, it's not a mere phrase, see it for yourself.

An advertisement in a newspaper caught his eye, for a trip across the Sahara, from Algiers and Ghardaia down to Tamanrasset. So he bought a rucksack and walking shoes. Twenty-three of them were on this tour, sixteen of them girls, and they had more or less identical new rucksacks and walking shoes. The company organising this tour was actually one man and his truck, with roof and sides of tarpaulins which could be reefed in. It was September, the heat was intolerable. Following for hundreds of miles a line of lamps which retained sunlight, they drove only at night. Passing trucks or lorries in the other direction, the girls sang and clapped their hands, to establish that in spite of appearances they were having a good time.

I loved Tamanrasset, Alexander says, and for a bit I wondered if I wouldn't study the Touaregs. I found someone to teach me what he knew of their script, very unsatisfactory though, you can't really date anything of theirs. Coming north again, I met that archaeologist, Graziella, she was working at Volubilis, that was a good dig. Then I spent a year or so on the west bank of the Nile at Luxor. My job was to pull in tourists and rent them bicycles to ride round the Valleys of the Kings and Queens. It gave Mahmoud a kick to have me touting.

My dropout years, Alexander says, my hippie stint.

He never wrote to his supervisor with the news that he was abandoning his doctorate. Long stretches passed when Mrs Ackroyd would ring up Dina in the villa, or Ursie in London, and complain that there was nobody to tell her anything of his plans, should she put sheets on the bed, or what. He might sneak into a Sheraton or an Inter-Continental to write a necessary letter, and to telephone Dr Golaz in Geneva about arrangements to forward funds.

In a hostel in Zaamalek, he met a talkative young Englishman, who turned out to be the nineteen-year-old Bruce Chatwin, already shaping any number of books in his mind, including the history of nomads and nomadism which he was to research on and off to the end of his life. Chatwin proposed that they go together to Afghanistan: the Hazara, he said, would be more rewarding than the Touareg, and besides he had an introduction to a tribal chief. They would winter with the man, they would see Herat, Kabul, Ghazni, find out if Robert Byron had told the truth in his earlier account.

As far as I remember, Alexander says, it was Bruce's friend in Rawalpindi who asked me to bring a suitcase through the customs for him at Heathrow. Of course we knew it was smuggling, but nothing dangerous, good heavens no. Only currency. You can't shift money legally out of places like that. Service with a smile, and Bruce hadn't a bean either. All I had to do was hand the suitcase over to a man in a turban in the Terminal Three car park. Twelve-and-a-half percent was my commission. It was a fortune. Daddy liked to boast about stuffing fivers into the Armstrong-Siddeley to beat exchange controls, he'd have approved, why not?

What can we do, Ursie used to ask, if that's how he wants to spend his life? It's his choice. It wouldn't suit me.

With her Italian and French, she worked as a translator in an agency. She moved to a public-relations firm, then into the City. She bought a flat. She had affairs, not many, more like consummated friendships.

'What's wrong?' Val used to ask her. In much the same spirit that her grandmother might have undertaken charitable activities, Val had become a social worker.

'Better than to be like you,' was the answer, 'divorced, and with two children you positively dislike.'

On occasions when she ran into Simon, he used to say that the greatest shock of his life was that Alexander had turned out a dud. Just to think how we teased him as the future Professor Sir Alexander Lumel, OM, and he's incapable of getting his act together. You know what, Simon says, I have a lasting image of him, it was one evening after a garden party somewhere behind St John's, I think. There was that girl in your college, the one who looked quite pretty from behind, and then you saw her face. They left together and when he thought nobody was looking Alexander bundled her into a ditch, her shoes flew off, he got on top and did her. Farmyard stuff. Didn't I warn you that he wasn't taking the Connolly lessons to heart?

'It's a question of finding the courage to horsewhip Lionel,' Ursie said. 'That would make a grown-up of him.'

The Sixties were like that, the Swinging Sixties, when doing one's thing had replaced the socialists as masters.

SEVEN

Usually Dina is awake before dawn. The thin beige curtains on her windows scarcely keep out the light. Whose rooster is it which has the same sort of effect on her as an early-morning telephone call? Why hasn't its neck been wrung? Round about seven, it is that tinny church bell from Sant' Ambrogio, on Sundays the deeper one. To pass the time, she listens to the radio, its earpiece a close fit. Foreign correspondents have the run of the airwaves at that hour. From all around the world, she absorbs reports of ministerial changes, attempted or real coups, threats, preparation for war, significant trends, the latest statistics and the shining rainbow's end of sociology. Unknown though they are, the correspondents come through as reliable, dull, trustworthy, or venal and poorly informed and plain stupid, just on account of an inflection or the rise and fall of the voice.

In winter the cental heating in her room taps a Morse code of its own, drip-drip-*drop*, recognisable but not quite intelligible, like the conversation of a senile friend. Closer, under the skin, is the tick of the pacemaker, with a timing all its own, to be sensed lying like a bullet slipped into the chamber of a revolver and waiting for someone to pull the trigger.

I shan't want to see you for years, Professor Vierchowod had said. Rejection of a pacemaker by the body is almost unheard-of, that little gadget will be your willing and humble slave, laying down its life long before there's any question of you laying down yours.

Visit your friends, the professor said, and didn't you tell me you used to go on those organised Hellenic tours?

Yes, she had invited Anna Karcz to the Dodecanese, and

64

she and Una Macleod had sailed in the Aegean on a ship with several hundred others. Never again; there were too many old ladies like themselves. And yes, Elsie Crane-Dytton rented a flat on the Grand Canal every September, and used to press the beauties of Venice on her, but a little of her went a very long way.

After the rooster there is a period of whining *motorinos* and Vespas, as the village prepares for the working day. Sometimes the revving and backfiring sounds wanton, deliberately to disturb, but nobody would dare to roar up the drive, to set the gravel scattering under her windows. Behind her are two square pillows, and a bolster under the neck. On the bedside table, in due order, is a clock so that she can pace herself to the moment of Chantal's tactful knock, a glass of water, the photograph of the children at the age of seven and five, still mercifully obedient, smiling in grainy but absolute innocence of the world's disorder surging in through the earpiece of the radio. To her at least the ebb and flow is predictable, a sort of mill-race which surged in a narrowing channel between Presidents Kennedy and Nixon, Khrushchev and Brezhnev. She has a soft spot for Suslov the Soviet ideologue, and for Castro and Muammar Gaddhafi, mainly on account of their style or looks (she is the first to admit the irrationality). On the writing table shipped from Maydeswell are the latest books by such personalities, or biographies of them, from the scholarly to the downright scurrilous: she reads everything relevant.

The knock on the door might signify a mouse scurrying, so tactful is Chantal, balancing a tray with the pills prescribed by Professor Vierchowod, and a fresh glass of water. On the counterpane, the nurse places yesterday's newspapers, because the post arrives so uncertainly. *The International Herald Tribune*, the *Corriere*, *Le Monde*, the *Neue Zürcher Zeitung*: early morning is the moment appropriate to lighter features, gossip even, in the aftermath of the radio and the news.

I've never met a woman with a better brain, Pippo Piccolomini likes to tell everyone, there isn't anything on

65

which she is badly informed. She is, he says in his special English, a geyser of knowledge. Nobody likes to contradict her either. Anna Karcz has the reputation for being the only person ever to have convinced Dina to change her mind. 'A.J.P. Taylor's book on the origins of the last war is a disgrace,' she said, '*I* knew Lipski, *I* worked with Beck, and when I read that horrible Taylor it was like being persecuted all over again.'

In the months of Dina's convalescing after the operation, Una Macleod used to come often, and sometimes early in the morning, too early for Dina to have finished with the papers, and to be dressed and downstairs. Daughter of a Scottish earl, Lady Una is also the widow of a diplomat, whose last posting had been as ambassador to Bucharest. Tall but with a stoop of the shoulders, Lady Una has clipped white curls with the look of a terrier. Almost invariably she is in a cashmere jersey, a polo neck, and a pair of trousers. Even at La Grecchiata, in the bedroom too, she likes to be accompanied by her Alsatian, and she shouts 'Lambkins!' at it, in a way which unmistakably encourages it, even when the dog lowers its muzzle on the counterpane and leaves an outline of saliva slow to dry.

'Can't be bothered with clothes myself,' Una says. Dina has her distinctive style: a skirt in a range of grey and chestnut brown or maroon, thick in winter, but in linen for the summer, with the hem to the mid-calf; and a long-sleeved shirt with a tie as part of its collar. Every so often she drives to Rome for more of the same clothes, and likes the company of Una or of Sandra Piccolomini on these shopping trips: they pick out shoes with heels too low to be in any danger of tripping, and handbags to match. 'I never buy anything for myself,' Dina says, which really only means that she hasn't the patience to be selecting this rather than that, saving time and energy by eliminating novelty.

Po'ra baronessa, Luciana sighs, sometimes even to Dina's face as she comes downstairs, and certainly whenever she talks to Ursie on the telephone. It's terrible to be so lonely, she insists, to have nobody to talk to, to be alone at meals. Luciana has italianised Chantal's name into Chiarella, but appears to think that the nurse hardly rates as a person.

She is sure she is being kind, just as Ubaldo believes that he is expected to wear white gloves in the dining-room, and black gloves in the Armstrong-Siddeley.

This loneliness is a matter of perception. Dina feels that huge demands are made on the time when she might be reading, what with all the entertaining and telephoning done by the neighbours, kind and well-intentioned as they are, Nini Canavese and her deaf husband Roberto ('I'd rather have Lambkins slobbering over my hand than him,' Dina says), and Jacques Lemasle with his lunch parties and impossible French friends, the Francks, she from the Argentine and he an industrialist whose company had done business with Andrew, Leonora Pigri the Milanese art dealer whose ideas make headlines, Roddy Berkeley and the Whitakers, the Hagelunds, Martin Cammaerts who had spent his life as an administrator in the Belgian Congo, and who likes to relate in grim detail how whatever the Europeans did to the Africans has been nothing like so harmful as what Africans have done to themselves. '*Tshombe,*' he once said to Dina, '*était joyeux comme un bébé éléphant.*'

Lawyers and doctors besiege the elderly. Avvocato Bellini is the successor of Dr Grazioso, and he is top-heavy with a centre of gravity somewhere around the hips. His large face is the livery hue of putty. No matter what the time of year, he wears a three-piece suit. On the occasions when Dina used to go to his office, a cell of a room fit for a monk, she would be distracted by the width of his desk, with to one side a photograph of himself on a grouse moor, ponderous amid cartridge bags and bandoliers enough for a guerrilla, and on his head a tartan bonnet complete with woollen pompom. In the exercise of his legalese language with its past tenses and subjunctives, she would lose the meaning. Since she has been ill, he condescends to sit in the *salone*, graciously refusing anything to eat or drink.

He has power of attorney, and pays the servants every month, as well as the utilities and taxes, standing protectively between Dina and the demands of the Italian state. Acronyms such as INVIM and ILPEF and SIPA clutter his speech.

One longstanding topic is an ancient right, or *servitu*, whereby the drains of the villa are carried under the olive orchard, to empty into a septic tank which happens to be situated in an adjoining field belonging to one of the Sant' Ambrogio villagers. Every so often, this man deliberately breaks the pipe, causing seepage and a stench for which he then claims compensation. His suggestion is that Dina should resolve this point of contention by buying the field, each time regretting that she has not taken advantage of his previous generosity and now he must ask for millions more lire. Avvocato Bellini is quite as stubborn. According to him, this man is only one among several with claims to ownership of this field, and in addition everyone is watching to learn if money will change hands. Who knows what other *servitus* might emerge, what historic claims there might be on the villa and its land? Cheaper by far to have Armando and a friend repair the damaged pipes until the next round.

Those with property, Avvocato Bellini likes to emphasise, must be aware that everyone covets that property, and they have to protect themselves. He has her will locked up in his safe: an Italian will, whereby under a law inflexible since Napoleon first formulated it, the villa must go to her children. Codicils are something else. Who is to have the Golovin portrait, or the black sable fur she never wears?

As for Dr Melegnani, he conveys urgency. It is his habit to hop out of his car on arrival, involving himself with whoever is about in the kitchen, sitting on the sofa next to Ubaldo and dipping Luciana's homemade biscuits into *vin santo* provided by Armando, while looking at his watch and rebuking himself for idleness which is evidently to his credit. His tie never quite knots into the buttoned collar of his shirt: his hair is stalky. His jackets are so humped and creased that he seems never to have removed them, certainly never to have sent them to be cleaned or pressed. A bachelor. Sandra, Una, Nini, Mrs Franck, they swear by him. By the time he is ready to attend to Dina, he leaps up the stairs two at a go, cultivating Chantal by trying to give her a series of quick little slaps on the behind. 'You Italians,' she fends him off. He answers, 'I wish I had nurses as good as you working for me in the hospital.'

Wonderful progress, he always assures Dina, we're back to normal. You ought to exercise more. Not always sitting and writing. Walk, bend and touch your toes. Then you'll sleep better, and won't need your radio.

Once a quarter, year after year, Dr Golaz has travelled down by night sleeper, to bring in person the accounts and statements of the portfolio, and they have analysed them together. The sight of the Quarretti ceiling is enough for a string of exclamations. Fidgeting, he runs his hand over his face, as emaciated as an army veteran's, and he is prone to whip off his spectacles to polish them with the handkerchief from his breast pocket. His appetite is not just for food, but for literature and Italy, and Dina's ideas about history and politics.

For the spring and summer visits, he likes to be accompanied by Isabelle, his wife: this is something of a tradition. The two of them converse about the villa and its interior and the garden and even about Dina, as though she weren't actually present and listening. *Oui, ma chérie*, he says, *quelle culture générale*, and she sighs, *une personne tout à fait exceptionelle*. Part of the routine is to undertake each year a major piece of sightseeing, to have Ubaldo drive them in the Armstrong-Siddeley to Siena, Perugia, Monte San Galgano, on a search for Caravaggio or Pontormo paintings. For these expeditions, Isabelle Golaz wears walking shoes suitable for the Alps, with white socks rolled down over their uppers. She sports a green hat in folk-costume style. She buys postcards of places where they stop, and accumulates them in a square shoulder-bag containing first-aid items for an emergency.

Another regular guest has been Holly Strickland. A bad

penny, as she puts it, always turning up. Well before the pacemaker operation, Holly Strickland had written out of the blue, to introduce herself. An art historian, she had been the advisor for the British Portraiture exhibition held at the Royal Academy in the winter of 1971. Thanks to her, John Napier's portrait of Queen Marie of Romania was included, the first occasion that this picture had been allowed by the Communist authorities to leave the former royal palace at Sinaia.

In her letter, she explained that she had understood that the contents of John Napier's studio were now at La Grecchiata. This was the moment for a revival. Taste was changing, the public was rejecting non-figurative painting in favour of professionalism like his. Could she be allowed to look at the collection? She might embark on the long-term project of a *catalogue raisonné*. Dates were proposed.

Holly Strickland is compact, she has no figure to speak of, her dresses a shapeless cotton in some vaguely oriental style. It was all Dina could do to stop herself from asking the woman never to wear her sandals, because they clacked maddeningly on the floors. A necklace of semi-precious or at least polished stones dangles on her flat chest. When she speaks, she adds emphasis by moving her head from one side to the other, thinking to please, and this necklace thumps on her ribcage. In her excitement, what she says can sound winsome, even precious. She talks for two.

'How could you leave such a treasure trove up here?' was her shocked reaction on being led up to the attic where the paintings and drawings were stored. 'A tile has only to slip in a storm, and you've lost the lot. Water damage.'

With Ubaldo and Armando to help, she transported the collection to the guest room in the centre of the corridor. This became her office; the bed a desk of sorts on which to lay out whatever she was working on. She herself slept in Alexander's room, with its posters of Gina Lollobrigida and Fausto Coppi.

In the light of what was to happen, some people were to say that Dina had simply been lonely. The claim to a vision: what else is that except escape from solitude? A widow, they said, and her children never there. Luciana, for one, thinks that this is the complete explanation, and she is always saying how much better it is when the *professorina* is around, taking the place of the children and what ought by now to be grandchildren as well. Yet the villa did not really offer some kind of living death. Lovable, fascinating, a phenomenon – that was the kind of language used about her by the neighbours, cosmopolitans receptive to a character like her, and also in search of anyone who could help them to entertain their guests.

October 10th happened to be the day to mark the break between what was past, and what was to come. Since every detail was to acquire such significance, no doubt it was not a coincidence that it would have been Andrew's seventy-fifth birthday. Since the April vision in Assisi, she had recovered: everyone said so, not only Professor Vierchowod and Dr Melegnani but Luciana and Chantal and her friends – Jacques Lemasle had told her he was positively looking forward to having a pacemaker by way of rejuvenation.

That night she checked that as usual the photographs and glass of water were in their due place. She slept normally, and woke some time before dawn, to turn to listen to the radio. Recently Martin Cammaerts had been drawing her attention to the wholesale looting of Union Minière in the Congo, and now some commentator was describing the condition of that once-great company, and its trading difficulties with the price of copper as low as it was. Martin Cammaerts evidently could be relied on. And then followed an account of the efforts of the Tupamaros to destroy the state of Uruguay; this would lead, she heard, to military dictatorship.

The wavelength, she was almost sure (and slightly riled by the small element of doubt), was the BBC World Service. The commentator's voice faded out, and without a break Andrew cut in. I'm here with you, my darling little May, my little Miss Naps, he said, in that crisp Cole Porter intonation he used when pleased with how things were going. Their snug vocabulary had been so private that

71

nobody besides them could have known it. Not for a second did she doubt his presence. There was nothing to fear.

We have work to do, he continued, to Unite the Impossible.

And what might that mean?

It was possible that interference silenced the radio temporarily, or that her sense of time became disturbed. At any rate, a lengthy period seemed to ensue before he explained himself. Remember that flat you were living in behind Sloane Square, he said, when you'd just escaped from occupied France. How the bathroom was so cramped you practically had to be Houdini if you were going to squeeze past the basin to the loo. I used to walk from the Air Ministry or my club. How I kept you waiting. And there'd been that frightful raid the day before we got hitched at the Chelsea Registry Office when they flattened the church, which one was it? Glass all over the streets. No honeymoon, not then and not after either. There was a war to win. An unlikely couple, you'd have said, but it worked, after its fashion, wouldn't you agree? That's what we have to teach the world. Unite the Impossible. We showed that with Iris Warren too. It can be done. People *are* reconciled.

That morning she had missed the insistent rooster and the church bell. It was highly unusual for Chantal to have to wake her up, to lift the radio off the bed and tidy it away.

'Madame is tired?' and at a second glance, 'Is something the matter?'

'Ha h'm.' This singsong answer – a sharp high note, then a low hum – dated from that night, a characteristic intimation that she possessed a secret whose significance couldn't be shared.

A look at Dina's fierce black eyes, and the pouches like moats below, told a story. In the kitchen they tried to guess what might have happened. It couldn't be said that Dina was ill and Professor Vierchowod or even Dr Melegnani ought to be summoned. She ate properly, she read

72

her newspapers with the same attention, accepted an invitation to lunch with the Whitakers and had a long telephone call with Jacques Lemasle which included some remarks from him about the merits of Bernard Shaw as a music critic, to which she listened patiently.

At one level she's functioning all right, Holly Strickland said to Chantal, but at another level she's gone absent.

In that early period of his communicating, Andrew was loquacious – this was not always to be the case. Dina went to bed early in order to be sure not to miss him. It was on the American Forces network in Germany that he repeated his instructions about Uniting the Impossible. On Radio Monte Carlo, he interrupted a programme devoted to Glen Miller and his dance tunes, to give her another key phrase. The world is harmonising, he said, and it will do so to a greater extent once you spread the word. Ordinary people can't follow the process, they're too caught up in trivialities to see the grand design. Some things are pushed to happen, others are blocked from happening.

Pushed and Blocked. So there was a universal purpose, and Andrew and Dina were to be its agents. History was leading mankind back to the Garden of Eden. You've been reading the papers, Andrew said, you can draw the right conclusions.

It isn't a dialogue, though. Andrew does not answer questions. On Italian Radio, on the BBC, out of Moscow or Madrid, he gives orders and has his way, as had been the case in life. The autocrat still.

All human life is one, Andrew says, distinctions between the churches are man-made and irrelevant to our needs. The churches will help her to Unite the Impossible.

'I want a notebook,' Dina said to Chantal, 'for my ideas.'

In Sant' Ambrogio only floppy school pads were available, with chequered pages of close-knit vertical and horizontal lines. At the sight of one of these, she had one of her classic rages, ripping the pad in half and ordering Chantal out of the room. That was also the morning of one of the small coincidences which extended this whole

chain of events. Still angry, she set off to the Whitakers'
for lunch. They lived on the far side of the Valle
Tremaldi, and the way there lay through Ponte a
Maiano, a market town where in the past she and
Andrew had bought things for the villa. It was not like
her to wish to visit the antique shop but all of a sudden
she insisted on it. Ubaldo dropped her there on the
pavement while he drove off in search of a parking place,
and she walked in, as though inspired, to pick out
straightaway the notebook she had had in mind, a
nineteenth-century affair with a blue velvet cover and a
gilt clasp. Pushed and Blocked had had its first practical
demonstration.

This notebook was to contain what she called her
Flowers of Meditation. These seemed to spring up fully
formed, as though a line in a poem or a musical phrase.
The very first one in the notebook, written on her return
from lunching with the Whitakers, reads, 'In a mystical
union, there is the bliss of final serenity.' Also written at
this time before Unite the Impossible was out in the open
is, 'Everything except God ends in disillusion.'

Something's up with our friend, Leonora Pigri said to
Peter (actually Mrs) Whitaker after lunch, but I couldn't
worm it out of her. She looks like someone who's won the
lottery. Can that good-for-nothing son of hers have got
engaged?

Some people spread the rumour that Leonora Pigri is
the bearer of the evil eye, and they say that after an
encounter with her they have lost a brooch or heard bad
news. She's altogether too fond of anything occult. Other
people of course point to the success of her gallery, and
the many articles in the press about her influence on
contemporary taste. Holly Strickland, for one, says that
few people have done as much as Leonora in promoting
fresh ways of seeing the familiar. After that lunch, at any
rate, Leonora telephoned whomever she could think of to
pass on her impressions of Dina. She's changed, she said,
even the voice is different, she's in touch with the
beyond.

And still it might have come to nothing if it hadn't been for Sandra Piccolomini who took seriously Leonora's telephoning. It could well have been a matter for the doctors, schizophrenia to be treated with pills or a prolonged stay in the *casa di cura* to rest the body after the pacemaker's insertion. Or it could be Pushed and Blocked on its predetermined path.

Sandra Piccolomini in old age still believes the best about people, it's an almost constitutional inability on her part to imagine that anyone's life could fail and fall apart. The optimism is as admirable as the curiosity – qualities which have given her the looks of an extremely bright hen, brilliantly scratching. Generous with time and money, she races and squawks all over the place, the patron of charities and good causes. Her favourite priest is Monsignor Silvestri, and she invites him to hold Mass in the chapel at Mugniomaggio (the fresco on the west wall is sometimes attributed to Il Sodoma, presumably because the faces of the Christ and his disciples look so soppy). Have you ever seen eyes like his? she asks of the monsignor. It's all in the eyes.

Monsignor Silvestri had known the *squadrista* who once lived at La Grecchiata, and has heard that the man successfully set up in business in Genoa, in the docks, breaking up ships, notably surplus American destroyers. He's not someone to forget a significant detail. The *Campo*, for instance. That was a gift to the children of Sant' Ambrogio which made a huge difference to their health and happiness. Indeed he'd heard of the English benefactor, and would be delighted to meet his widow.

In his youth, the monsignor had not been your ordinary seminarist but something of a sportsman. A paunch now slips this way and that under the buttons of his cassock, hardly restrained by the wide sash. Sideways on, he has the profile of a small bear. The head is intelligent, the forehead high and the jaw like a prow, altogether in the cast of a man who senses his success and relies on his charisma for further advancement. His writings are part of the career. *Crisi del Cristianismo* describes how the

Church overcame the Reformation and the so-called Age of Enlightenment, and today must rise to the challenge of nihilism and atheism. The succeeding work, *La Chiesa di Oggi*, is a passionate advocacy of the ecumenical movement. Christians have to join forces to survive, then to conquer. Whoever he is addressing is pinned in that intelligent gaze which Sandra so much admires.

Luciana recognised the monsignor although they hadn't seen one another, they calculated, for thirty-three years. And this villa, he said, always so beautiful, and this ceiling is perfect. Who plays the piano, he wanted to know, flicking over the Diavelli scores. Your husband did – and he bowed in Dina's direction with the sincere respects due from one music-lover to another.

Explaining why the monsignor was accompanying her, Sandra said, 'Leonora's insights can't be resisted, my dear. She *feels* these things. Lunching with Peter the other day, she had one of her intuitions about you.'

As Sandra tells the story of that afternoon, it all came pouring out of Dina. How she could never have imagined such a development. How Andrew had been contacting her that day at Assisi, it was his first move, and quite obviously she hadn't collapsed and didn't need the pacemaker. Why ever had she allowed that to be inflicted on her? Only because of helplessness at that moment. You never knew which wavelength he'd be on, you twiddled the knobs and there he was, he might have been in the room.

We went for a walk in the garden, Sandra says. It was a marvellous sunset, so to speak painted by Tiepolo, the way we sometimes have them in late autumn when everything just seems to be in its right place. I'm not usually one for anything mystic, that's not my idea of religion, I'm a practical person. And I don't care for religious mania, you know my grandmother – she was a Gaetani – she almost ruined the family with building churches all over Italy. But a glance at Dina's face showed that it was all true to her, she believed every word of it. I hadn't the heart to do anything except nod.

Pippo says, 'It's not in Sandra's nature to play spoil-the-games.'

If it makes her happy, they think, then it can't be wrong. It's doing nobody the least harm. Better than taking to alcohol like Betty Hagelund who can't really be asked to dinner any more, and certainly can't play bridge afterwards without sliding off the chair. Monsignor Silvestri was highly impressed, and that was a factor too. The Church needs reinforcements in the fight against materialism and consumerism, he said, clasping his fists together militantly, it doesn't matter where our recruits come from, they all help. He took Dina's arm, and they walked and then they sat on that seat where the old well is.

Shown the Flowers of Meditation, he ran his fingers over the velvet covering of the book. Not an English speaker, he had to have the entries translated. They lose a lot in Italian, Dina told him, as she struggled to render, 'My sweet one tells me that to be pessimistic is devil's work.' Also, 'Do not criticise, only love.' The last to have come to her at that point was 'Loving has a reality unknown to thinking.'

You are the new Joachim of Fiore, the new Teresa of Avila, he told her, Your gift is of the highest order, I shall make it a duty as well as a pleasure to tell the cardinal. This must be preserved and published.

Sandra says that on the way back to Mugniomaggio, Monsignor Silvestri was lost in his thoughts, repeating from time to time what a truly remarkable experience the return to La Grecchiata had been, how unexpected. In what people and places, he sighed, faith was renewed. It never failed to amaze him.

Now it was Sandra's turn to telephone. Unite the Impossible became common property. My old friend, my old canasta partner Andrew, Sandra spreads the news, has taken to becoming a radio star in the afterlife. On wavelengths of his choice. Dina says she hears him, and he's a prophet in his way, he tells her what is about to happen. Even the weather. She doesn't have to worry any more about carrying an umbrella. If it's fine, it's because he's smoothing things out for her. Monsignor Silvestri, such an angel, he's terribly impressed. Can you believe it?

Anna Karcz sounded doubtful, but Sandra warned her not to upset Dina.

I don't think I'd be too welcoming to my Harry if he spooked me in the small hours, Lady Una said, but darling, you and the monsignor must know best. It's really easier to believe in Unite the Impossible than not, isn't that so?

Among those who believe that the monsignor egged her on to the next and irrevocable stage is Jacques Lemasle. A sceptic, a good old-fashioned Third Republic anti-clerical, that's me, he says, and he remembers how his father had campaigned to have the Jesuits slung out of France all those years ago. 'They've got their eye on the main chance, the whole pack of them, I shall have it out with Dina,' he promised, but he didn't. The Proofs put an end to that. After the Proofs, nobody could imagine confronting Dina.

She had been listening to the usual German comment-ator pontificating about the wickedness of the United States, and in particular the stationing of foreign troops in his country, when Andrew silenced the man.

In my room there's a present for my Miss Naps, he said, and when you find it, that'll be a proof.

My Proofs: Dina was to sound combative speaking of them. The word itself seemed to burst out of her like a bullet from a rifle. Tell me about your proofs, friends and visitors used to ask, looking in some trepidation at the panda-like whiteness of her face with its two black rings for eyes, and intimidated by the humour which infused the conviction. Were you to laugh or cry?

Naturally I couldn't wait, Dina says to her friends, not after hearing that. So I got up, and put on my dressing-gown and went to investigate. Luckily I'd preserved his room the way it was. The Golovin portrait fills it with his presence. But I had no idea what I was looking for. A present, he'd told me, but not where it was, nor what it was.

An early riser, Chantal immediately understood that something was amiss. Dina's door was open, while down the other end of the corridor the lights were on in Andrew's room. Burglars, she concluded. Going barefoot in order not to be heard on the stairs, she ran to find Ubaldo and Luciana. The three of them whispered in the kitchen. If it were burglars, how had they broken in, and what about their getaway. A shaking Ubaldo took a kitchen knife, and Luciana brandished a useless torch.

None of us like to go into that room, Luciana confides, We all feel the same. Even Giulia, and she's got a will of iron. Those yellow curtains, and the dreadful picture of the *barone* which is always looking at you, you can't hide from it. We don't even want to dust there. Someone's over your shoulder. You could give me a billion lire and I wouldn't sleep there, no, not for anything in the world.

'*Madonna!*' Ubaldo said. 'What is the *signora baronessa* doing?'

'And why are you waving that knife?' Dina answered. Then she sat back on Andrew's bed, and repeated, 'Ha h'm. Ha h'm.'

Behind her, the room was disordered. To begin with, she had examined his suits one by one, and jackets and trousers lay over the red tiles of the floor. Comb and hairbrush, pocket diary, slippers were now in the centre of the bed.

'Let's go to our room,' Chantal helped her.

She's very easy to deal with, the nurse's pretty smile implies, like a lamb once she's understood that she's going to have things her way. It may have looked mad, but not once she'd explained to us what she was looking for. That was the first time any of us had heard about these Proofs. I knew about the Flowers of Meditation, yes, I had to make sure the notebook was safe after the fiasco of trying to buy one in the village. But Proofs were still new.

In the middle of the morning, they returned to Andrew's room with Holly Strickland in tow – Signora Strigi, is the best version that Luciana can offer of the harsh English consonants. Everything had to be searched for this present, whatever it might be.

I have not the slightest doubt we'll find it, Dina says.

One of the pieces bought from the shop in Ponte a Maiano was the chest of drawers which has a bow-shaped front. In the third drawer down, shirts had been folded away. As these were being lifted out and examined, a small packet wrapped in tissue paper slipped to the floor. Inside were polished stones, the colour of treacle. A dozen in number. Polished, lumpy in a beetle shape.

'My witnesses!' Dina exclaimed. 'You have all seen this Proof, you can all swear to it.'

'Are they valuable?' Luciana asked.

Beyond price. Nobody had dreamed that these stones might be here until the *signor barone* had told her about them. Proof, he had said, and proof they were. She paid no attention, perhaps did not even hear, when Chantal suggested that it might be a case of forgetfulness, the stones could have sunk into subconscious knowledge.

Where, Dina wondered, had the stones come from, in all likelihood Kenya, unless it was South America. She was to ask Barigliani the jeweller on the Ponte Vecchio in Florence, and he confirmed that the stones were agate. Not the best quality, he added, but that may have been because he feared that he would be asked to buy them and had no intention of doing so. Inexpensive cufflinks might be made out of them.

As for the written account of the discovery, Dina insisted that her three witnesses sign it. This she sent off by registered post to Monsignor Silvestri.

Before he could reply, though, Andrew had spoken again, interrupting the announcement of one of the first murders perpetrated in the country by the Red Brigades, still largely an unknown quantity, of an industrialist in Verona, his body dumped at night on the steps of the distillery he had owned.

The flower in my room is also for you, Andrew had said. A flower for my May in this December.

This particular Proof came to light more quickly, in a plastic measuring beaker, in the medicine cupboard in Andrew's bathroom. A rosebud, hard and dry as a nut, possibly all that was left of a buttonhole once picked from the garden. Chantal said, 'Monsieur must have looked so handsome.'

'Ha h'm.' Uttering this know-all noise, Dina can wrinkle her nose, as if literally smelling out truth.

Such resistance as there was to the Proofs was organised in the kitchen by Luciana and Ubaldo. Early in the morning they began drinking grappa, and as they did so, their suspicions of Chantal hardened. The woman was too good-natured, and therefore must somehow be taking advantage of the *baronessa*. This whole thing would finish badly. If you won't fetch Don Alvise, she said, I will. And so she did, by herself after dark, with a shawl wrapped over her coat, a padded figure more fit for Siberia than the nearby village.

In recent years Don Alvise's air of self-martyrdom has shifted, as though he has internalised his suffering and can almost take pleasure in the good it is doing him. In spite of his appetite, he has not put on weight, still the scarecrow, still that eggshell of a skull, the Adam's apple bobbing with all the animation of a rubber ball up and down in his scraggy neck. Those frightful teeth have a graveyard flash whenever he smiles, as he does more frequently, a new spectator of the world's comedy. The eyebrows have thickened and as a result the brown eyes have a marvellous spiritual look. Nobody could possibly mistake his sincerity as a man of God.

'Monsignor Silvestri has been in touch,' Don Alvise said to Luciana. 'What can I do?'

'I can't be watching Chiarella and Signora Strigi all the time,' Luciana protested. 'Ubaldo helps me, but neither of us are as young as we were. My legs, I have circulation problems, Dr Melegnani recommends me to take the weight off them.'

Change has come about in Don Alvise's life through his literary success. Modest about it, he says that he began to write because the evenings all by himself dragged on and on, and he couldn't bear the loneliness. *Pier Paolo and his Friends* was his own story, he might have been just such a teenager, coming from a community in the south, poor and uneducated, with no prospect except crime. Organised local criminals treat his Pier Paolo as their mascot, and he happily falls in with them and their crimes. The priest awakens his conscience, and with his help Pier Paolo finds release from his racketeer employers. *Benedetta and her Friends* is a companion volume, about another fortunate escape from poverty and deprivation.

Agitating his beautifully shaped hands, he likes to say that it was his good luck to have sent these two stories to the right publisher, a firm specialising in uplifting literature. Simple morality tales, that's all they are. Printed on paper so cheap that it starts to brown at the edges even when new. By the terms of his contract, he has been delivering two stories a year, and these flimsy paperbacks sell well – *Neri and his Garden, Guggo who Loved Animals, Gelsomina and the Butcher's Shop*. The intention of the series is to have a story about every boy and girl in his imaginary village.

'Shouldn't we inform Alessandro and Ursie?' Don Alvise asked. 'But what can *they* do?'

Don Alvise makes no bones about it, that he had been postponing a meeting with Dina, and had simply put out of his mind the need to respond to Monsignor Silvestri. I have a tendency to escapism, he admits, and the *baronessa* is sometimes, what shall we call it, alarming. I shall invite myself to lunch, and don't you laugh at me for tucking my napkin round my neck, I become nervous in a house like that and the food spills down my front, especially if there's *sugo*.

I asked the *baronessa* – Don Alvise continues – how the voice is when she hears it. And she answered, 'It's as if he is with me in the room, he might just have come in.' That's exactly what she said. Of course I don't know anything about wavelengths or broadcasts. Sceptics will say that you want to deceive yourself, I told her, or that this is an after-effect of your operation. Remember the vision at Assisi, she replied quite sharply, he's obviously trying to communicate.

In fact he had sat on one of the leather chairs in the *salone* and listened intently while she explained Unite the Impossible. Nothing there was in conflict with the policy or teaching of the Church. Pushed and Blocked: a sound metaphor for the will of God. Standing up, he had moved to the window to stare absent-mindedly at the dark cypresses outside, his head at a submissive angle.

Finally he bent over Dina, to take her hands in his and declare, 'I am a man of faith, I believe in Proofs like yours.' He would hold a service in Andrew's room, a service of dedication and prayer. The good people in the house would be glad of that. On the very next day, what's more, before lunch.

So they prepared for it, placing on the chest of drawers the agate stones and the dried rosebud, Andrew's pocket diary and even his slippers. Winter had set in early that year, and the morning of the service was overcast. Electric light had to be on, and everyone in the villa gathered between Andrew's bed and the Golovin portrait, including Giulia and Armando, who never made a secret of their anti-clericalism. Don Alvise swung his incense burner to and fro until the room was hazy. Praying aloud in Latin, he asked for divine blessing on the *baronessa* and her purposes.

The first that Ursie and Alexander heard of what had been happening was from Sandra Piccolomini. Head-strong, Sandra said, there's no arguing with her, and I'm not sure I want to. My friend Monsignor Silvestri has full confidence in her, they're in the closest touch. But I'll tell you why I'm ringing, it's that she feels she must have a Christmas present for your father, he deserves something back for what he's given her. We've made one of our expeditions to Rome, and chosen for him a bolster to place on his bed. It's got strips of blue ribbon at the ends.

I can't leave the office, Ursie said to Alexander, I'll take extra time off at Christmas, but meanwhile you'll have to go and suss it out. There's a whole new vocabulary that's dead tricky to follow. The doctors assure me she's okay physically, this is all in the mind.

Chantal has always refused to talk openly on the telephone, for fear of being overheard by Dina. As usual, Luciana is overcome by her emotions and pleads for Ursie to rush to the villa. It's her remedy for everything. Returning home for Christmas, Holly Strickland was in contact. In every way, she reported, Dina was herself, as politically informed as ever, as bright, still visiting the neighbours, but on this one subject she was, well, disturbing. You didn't quite know what to do with yourself when over lunch, for instance, she might get into her stride to explain Andrew's latest directions. You squirmed.

'Business responsibilities', as he called them, kept Alexander in London. The latest of his ventures involved Pet, who parted her hair in the middle, forbiddingly Victorian. A textile designer, she had ambitions to launch into fashion, starting a shop of her own, another Biba or Mary Quant. Nothing about her appearance suggested colour or style or flair: like Alexander she wore jeans with a tear at the knee, and a leather jacket. If we do go, Alexander said to Pet, I'd better warn you that practically none of my friendships have ever survived a visit to the villa.

Actually, Alexander likes to say, I broke off with Pet in the end because she was always pestering me to give her a child. Thirty-six or whatever she was, and if she didn't have a baby then, it would be too late. How she banged on about it! I had to tell her that I wasn't interested in releasing unmarried mothers into the world. Then we had hysterics about abortions. That's the crap that marks the end of a relationship. Time to run for cover. But that Christmas at the villa before it all blew up was terrific. Pet was in the big spare room with the Napier drawings and things all stacked up everywhere. And Dina couldn't have been nicer to her. The two got on like a house on fire.

Cold weather had set in. As a result, the harvesting of the olives had been mistimed. At first light, the pickers assembled, elderly men with their wives and as many grandchildren as they could muster, embedded in jackets and scarves and mittens. Under the trees they spread tarpaulins. Hand-made, the ladders had wobbly rungs on which it was easy to lose footholds. Alexander loved to join the others, to climb those ladders and sit astride the fork of a tree, shaking and stripping the olives until they pattered like hailstones on the tarpaulins, rolling deeply into the folds of canvas. Once in sacks, the olives were loaded on to a handcart and lugged round to the *podere* behind the villa, dumped under the arches outside the *camera del Tedesco*.

Dina and Pet walked together to the orchard, figures as shapeless as any of the pickers, their breath visible in the cold even at midday. Even such limited physical exercise as this seemed out of character for Dina, a lady-of-the-manor act. But afterwards she accompanied the others to the kitchen, where Luciana had prepared a meal.

We'd finished the harvest, Alexander says, and I think it was still before Ursie had managed to come out. Dina was suddenly so affectionate, making the effort with Pet, that I couldn't help feeling sorry for her. Those who know the family have always pointed out how sentimental we are. Maybe sentimentality was just the obverse of Dina's frightful temper in old days. And that Ha h'm of hers, it was the first I'd heard of it. There *was* boasting in it, that she knew more than we did, but I could detect a sort of plea not to probe too deep. Aren't old people vulnerable? Yellowy teeth and skin like a sponge-bag, and all that. I couldn't help noticing. One evening I was in her room, and the boiler downstairs was conducting that maddening dialogue it has with the radiator. I asked if she wasn't cold. No, never, I've got my Flowers of Meditation and my Proofs to keep me warm, that's how she answered. Tell me, I said. So she did. I had the book in my hands, it's rather handsome in its Victorian way, and I read the entries through. They were better than I'd expected, that was a surprise. If only she'd had any formal education, some kind of intellectual standards by which to judge herself. On that occasion she must only just have written, 'The freedom most needed is the freedom to love.' You can go and check it in the book, but I think I'm probably word-perfect. Why, I said, that's very contemporary of you. I expect I got a Ha h'm winging back, and then she was away about how Monsignor Silvestri or Cardinal Suenens or some big shot had written an article she approved of. You never could tell if her head or her heart would come out on top. She could be awfully touching, couldn't she? What a battle she fought with herself.

Christmas at La Grecchiata had always been low-key. Armando used to buy a tall tree, and it stood undecorated except for candles at the foot of the stairs. There was a whole day of rain, and the temperature then dropped to leave a glaze of frost on the ground, such a frost that in the morning icicles hung in glittery spikes below the gutters and the tops of drainpipes. Then snow began to fall in flurries. This weather delayed Ursie's flight.

I walked straight into it, Ursie says, I'd been listening to Ubaldo all the way from Fiumicino. It was Christmas Eve, on the autostrada it was all right, but the backroads were more or less white. I don't remember ever having seen the cardinal's arms above the front door under snow, sort of eyebrows on the stone. Anyhow I was terribly late, and the others were all getting ready to go to Una's. I was exhausted, and longing to get out of it. The trouble was that they'd arranged to go on to midnight Mass at Mugniomaggio. You can't just say you'd prefer to curl up in bed with a book. Dina had had fetched this famous fur coat of hers, it had been stored for ages in a zip-up cover with camphor balls. That's a smell which depresses me. Anyhow she had made up her mind that she was going to wear it to go to Corubbio. Russian fur, very black, it must have been gorgeous when it was new. Giving it to her, my father must have been in one of his post-war moods of extravagance. She couldn't have worn such an ostentatious coat in Italy then, with everyone else in cheap mackintoshes. She'd had it fetched out of store just to make an effect at Una's.

What had happened was that Dina had put her hands into the pockets of the coat, only to find a scrap of paper, about two inches square, with the words written on it,

'Happy New Year, Darling,' in Andrew's unmistakable jagged scrawl. This fragment had been torn, evidently with care, from an old sepia postcard, and the picture side of it showed what must have been part of a cottage, and the word 'Devon' in the kind of white lettering aimed at tourists.

Dina looked radiant. 'The timing,' she said. 'You have all seen how this happened, you are all my witnesses. My own children can't deny it. He used to go to Devon, there was some War Ministry establishment at, I think, Barnstaple. What was the reason for tearing off this corner, I can't for the life of me imagine, but it must be so that I could show you Pushed and Blocked in action. Here's another Proof. How blessed we are.'

Because they didn't seize the opportunity then and there, so they agreed afterwards, they never could. In retrospect, they ought to have decided against driving over to Una's, and sat down instead to have things out. As her children, they had a duty to look after her and to explain what others were too frightened or amused or self-interested even to hint at. Would she have listened, come to her senses, been able to analyse the underlying causes, whatever they were? Wasn't it more likely that one of her volcanic rages would have exploded, the eyes deepening into bags of hate and resentment, to throw them out of the villa on Christmas Eve itself, to excommunicate them, and cut them off without a penny. Admit it, Ursie and Alexander have concluded, we were cowards, we *are* cowards. Not just cowards, humbugs.

It was like some mad game of hunt-the-thimble, Ursie says. Oh, she's made me feel such a hypocrite. If really we'd loved her, we'd have spoken our thoughts.

We did the right thing, says Alexander, the *only* thing. What would have been the point of depriving her of hope and comfort? If she needs fantasies, so what? Where's the harm in it? Of course the phenomenon must go back deep into the roots of that marriage. Having to do with guilt, frustration, lack of fulfilment of some fundamental kind, probably founded in the prolonged absence of my father, and the way they lived apart, in different countries even. It can't be coincidence that they were so polarised between Maydeswell and here.

It had been the fear of death, according to one of Ursie's theories. The pacemaker must have seemed like the eternal footman taking her coat. And they'd noticed how sometimes her hand used to creep up to feel that the pacemaker was still in the right spot, keeping up the good work.

'Dangerous,' Dina said, 'a few snow flakes like this? Una's asked everyone, it would be unkind not to go.'

Corubbio has long since been divided into flats. The entrance turns under a gatehouse leading into an interior courtyard; and through yet another arch are the former stables, where Lady Una Macleod lives. At night, lamps along the outer walls throw a dim saffron flare which makes the house seem massive, its walls like spectral cliffs, its scale that of a whole village. Cars everywhere.

In her evening black trousers and black cashmere sweater, Una displayed the vanity of someone who doesn't want to be thought vain. Leaping and barking at new arrivals, the Alsatian streaks through the door as if making for a throat, and 'Off, Lambkins, down, you good boy,' Una shouts at it. She looks a bit like a dog herself, as lean as a greyhound, or a Dalmatian. In a hurry that evening, or in the poor light of her bathroom, she has applied white powder in streaks, with her finger-tips, any old how. Already a number of friends are present, but they can never be enough to spoil the perspective of Una's long room downstairs, presumably built to house carriages, and now with at its far end the outsize Allan Ramsay portrait of the fourth earl in regimental uniform. 'My nephew badly wants it back,' she likes to laugh, 'but fortunately the Italians don't dream of letting it out of the country.'

The Buonaccorsis were there, with cousins of theirs, and the Francks, Nini and deaf Roberto Canavese, so much older than his wife, the Hagelunds and two Americans all the way from I Tatti, and Una's daughter Sally and her husband Tom. Dina's looking terrific, they said, she's so thrilled to have her children with her. Now that's what I call an exceptional woman. Eccentric, if you like, there's no need to go all the way in accepting her ideas, but there's nobody quite like her.

'In Foligno,' Nini Canavese said, 'there's a mother and daughter who are clairvoyant. We visit them regularly. All they need is a sample of your handwriting, though they do like to hold something of yours in their hands, a comb will do, or your pen, even a shoe. *Stupendo*. They're nearly always right, they foretold exactly what would happen to my uncle Claudio last year.' And what did happen? 'Lost his money. He was cheated of his fortune.'

'To my mind, Dina Lumel is the most extraordinary character it's been my good fortune to meet. She's just been telling me about her latest Proof, she found it just this evening. It's been in a handbag where her late husband left it.'

'In some clothing, you mean.'

'Yes, I said her handbag.'

Out in Africa, Martin Cammaerts thought, they'd make a cult of her, they'd build shrines. That's how public opinion forms out there.

The snowstorm passed. Behind the last of the fleeing clouds were stars and a moon to throw a relief over the silvery landscape. In a procession, the cars drove to Mugniomaggio. Along with Pippo and Sandra in the chapel were Nico and his wife, and their three identically dressed little daughters. In her hand Dina held on to the latest Proof, and in her mind she was calculating when exactly she was going to place on Andrew's bed the bolster which she had bought him as a Christmas present, and quite what would be appropriate to mark its dedication. Christmas, said Monsignor Silvestri in his brief address, was a time for a new vision which was also a most ancient one, and he stared at Dina when he said that this was a moment to Unite the Impossible.

EIGHT

Proofs had a timing all of their own. In a week there might be two, or months could pass without a new one. In the pocket diary, Dina discovered the page on which Andrew had jotted down 'little Miss Naps' birthday', which happened to have fallen some ten weeks after his death. So he had been thinking about her. Then his watch had been lying in a drawer, and its face had become discoloured or tarnished, so that she could pick out in the smudging an unmistakable profile, brow, nose, indentation for mouth, certainly Andrew's. 'Look at the command,' she said to Anna Karcz, savouring the word for connotations that were military, making of Andrew a commander, the leader. What a good-looking man he was too, Anna agreed, I'm not a bit surprised you ran off with him. Old-world courtesy is natural to Anna. There is nothing spare or out of place with her, the skin draws tight across the bone of her face stretching out wrinkles, and all you need to know about her past is resumed in the delicate and apologetic smile. After a lunch in the villa, or simply during an evening call for gossip and the news, Anna likes to lower her voice in her too-perfect Polish French to Chantal, 'It does her such good, one can only encourage it.'

The insurance certificate of the Armstrong-Siddeley, and the Green Card valid for the continent and issued for the original journey out to Italy, fell out of the *Guide Bleu*. The documents must have been there for twenty years and more, in spite of the fact that this guidebook had passed through so many hands on so many excursions. Among a pile of old letters, Sandra Piccolomini had unearthed one from Andrew, full of effusive thanks, and including the phrase, 'It's such a blessing to have you helping us move into this heaven-sent new home of ours. It will suit us down to a tea.' A private joke, possibly, or a misspelling, a lapse of his English. He was brought up in Holland, Dina explains, but he never had a trace of an accent. Time to get ready to join him, Sandra laughs, time to put everything in order, I spend my day tying up parcels for Nico to untie the moment I'm no longer in the land of the living.

One of the most evocative Proofs was contributed by Holly Strickland. She had found a Napier drawing in quick and light strokes of a pencil, evidently a doodle, and whimsical because it can only have been done before the war when Dina and Andrew had still to meet. This showed the figure of an angel flying upwards, robes a little disarranged so that the legs extended bare up to the calves, and the halo was at an angle in a slipstream. Underneath, as for a cartoon, was the caption 'My son-in-law'. The Donatello look, Dina tells her friends, like on that statue in the Duomo museum, the one with the mouth open, it revealed his inner self, the secret man who was unreachable. Just how he had shown himself in Assisi. Whatever could have made my father depict an angel? If you ask me, Una Macleod told her, you must have had a row with him, and he was getting his own back with the idea that only an angel could manage you, and he'd be a flustered angel at that.

Dina was delighted. Happy as a sandboy, in Una's words. Ask any of the friends, and they will give the same answer, that Dina had never been better than when the Proofs first appeared, never so light-hearted. The Ha h'm could be a bit off-putting, especially if she said it in front of someone who hadn't known her before. Also she developed a little habit of humming, even tuneless singing under her breath, especially if she was out in the garden. We're all in need of a bit of consolation, they say, and really if it was a touch potty, it wasn't much pottier than the rest of us. Was it any odder than the way Una drools over Lambkins and keeps the wool she brushes off him because she wants to see if it's possible to card it and spin it eventually into a sweater? Any odder than Sandra siding with Nico against his wife when the whole world knew how he'd had a child with that woman in Positano?

Among ourselves we talked about her incessantly, Anna Karcz says, I loved her charm, I have to admit. One accepted the religion with a pinch of salt.

Soon the Proofs were too many and too vulnerable to be left on the surface of the chest of drawers in Andrew's room. Giulia and Luciana handled them whenever they dusted and there was a risk of spoiling them; the light might also cause fading.

'Only you can really provide the meaningful explanations,' Monsignor Silvestri said, 'for posterity's sake you have to write a precise description of each, with its significance, and then we must find a safe deposit.'

Someone who did regular work for the Church was the owner of a small leather business in Florence. He and his brother and three elderly ladies occupied a ground-floor shop with a roofed-in yard off the Lungarno, and there they made boxes or cases for chalices and silver plates and objects of worship; also for surgical equipment. The street was too narrow for the Armstrong-Siddeley. Dina and the monsignor shook hands with the brothers and the ladies of the staff. It was an honour to be chosen, the owner said, the monsignor had explained already what was required, and he would certainly be able to provide what was wanted, something appropriate for the Proofs of Unite the Impossible. Samples were laid out. Carefully Dina chose a dark green leather for the covering, and a velvet lining to match on the interior. The Proofs were to be contained in a box the size of a small suitcase, fitted with trays, some of which were to have lids, to contain more fragile Proofs, the rosebud for example. Right across the top of this case, the words 'Proofs of Spiritual Realities as Experienced by Andrew and Edwina Lumel' were to be inscribed in hand-tooled gilt lettering about an inch high. The monsignor thought this appropriate, the owner of the shop gathered his sketches and notes, the listening ladies nodded at Dina with approval.

Ursie heard of this development only after it had happened. She had forced herself out to the villa for a long weekend. 'You should have been here ten days ago,' Chantal told her, *'quelle histoire, c'était affreux.'* The owner of the leather workshop had delivered the finished case in person. Certain of a triumphant reception, he had handed it over in the *salone*, and watched eagerly while Dina tore off the brown paper wrapping.

'I thought she was going to have a fit,' Chantal says, 'I've never seen such a transformation in anyone. The face went black. The colour of gangrene. She choked in her rage, she was far too angry to tell the poor man what was wrong. Like a scarecrow he just stood there, not understanding a thing, but sort of flapping his arms.'

The name had come out wrong, misprinted in the gilt lettering as 'Lumen'. I wasn't sure the pacemaker would stand the strain, Chantal said, she was all anger, in a pure state, a laboratory experiment in anger.

'The eyes,' said Ursie, 'don't tell me, I can guess.'

The others came racing out of the kitchen, they thought it had to be murder, but all of us together managed to explain to him his mistake, and to get her upstairs. He went away practically in tears, tears of fright, mind you, that's an afternoon he won't forget. By the time the monsignor arrived, Madame had quietened down, he's awfully clever with her and reads her moods marvellously. And it hasn't been as bad as expected. The case came back within the week, with the error corrected. The monsignor brought it, I don't suppose the other man had the courage for it.

'You are wonderful,' Ursie told her, 'I don't know what we'd do without you.'

'I like Madame, I admire her. I've never met anyone like that before.'

That Chiarella, Luciana chattered in the kitchen, Ubaldo and I don't trust her, nor the monsignor either. What are they up to? They want to get their hands on the *baronessa*'s fortune, that's their game. You listen to me, if they have their way there'll be nothing for you. Where's it all going to end? Do they think we haven't eyes in our heads?

The case with the Proofs was bulky on Andrew's chest of drawers. I want you to see it, Dina said to Ursie, Unite the Impossible is spreading, and Monsignor Silvestri is one of the Church's coming men, he's supporting me.

If you'd been in my shoes, Ursie says, what would you have done? She hauled me off to Andrew's room. There was that wretched and hideously expensive box, and you could see on the lid the outline of the N underneath the L. It's indented there, although they've done a brilliant repair job. She never mentioned it, so I hardly could. It would have been to spoil things. She opened it and lifted out the trays and showed me her Proofs. I simply can't decide if I'm to blame, and if so, for what. In actual fact I said that she ought to have the famous photo with Churchill blown up and put on an easel, to make a pair with the Golovin portrait. At least that kept her busy for a while.

In my opinion, Ursie argues, Andrew's voice was a projection of all manner of hopes she really had for mankind. Sincere hopes. She's a frustrated idealist, that's where Alexander gets his character too. She ought to have been in public life or politics or somewhere where she could have put these kinds of ideals into practice. Andrew came on call, don't forget, in the aftermath of the 1973 war and the collapse of Vietnam. Fighting of that kind shook her because it negated everything that Unite the Impossible stood for. For some reason she hated Kissinger, she was irrational about him although as far as I could see he ought to have been the perfect agent for Pushed and Blocked. The doctrine meant that even if appearances were to the contrary, everything coheres as it advances towards reconciliation. A retrograde step in some part of the world might well be activating progress elsewhere. What a lot of mileage she got out of coincidence. In fact I've come to think that coincidence is the basis of religion. Pattern-making out of what's random.

Whether this argument was right or not, at least it rationalised Dina and her activity, making it possible to come for these flying weekends and for longer holidays, to insist that Alexander take his share of responsibility, and at meals to listen to her approval of Jimmy Carter's linkage of human rights to foreign policy, to the bias she showed in favour of Anwar Sadat, Samora Machel in Mozambique, Bishop Muzorewa in Rhodesia. The Camp David business was Unite the Impossible in real practice, analysed as though she herself had brought it about. The Cold War, she was saying long before anyone else was doing so, would soon be brought to some such ending.

'Monsignor Silvestri is on the left,' Sandra Piccolomini told Ursie, 'and Pippo laughs when he hears your mother talking to him like a parlour pink. But this is Italy, and you can't be disinherited. *La famiglia*. She can afford a green box, and you will have the villa. Don't worry.'

The box could not stay where it was, though. People must already have heard of the Proofs, Monsignor Silvestri said to Dina, and were probably imagining them to be fabulous treasures. Any burglar could make away with it under his arm. Then where would we be without proofs?

There would have to be a safe, and he found the exact spot for it, in the space at the bottom of the stairwell, on the flagstones leading to the back door out to the terrace and the *podere* beyond the rose garden. Right at the centre of the villa, the safe was to provide a reminder of its contents to whoever passed by. As protection, it was to have an appropriate dark red brocade cover, and a pair of candlesticks on top. No burglar would dare crack what looked like an altar. Things were bad in the country, but not that bad.

More, the monsignor presented her with a crucifix, in a majolica of the palest whites and ochres, on which the wounds of Christ were brightly stylised and splotchy. Ubaldo fixed it to the wall, and did not stay to watch as Dina and the monsignor knelt in front of it in a moment of prayer which served as a dedication.

'Your admirable work,' the monsignor said to her, 'is in keeping with the spirit of the times, is advancing that spirit. Unite the Impossible is attracting the attention, the keen attention, of the powers that be. We live in times we could hardly have imagined, when historic enmities are being reconciled. We must assure continuity, find a way of presenting and perpetuating your Proofs.'

That summer of 1975 was particularly hot. The rooms under the roof of the villa baked up by day so that it was hard to sleep at night. Visitors to La Grecchiata asked for nothing better than to swim in the pool at Mugniomaggio. During his short stay, Alexander slung a hammock out of doors for himself and the two girls he was taking on to Brindisi and the ferry to a Greek island. Albert and Isabelle Golaz made an excursion to the sea. The recent collapse of world markets in the wake of the rising price of oil had depressed Dr Golaz; he was advising Dina to consider cutting down on expenses. Multinational companies might well go broke, and now was the time to be as defensive as possible. Ha h'm, Dina said, but she felt too drained at that point to put an alternative view. In those sultry nights, Andrew was silent. Sending Chantal on holiday, Dina caught the train by herself to Venice, to be with Elsie Crane-Dytton. An errand of mercy too, for Michael Crane-Dytton had recently died of cancer. It was at moments like this for Pushed and Blocked to demonstrate what it could do.

The post brought the letter in which Bishop Harold Satterthwaite introduced himself. The Bishop of the Mediterranean, no less, *in partibus infidelium*, without a diocese, but on a roving commission round what he called the basin of civilisation. He had been hearing from many a mutual friend of her activities, he wrote, and he found them inspiring. Might he and his wife Catherine call next time they were passing anywhere near the region? Unite the Impossible sounded to him a concept whose time had arrived.

Over the coming two or three years, the bishop and Catherine were to be the most assiduous of guests, very much at home in the villa, not only friends but courtiers, and as such able to telephone from Rome or Siena to ask Ubaldo to fetch them, and to go straight through to Luciana to remind her how fond they were of roast veal and her pasta speciality with mushrooms. From Armando, they were to receive with many thanks flasks of olive oil and bottles of his *vin santo*. But at the end of that September, they appeared in a small hired car, in a countryside still parched, burnt to a dung-brown, with even the cypresses wilting.

'What a place,' the bishop immediately greeted Dina. 'What a view,' Catherine added. 'How they cultivate every inch of land in these valleys. Think of the centuries of husbandry. I don't suppose much has survived this frightful heat?'

The bishop wore a jacket once white linen but now a curdled cream in colour. On the cuffs of the sleeves, some of the buttons were missing, others broken. His panama hat had a black ribbon round it. A marmoset of a man, he had a low forehead and an exceptionally receding chin, with its characteristic suggestion of weakness, an elderly version of the boy who is always picked on at school, so physically defenceless that bullies long to see how far they can go. Shoulders rounded, he was bent with his eyes downward as if looking for something, on the trail.

'She doesn't mind being called Cath,' the bishop said, 'she even prefers it. Intimacy, you know.'

Catherine was a head taller than her husband, and would in any case have dominated; big-boned and short-haired, accustomed to contradict without being contradicted. Her dresses, in some floral pattern, seemed to have been made for someone else, and the hem of her petticoat often hung at the back of her legs, or its straps showed at the neck. 'She cuts up old curtains and chair-covers,' Una Macleod was to say of this appearance (but not, of course, in front of Dina). By training a chemist, she had taught at Cambridge, but now, she explained, 'I never think about my subject, I'm so completely out of date.'

'Don't you bother about that pipe of his,' Catherine said, catching Dina looking at it. The bishop had a habit of digging a grey thumb into the bowl of the pipe, then sucking on the stem as a baby does on a dummy. 'He only does that to give himself time to think out what he's going to say next. If there's any smoking to be done, he goes out of doors.'

'Good chap, Silvestri,' the bishop said, 'one of the best they have. Keen. And I'll tell you who else I've been talking to about you, our ambassador, Sir Gordon, he's interested in Unite the Impossible.'

On that first visit, as afterwards, the bishop could not have enough of the Proofs, questioning about the doctrine of Pushed and Blocked, and making her describe minutely how Andrew had appeared at Assisi. The timbre of the voice over the radio concerned him, and like others he asked whether this constituted a monologue or a dialogue. In Andrew's room, they stood in front of the Golovin portrait and the Churchill photograph. Dina unlocked the safe for them, and brought out the case of Proofs.

'You'll really have to write up the histories of each of these,' the bishop said, 'for posterity. Silvestri told me something about them, he's awfully taken with your ecumenical outlook.'

Nobody before the bishop and Catherine had been allowed to study in private the Flowers of Meditation. 'Some of these are outstanding, really good, like this one here,' and he read out, 'Miracles are the events of Truth'. One which he copied on to the back of his chequebook was 'What happiness it is to be completely humble before the sublime element in oneself'.

'It's remarkable that you manage to be humble,' Catherine said to Dina, 'considering this gift you've been given.'

'Nothing to do with me,' Dina's eyes were shining. 'I only report.'

Could the bishop copy out the whole of the Flowers of Meditation for himself? The original one day ought to be deposited in Lambeth Palace library: might he ask the librarian to contact her?

'Our friend values her privacy, she's not a missionary like you,' Catherine said.

'If I've learnt anything in life, Cath, it's that even the best work gets nowhere on its own, it has to be institutionalised. May I have your permission, dear lady, at least to look into the structure, the support system, you need for Unite the Impossible?'

A public lecture, he thought, or possibly an interview in a colour supplement, or a little book, going beyond his usual material, by Don Alvise. With the monsignor, he himself might organise an ecumenical seminar at the villa. Perhaps she would consider ensuring the future of Unite the Impossible by setting up a foundation in the villa to perpetuate it, complete with a secretariat, non-denominational, clerical as well as lay – he had ideas, he had contacts, he would take the matter up with the powers that be. Would it not, he asked, be tremendously exciting for her children? Surely they'd welcome the spread of her ideas and values, and Alexander might even want to be curator? Who better?

Sometimes Bishop Harold and Cath were able to stay only for a weekend, but on other occasions they invited themselves for a week or two. Playing truant, they said, from their other duties, but nothing was so important as this. When I have the privilege to be here with you, the bishop used to tell Dina, I feel made anew, I am reminded of God's purpose.

No doubt about it, Chantal is to say, Bishop Harold and his wife brought Madame a great deal. I would say more than Monsignor Silvestri, just because they were English, they spoke the same language. She used so much to look forward to their arrival, she wanted to look her best for them, and took trouble with Luciana to see that the meals were just what they wanted. Company for her. We were a happy family circle. She had people she could confide in. One strange thing, I noticed that Monsieur used to go off the air when they were here, you could maybe say that she didn't need him, she was too busy with them and their plans. As good as gold, she'd let me put her into bed, no fuss, straight to sleep, and the radio mightn't have been even touched in the night. For my part I was tremendously grateful to them for introducing Adela, once she'd joined our circle I had much less work, I could stick to nursing.

Originally from Haslemere, Adela Brockett had been engaged as girl groom to the Milanese biscuit manufacturer who had bought Roddy Berkeley's house at Bagni di Lucca, and spent millions on it. Soon she had married an officer in the carabinieri, and he considered a groom's job to be below their status. Part-time employment with the dean of the Anglican Church in Florence had brought her into the bishop's orbit. It was a long drive for her every day from her home to La Grecchiata, but she would consider it on condition that she received a travel allowance on top of her salary. The carabinieri officer insisted on meeting Dina and judging the set-up before he allowed her to accept.

Thanks to Adela, Unite the Impossible could find a shape. In Ponte a Maiano, she began by ordering a functional office desk, metallic and drab, and filing cabinets and adjustable shelving. These she installed in the library, hitherto a room which had been little used except for telephoning. Shifting the small desk already there, she arranged it so that she and Dina could sit side by side, if desired, with their backs to the window for the sake of extra light. A typewriter was bought, and a copying machine and afterwards a computer and word-processor. The record could now be properly maintained.

Unreliable, as late as noon sometimes, the postman chugged up the drive on his *motorino*, to deliver newspapers in four languages. It was Dina's habit to mark those articles which supported her view of the planet's development, and her prophecies of unity and harmony and peace: underlining in red pencil of the heading for politics, underlining in blue pencil for church affairs. Also three asterisks for those articles which were of major significance, and therefore to be photocopied and cross-referenced; two asterisks for something urgent, and a single one for the routinely progressive. Folders began to swell, marked America North and South, Africa, the Middle East, Third World, Industrial Nations; also individual holdings for those who held a key to Uniting the Impossible, the Secretary General of the United Nations, Pope,

Archbishop of Canterbury, Metropolitan, Catholikos, Patriarch, Sheikh of Al-Azhar, Ayatollah Khomeini (on the move from Iraq to Paris, where he was to be encouraged by Giscard d'Estaing, a cause for enthusiasm at first, though Dina later turned violently against him). Through Adela's files, Dina could track the current global pattern of international meetings and conferences, detecting in the movements of heads of state and their foreign ministers the outline of what was to come, on the lookout for appointments and demotions, the advances and setbacks that denoted Pushed and Blocked, the manifold jostlings and clamourings of mankind pressing in spite of everything towards the reconciliation which Andrew heralded into her ear in the night.

Adela has her hair cut short up to the nape of her neck, and butch it is too, with a sort of tuft on top, almost spiky, which she dyes blonde to reveal darker roots at the scalp. She exaggerates her mouth with lipstick of a modern scarlet, and her nails, painted the same colour, are like caps at the end of stumpy fingers. On fingers, wrists, neck, she sports what seem to be ever-widening circles of gold jewellery, because, she says, her husband is very particular about the way she's turned out, and she has to keep up appearances if she's to earn the promotion he deserves. Until then, they have resolved not to have children. Broad in the beam, she is in danger of putting on weight, especially since giving up horse-riding, but she conceals her figure in Italian versions of English tweed suits, elaborate with braid.

Kissing Bishop Harold and Cath, she leaves more than a smear of that lipstick on their cheeks. That doesn't work with Don Alvise, who shrinks back from her, priestly hands upraised, as though physical contact with her was a violation. To Holly Strickland, she makes herself extremely useful, taking shorthand notes and typing them up, helping with the classification. The first Ursie heard about this enlargement of the court was when she received a typewritten letter from her mother, with the initials EL/ AB in secretarial efficiency at the bottom left-hand

101

corner. Telephoning to ask about it, Ursie found herself questioning Adela, and on a day and at an hour when Bishop Harold and Cath, Una Macleod, Don Alvise, Holly Strickland and Chantal were already gathered in the *salone* before lunch. Quite a party, Ursie said, only to hear Adela replying that she 'would get back to you as soon as possible', office-style.

With the daily newspapers in the post come books, a good many of them sent by Monsignor Silvestri or the bishop. Works by Hans Küng, Reinhold Niebuhr, Father Schillebeeckx, liberation theologists such as Father Boas, Teilhard de Chardin and the commentators so faithfully chewing him over, Roger Garaudy, Cardinal Bea, the Hindu thinker Gupta V. Sen, the mystic Abdara, as well as the founders of Subud, the Panchen Lama, Professor Isakowitch the populariser of modern Sufism, Ellen Hitchcox Hierl and her Heralds of the Latter Day, Arthur Koestler and Sir Alistair Hardy's *The Divine Flame*, and *The Cloud of Unknowing* newly edited by the man who also wrote a biography of Evelyn Underhill. For the moment abandoning history, Dina reads what she can of these in every spare moment, scribbling her thoughts in the margins or on endpapers, sometimes writing longer appreciations which Adela has to type out too, and keep safe. Bibliographical details are also stored in a series of librarian's boxes made of a purple-coloured cardboard.

'Now that we're on a proper footing,' the bishop persisted, 'we ought to find our way to the public. Plant the acorn from which the oak will grow.'

The idea of the Newsletter came to him in an inspired flash, he was to tell her, out of the blue when he was sucking at his old pipe and casting about in his mind how he could make himself useful. You can issue them when and how you see fit, he said, it'll be your choice. A list of subscribers and interested parties will build, you'll be amazed.

Did she feel some hidden doubt or even shame? Is that why she was so secretive? Ursie thinks so. Christmas 1976, another Christmas when I schlepped myself out there,

Ursie says. For some reason I've forgotten, Alexander didn't make it that year. I hadn't twigged how swiftly the bishop had dug himself in, it was already far too late for me even to raise an eyebrow, never mind outright objecting. I couldn't have said anything except yes sir, no sir, three bags full. Cath never let me out of her sight, and the chinless wonder was closeted with my mother day in day out. He'd arranged for a printer in Milan, the man came down specially to do the layout and the artwork.

Volume I, Number One. Nothing if not ambitious. The Newsletter was to be more like a stiff card, folding in the middle, capable of being stood upright. Its outer page was almost completely filled with a photograph of the church of Assisi, though at each corner was a black-and-white design of a cherub, a head with wings but no ostensible body, apparently gazing in towards the church in the photograph. On the back was a selection from the Flowers of Meditation. In the centrefold was Dina's statement of faith, under the caption Unite the Impossible, set in bold – on the left in English, on the right in Italian, *Unire l'Impossibile*.

Whatever our religion, our colour or gender, we members of the human race are all one, brothers and sisters before the Sole Creator of the universe. I *know*. I have received the message from beyond the curtain which we call death, but which we have only to pull aside to reveal true life.

From 1941 to 1953 I was married to Andrew Lumel. An orphan born in Holland, he made his career as an aeronautical engineer in England, contributing in many fields. Nothing could have been further from my mind than the idea that a scientist such as he would make himself manifest after death. That happened! In the famous church at Assisi, so beloved and venerated down the centuries, he showed himself to me, like an angel, hovering overhead. Three short months later, he returned to announce that we have to Unite the Impossible. It is God's purpose for us. Ours is a time for

103

hope. Distinctions between one human being and another are invidious and man-made, destined to break down and vanish. This is true worship, this is the message of Unite the Impossible. As my angel has told me, we are advancing towards perfect peace. If blocked in some direction temporarily, then we are also pushed in another towards the universality of God which is to come. I have the privilege of speaking of these Spiritual Realities, as Andrew and I together and constantly are experiencing them. I have PROOFS.

The bishop was hesitant only about the expression 'hovering overhead'. That's how it was, he said, I quite accept that, but don't you think it may be too strong for your readers? After all, they'll come to you via cold print, not like me, in your beautiful villa where I can appreciate you and your works all around.

Monsignor Silvestri made himself responsible for the Italian translation. It was also his suggestion to add 'La Grecchiata', by way of signing off the statement. Of the five hundred copies printed, he and the bishop each took a hundred to distribute.

In the years following publication, correspondents have extracted the name and address from the Newsletter to write to her. The varied stamps from around the world have attracted the interest of the postman, and he asks if he can have them, for a son who is a collector. If he has a letter, he hangs about in the office until Adela hands over the envelope. One man has written from Jarandilla de la Vera in the Gredos mountains, and another from Un-quelleta in southern Venezuela. Four or five women, possibly members of a sect, appear to be supporters in Baguio City in the Philippines, but Adela has detected similarities in handwriting and paper, coming to the conclusion that it may be one woman using pseudonyms. The postman appreciates the colours and varieties of Philippine stamps, some of which are outsize, devoted to exotic flora and fauna, and unique in Sant' Ambrogio. There is also a married couple in Gatehorn, Arkansas, and someone in Iceland who claims to be a hermit, though in summer he guides tourists round the hot springs. An electrician has written from Donaueschingen. Some correspondents mail publications of their own which they propose to exchange with Dina. There have been requests for donations. Once a woman in County Cork claimed to have heard Andrew on the soundwaves of her radio, and this letter was considered a Proof. As Dina pointed out to Bishop Harold, the woman couldn't have learnt from the newsletter how Andrew chooses to communicate. A correspondent in Durban was angry, writing to complain that his reading of the Flowers of Meditation had led him to sell his house, thereby losing much of its value, and it is his understanding of Unite the Impossible that he ought to be compensated.

The literary style of the Flowers of Meditation prompted Iris Origo to write a kind note, congratulating her. Her favourite, she said, was 'The end of self is the beginning of God's love', and it reminded her of something very similar in a passage from St John of the Cross which at the moment she couldn't lay her hands on but would search out. (To Dina's annoyance, she never did so.) The Piccolominis asked for a dozen copies to pass on. In another age, Roberto Canavese went around saying, either she'd have been canonised or burnt as a witch. Anna Karcz mentioned the writings of Gurdjieff and Uspensky, both of whom she'd known at Fontainebleau in old days, but these rang no bell with Dina. Always original, Una Macleod told Dina that she could have done without the cherubs in the corner of the page. 'Little plug-uglies, you wouldn't want one of them coming for you.' She could get away with whatever she liked.

'I don't think I'll send one to my children,' Dina told the bishop, 'they're too limited, too caught in their own small concerns to be able to look up.'

'But you should,' Cath said sharply. 'They must be brought to face the future. Your work here has put down strong roots. It can't be interrupted now.'

I don't quite remember when I picked up a copy, Alexander says, but I must have been passing through, and I spotted the ghastly thing on Adela's desk. I couldn't bring myself to go to the villa very often or for very long. The madness felt infectious. You didn't know where to put yourself, it was embarrassing in a way I've never been embarrassed. Criticism was besides the point. You just had to listen. The grin on my face was as taut as a mask, and it used to set so that it was almost a muscular pain. Ursie took more of the brunt of that madness. She was quicker than me at realising that the priests ought to be considered babysitters, or perhaps more accurately attendants in the geriatric ward, they kept her mind occupied, and filled in the day. Obviously the priests were plotting to get the villa, and we couldn't imagine how to prevent them. Sometimes I had a fantasy of confronting the bishop, such a creep, but I knew he would go straight back to my mother and report what I'd said. Denouncing people, *fare la denuncia*, is the local sport in Sant' Ambrogio, the monsignor wouldn't have hesitated either. Who should I have turned to? The law? Lionel? You must be joking. Ursie and I decided early on that we'd lose the villa and nothing could be done about it. I don't even think I minded, except in a vague way that it was a pity. A chunk of the landscape gone.

Monsignor Silvestri brought the cardinal-archbishop to tea at the time when President Carter was convening the Camp David meeting with Anwar Sadat and Menachem Begin. That was a good omen. The outcome could not be in doubt. The world would be witnessing Unite the Impossible in action, even though as yet it might be unaware of that fact. All would be unfolded. With royal punctuality the cardinal-archbishop arrived at the villa at four o'clock, accompanied by the monsignor, and a secretary, whose words came out with a hiss of self-importance. On the steps of the house to greet this party stood Dina, Don Alvise and the rest of the household. Very frail, the cardinal-archbishop had a stoop, his eyes were watery, the hair fluffy and white under the scarlet skullcap, far more feminine in appearance than Dina, severe in her suit. He held one hand out to her, the other to Don Alvise. 'Not one but two such excellent writers,' he said, 'what is it about this place that has this effect? The climate? The water?'

Our ecumenical age had come too late for him. Look, he said, sitting on one of the tapestried chairs in the *salone*, I hardly have strength enough to raise the cup from its saucer.

After some dangerous rattling, he managed not to spill a drop.

Born in Fiume, he had been a boy in the crowd pressing into the streets to cheer the Archduke Franz Ferdinand and his wife on the fatal way south to Sarajevo. Who could have imagined the things he had seen? There was never quite time enough to sit down and write his memoirs, and besides he wasn't like the gifted writers of Sant' Ambrogio, he couldn't find the right words for his simple thoughts. Had Dina ever milked a cow? That was a dying art. Machines took away the pleasure and the skill of it. Sometimes he dreamed that he was back in the shed of his parents' farm, settling down with a three-legged stool and wooden bucket. The whole trick was to be regular in the action, neither too hard a tug nor too hesitant – and putting his cup and saucer down, he clenched his hand to demonstrate what he meant. Animals are ticklish. Stroke the teats wrong, hit the udder, and a cow will give you a nasty kick forward, and can catch you on the shins. He'd had friends in the Trentino whose kneecaps had been broken.

The stairs to Andrew's room were too much for him. Instead Adela fetched for him the 1943 photograph. 'A personality, evidently, as I'd heard,' he nodded. Then he walked with the others in a procession as far as the safe, and the leather case of the Proofs was lifted out for him to admire.

'It means he really trusts you,' Monsignor Silvestri confided to her, 'he talks about milking only to those in whom he has confidence. Sometimes he will describe how they used to make black sausage up in those parts.'

I never asked for an audience with the Pope, Dina says, that's not my style at all, I wouldn't have dreamed of it. But the cardinal suggested it, and it was an honour I could hardly refuse. Not that I thought it would really happen. At least not until Andrew warned me. 'Don't let this go to your head, Miss Naps, remember who is working for you, and why,' that's what he said several times between when the cardinal came to tea and I went to the Vatican. None of us, as the cardinal said, can do more than accept the love of God. I'd find his Holiness most accessible, he told me, and you know, that was true I admit, I was nervous. Who wouldn't be? Luckily I had Andrew.

Speaking like this, Dina never used to look as though she knew what it meant to be nervous. In full control of herself, you would have said. Possibly over-protected, purse-proud or at any rate cushioned by her fortune, but with not the least hesitation about her actions or the need to be justifying them. And there was humour in the expression, in the twitch of the nose, and in that mobile mouth, which made you wonder if in her inmost self she wasn't laughing at it all and surely wasn't going to be taken for a ride by any of this gaggle of priests? Too shrewd for that. There were also the ties to her children. In the last resort, conventional. Yet out poured intimations, hints, the matching of great ideas and trivialities, until reality itself wavered and melted, and she was left alone in patterns of her own making.

Four months were to pass before the date of her audience. In that time, she wrote in her Blue Notebook, 'History is not the offspring of Man but of God.' Also, 'I am of God, through God, for God. What then is the name of my religion?' And, 'I loved God in my angel, he loved and needed purity in me.' Of all the entries in that notebook, these were the only ones to be dated.

In those four months, Sandra Piccolomini planned everything for her, in a virtual campaign. He's a decent Pope, Sandra said, nice and jolly, you'll get on like a house on fire, in old days my mother-in-law found him a great help with her charities.

Together they drove to Rome, to buy a black dress of the proper sort, with a black hat complete with a veil. Of course the sable coat would have an outing. 'I'll ring up that Gordon what's-his-name, your tiresome ambassador, and I will have lunch with you there afterwards and Pippo if I can persuade him,' Sandra said. 'The post-mortem will be fun.'

'Are you going to talk about Unite the Impossible? Silvestri tells me he's passed on your booklet,' Pippo said.

Dina answered, 'I shall do what I'm told.'

On the day of the audience, a winter sun managed to break through a cold haze – 'it never fails,' Dina told Sandra, 'like a smile from Andrew.' Light reflected in a dazzle off the much-polished Armstrong-Siddeley. A special permit had to be fixed to the windscreen. Ubaldo stopped the car on the edge of St Peter's Square, outside the gate leading to the private apartments of the Vatican. Police and Swiss Guards saluted. Flocks of pigeons wheeled overhead at the comings and goings, and a noisy tourist group emerged from a charabanc. Sandra stayed with Ubaldo, while Dina was escorted down corridors, and into an antechamber lined with stiff-backed chairs. Someone in striped trousers and a tail-coat explained procedure and etiquette, how she was to kneel, how to address the Pope, how to kiss the ring on his finger.

Pope Paul VI then had not much longer to live. His steps were slow. The physical frame seemed to have not enough strength to support him. His face was oddly hairless, anatomical, an expanse of skin like old paper, but with folds and dewlaps at the neck. Since she had been born in France, as he had been advised, he proposed to speak in French, a language he loved especially, since he had been fortunate enough to be posted years ago to Paris as nuncio. And didn't she think that Balzac was the greatest story-teller of them all? *La Maison Nucingen*, for instance, that was magnificent. Ecumenical work like hers, he said, gave rich satisfaction, and he had heard of it with much pleasure and approval. Then he presented her with a medallion of the Virgin on a fine-spun silver chain.

To everyone who is inquisitive, Dina says that the audience was over almost as soon as it had begun, and she regretted not having had time to collect her wits. No time to ask the Pope if he had read the Newsletter, and also missing the chance to learn if he thought that peace would come to the Middle East, and what was his opinion of the Chinese initiative over Cambodia. The Pope, she observed, smelled slightly of boiled milk, with a whiff of eau-de-cologne about his hands.

'When she came out,' Sandra says, 'she looked adorable all in black, the hat we'd bought was exquisite. She's such a coquette, isn't she? I love it. She knew just how good she was looking. At the embassy they were dying to hear how it had gone, and that dim Sir Gordon asked her, so she stared at him and threw full in his face one of those Ha h'ms of hers, a noise like a rhinoceros snorting, and he didn't have a clue what to do next.'

You can't really blame them, Sandra goes on. It's human nature. They saw an old woman with apparently plenty of money and very strange plans about what to do with it. I mean to say. They didn't think I was listening but I overheard Sir Gordon plotting with the bishop. You might try and rope her in, he was saying behind the back of his hand, if only for the British Institute, she ought to be good for a few million lire. Put her on the board. Try out on her the appeal for St Mark's.

After lunch, sitting in the back of the car as they set off home, Dina showed off the Pope's little medallion. Rome slipped past in the wintry mist. Columns of cars edged impatiently towards the autostrada.

Were you listening to the conversation about China after Mao? Dina asked. And then Iran's in trouble, and Afghanistan soon will be, they go together. The Russians have Farsi-speaking divisions on the border. The *Herald Tribune* has an article quoting a speech by General Yepishev. Very threatening. Gold's gone up, of course, but it's still not too late. We should buy in.

Whenever Sandra is asked about Dina's character, she brings out the story of how she escorted her to the Vatican, and on to lunch at the Embassy, by any standards a big day for Dina. Pippo hadn't managed to come after all, and there they sat in the car, stuck in traffic, Dina taking off that hat with a veil and shaking loose her grey curls, urging a major investment in gold.

And did you plunge? they ask.

Yes indeed. Most of us doubled our money, Sandra says. I could hardly wait to pass the tip on. Pippo didn't believe in it, he's got no peasant mentality at all, but I did, I wish I'd bought more. The Francks were very keen, so was Peter Whitaker. And of course Jacques, like all the French, he's really only interested in money. Debussy's finances matter to him far more than the music. *Una strega infatti*, you know how Roberto likes to talk, but he hoarded krugerrands as soon as I told him. As usual Anna missed out, poor thing, she lives on the bread-line, but I've every reason to believe I know who paid for that trip of hers to America. It came out of our gold profits. It's not too much to say that Dina altered the economy of the whole region. All because of that trip to the Vatican.

The Pope's silver medallion hangs on a nail in the wall behind the candlesticks on the safe, and next to Monsignor Silvestri's crucifix. *Bondieuserie*, Jacques Lemasle sniffs at it, but only to people who he feels sure, one way or another, will not repeat what he says to Dina. Sell when the price reaches eight hundred dollars an ounce, Dina advised, that'll be a price we shan't see again for years, it's only the result of political fluke. If she was so clear-sighted, and if Popes and cardinals and bishops attended to her, who was anyone else to criticise? In Dina's library is the Pléiade edition of Balzac's collected works, and it is a source of amusement how often she comments on that writer's deep understanding of money as a human motivation.

Among the letters delivered by the postman is one from Père Destouches. It was with 'abundant interest', he wrote in his flowery French, that he had been informed of her visit to His Holiness. His delightful duty now was to keep in touch with her, and he was sure that they would find

111

topics 'conducive to mutual instruction'. Could he and his colleague Pater Auhofer visit her?

My policemen, Dina calls them. She looks forward keenly to their lunches in the villa. Usually the two priests refuse to stay longer, pleading pressure of business. Members of the Vatican Ecumenical Commission, they are assiduous travellers to conferences and congresses on the modern politics of religion, or, as they subtly distinguish, the modern religion of politics. In one of the journals of the University of Louvain, Père Destouches has published papers on ecumenism. Within a time-span measured in years, in his view, Christian churches one and all will have united in the opening steps of a great march of Christendom destined to mark the coming century. His hopes are high for Greek and Russian Orthodoxy. Ordination of women, celibacy of the priesthood, liturgical divergences, theological disputation, he argues, are so much committee work. The committees are already in place.

Vibrant with nervous energy, Père Destouches can hardly sit still, but springs up from his chair with the excitement of his talk, and paces about. He seems to be looking to see who might be arriving, who might suddenly enter the room. He creates the occasion. Everything about him is on the attack, hair that is cropped but still will not lie quiet on his head, gesticulation with hands and elbows as though clearing a space at the expense of enemies, spectacles like a visor. Always a double-breasted suit, what's more, like a successful businessman, and a white shirt with a tie in subdued stripes, browns and maroons. He sips mineral water. He's memorised the Newsletter.

'How did you obtain it?' Dina asked.

Waving the question away, Père Destouches thought there ought to be a second number. The ideas she was presenting to the public were exactly those ideas now taking shape in the conscious minds of thoughtful people everywhere. Unite the Impossible was 'intellectual vitamins'.

112

Large-faced, with heavy blank cheeks, Pater Auhofer sometimes checks his colleague, warning that things may not fall quite so quickly or smoothly into place. He's a man who's never going to have an accident, not even stub his toe. Just as contemporary, he also wears a suit, and in his case his belly drives his waistcoat out into multiple ripples. Flat-footed, ponderous, a schoolteacher's son with a sense of order bred into him in Habsburg Bohemia where he was born. In deference to Pater Auhofer's weak English, French is the language they all speak together. Both men vigorously approve of the phrase 'pushed and blocked' as the closest approximation in any language to the historical record of God's will in action. From Pater Auhofer the words emerge as 'bushed and plocked', and try as he might to translate them, he has failed. A number of his sentences end with *'Que voulez-vous?'* which explodes as 'che foollie-foo?' as he propels his accent the way a gun fires a shell. The whites of his eyes are livery, an off-putting yellow as he rolls them to avoid looking Dina in the face.

Sometimes the two priests can plan their visits ahead of time, but sometimes they telephone at the last moment, improvising, breaking away from some other engagement. Lunching with them is Dina's newest and keenest pleasure, and she grows impatient if more than a few weeks pass without these kindred spirits calling on her. At such lunches, Adela and Chantal and Holly Strickland (if she's there) and Don Alvise, are expected to listen and learn in silence, marvelling at the unfolding of Unite the Impossible. The Soviets are overextended in Ethiopia and Angola, their enterprise is doomed. The invasion of Afghanistan has occurred as Dina anticipated, but she is convinced that the country cannot be held, and evacuation is only a matter of time. She expects them to live long enough to see the Berlin Wall dismantled and the two Germanies united. As a free man among free men, Pater Auhofer will return to his birthplace. Look at Lech Walesa in Gdansk, and Vaclav Havel in Prague, both the epitome of Unite the Impossible. Inclined to be sceptical, Pater Auhofer draws on his acquaintance with Bishop Desmond

Tutu, and the successors of Martin Luther King. *Je suis africainiste*, he said. Libraries all over the world would fight to have her newspaper cuttings deposited with them. The two priests tell her what she wants to hear, a judicious mixture of news and gossip, concerning Cardinals Ottaviani and Willibrands, Archbishop Feltin in Paris and Cardinal Koenig in Vienna, Professor Horsburgh of Notre Dame University, the prolific Roger Schutz and the Protestant community he has formed at Taizé, the Ecumenical Centre at Tantur on the road between Jerusalem and Bethlehem. For Dina, the great men about whom they speak have the aura of secret agents, as unwittingly they carry out the plans she has conceived for them. Belief itself is at stake. Unity is survival. How the individual today comes to realisation of God's purpose, that is the significance of the work done in the villa.

In the course of their duties, the priests bombard Dina with literature. Books and pamphlets and ephemera of all sorts pour in, to be duly catalogued by Adela. To keep abreast of so much print is a full-time occupation. And would Dina mind, Père Destouches wanted to know, if he consecrated an article to her and her work in the villa? Out of the question, she replied. She had never sought the limelight, and if there was value in what she did, then it could only be in anonymity. Nonetheless Père Destouches published an article in the *Osservatore Romano* on 13 September 1981 about her but without mentioning her name. Among the figures of speech which he used to get round this obstacle were 'a thinker', 'an English lady of distinction', 'a person of wide religious perspective'. He alluded to the audience with the previous Pope, and he summarised Unite the Impossible as the sort of contribution to the ecumenical movement which it was well within the power of each of us to make.

'I can't have you coming here if you're going to betray confidences like this,' Dina told him.

'What could I do?' was the answer. 'The editor insisted. That's the power of the press.' And the lunches continued as before.

A casual question about Dina's background revealed that she had known the Huxleys in Varendy days. Père Destouches at once made the connection that she must be the daughter of the artist of the Aldous Huxley portrait so often reproduced. Pushed and Blocked, *alors*! This has to be altogether beyond coincidence, because for more years than he likes to recall he has been preparing a *doctorat-ès-lettres* at the Sorbonne, under the title 'Aldous Huxley and the Implementation of the Transcendental'. If only he could find the time! Dina can be of the greatest help, putting him in touch first with Lionel, and then requesting Holly Strickland to extract from the archive over which she has control any sketches or correspondence. There must be, there are, letters. Père Destouches sighs that he needs only one good push, and now he has it, with this thrilling new material. And in those days of the red Bugatti and picnics on empty beaches, was Huxley more than a pacifist and idealist, already a visionary?

One day Aldous kissed me, Dina tells him. The only warning I had that this might be about to happen was that he removed his glasses, not to bump them on my face, I imagine. Then he dropped them, so that afterwards he had to get down on his hands and knees, and search for them on the floor. Who knows what might otherwise have happened? I was terribly in awe of him, I told myself this was love. My father became suspicious at the way I was acting, he stopped taking me there, he knew more about life than you might have guessed from his reserved manner. So English. Then the Huxleys disappeared to America, and that was that.

Once Una Macleod asked Dina, to test the water, so to speak, if she didn't think the two priests were too friendly. Were they really coming for the colour of her eyes?

'My policemen,' Dina smiled. 'They protect me.'

We have to face it, those two priests made her happy, Una was to say. Dina's friends agree. It was a time when everything appeared to be going right. The children kept their distance. Holly Strickland reported the wonderful news that the Getty Museum had offered to buy the Napier archive. Whatever conditions Dina might choose to make would be acceptable to them. For instance, they were willing to pay the entire sum now but to postpone delivery until the *catalogue raisonné* was complete, or even to wait until after Dina's death. The proposal originated with the Getty people, Holly Strickland told her, they were excited by that Royal Academy show I put on, and I think this might be the solution for John Napier, long-term.

Pushed and Blocked could only have widening repercussions. For instance Lionel was writing to ask about the future. Retired now, he still used head office in Berne as a base. There, the Papal Nuncio had approached him.

What he was after [Lionel wrote] was to know your intentions in regard to the eventual disposing of the villa. He seems to have been approached by a couple of priests from the Vatican, but I didn't get their names, or else he didn't tell me. You can't be surprised that they might want to clarify the matter, you do give them lots of encouragement. The Nuncio informed me that you are considering setting up some sort of foundation of Unite the Impossible, but I had to tell him I have nothing on which to base an opinion. What he was after, I think, were facts and figures, notably whether the means are there to endow such a foundation, and in that case whether you are contemplating making these means available.

Some course of action had better be decided soon. Not only are we not getting any younger, but testamentary muddles are expensive and unnecessary. The Nuncio, I gather, had sounded out Albert Golaz about your fortune, and this is *ultra vires*. Albert naturally answered that he was bound by banker's secrecy, but I mention it as an indication that the matter is too urgent to be left in a lot of loose ends. There are a number of possibilities. You could create a family trust, tying it up properly. Let me know as soon as you can, and we'll both come down and visit you to finalise this.

Lawyer's work. Such matters would arrange themselves, the day would come when Andrew would instruct her. The future would run its course. He encouraged her, he supplied the Proofs and decided the weather and the Flowers of Meditation. So far he had made no selection, but after lunch, on her way to a siesta or going to bed at a regular ten o'clock at night, she anticipated that voice and a definitive statement.

Chantal grips her left elbow as they climb the easy treads of the stairs, helping her, but also ensuring that Dina doesn't stop and by some mischance look back over her shoulder. On days, that is, when there are no guests to lunch, and Adela has returned safely to the office. For if she were to turn round, she might catch sight of Armando the gardener, who has become more and more reckless as he slinks into the house to leer up at Chantal, gesticulating towards the open flies of his blue trousers, pretending to wag his member as if he were a small boy. At the mere thought, it is all that the nurse can do not to burst out laughing, the whole situation is so ludicrous. She's all attention to her charge. Dina must suspect nothing. When the two of them reach the landing, and pause in order to steer towards the final ascent up to her bedroom, Chantal does her best to stop Dina so much as glancing down the flight which they have just climbed, just in case Armando has gone the whole hog, he simply can't be trusted when he's in this mood. Everything depends on keeping Dina insulated from reality.

Medicines have to be administered, and clothes tidied; the Blue Notebook must be left just so, and the wireless too, on the bedside table, with paper and pen in case she has to jot down anything of Andrew's. Then, as soon as decently possible, Chantal slips back downstairs, if it's in the afternoon making sure to avoid Adela, and if it's in the evening then dodging Luciana and Ubaldo in the kitchen. Safest is to let herself out of the front door, hug the villa in order to avoid crunching footsteps on the gravel, and round the corner to the *podere*, where if anyone should see her, *eh bien merde*, it's none of their business. Then it's a dash under the brick arches and into the *camera del Tedesco,* her mouth dry with the thrill of it. Armando has tacked black plastic refuse bags over the grimy windows, nobody can peer in, the room is a proper hideout. Behind her, she pushes a bolt into place.

Waiting, Armando is impatient. Otherwise naked on the hard and scraggy blankets of the truckle bed, he refuses to take off his socks. A man who does that, he says, is at the mercy of anyone who might rush in to catch him unawares. There's always time to pull up trousers and shove on shoes, but socks in the dark are the very devil. At least, she thinks that this is his explanation, because although she tries hard to improve her Italian, she has trouble following his dialect. Also she hopes that she has understood him because it would be almost folklore and delicious. His arms are hard and sunburnt. Now it is her turn to undo her skirt; she likes to scatter her clothes any old how, as they come off, inside out if need be, on the floor, on the bed, by the shabby washbasin.

'*Viene qui, ciccia.*'

And what does Giulia think of it? What would she say if she knew of these urgent meetings?

She thinks that Armando's answer is that Giulia has always been incapable of satisfying him, and she would take justified pride in his virility. Her man is a proper man, in need of all the women he can get. He grips his whip-like arms round her waist where there is no fat at all, only firm flesh. Caressing, she feels his bones so close under the skin. His hands are calloused and cracked, too hard to be clammy even in summer. Shoving at her, he can be rough, but unlike her, he never seems to become hot and sweaty.

'*Tu veux que je fasse le jockey?*'

She bends over him. Once one has a taste for lovemaking, as she has, she breathes in his ear in French he cannot understand, one's had it, *on est foutue, quoi.*

NINE

Turning thirty was grim, Ursie says, but I've got used to the run-up to forty. One minute the whole of life is ahead of you, and the next thing you know you can hardly bear old photographs of yourself, let alone sprint to catch a bus. Goodbye to the waistline. Maybe I'll throw a party.

At least I don't owe anyone anything, she tells herself, the life I've made for myself is all my own.

Crows' feet have a way of catching her attention when she looks in the mirror, and she has begun to read articles about face-lifting, which previously she would have skipped. Once she used to search in her dark curls for wayward grey hairs and hoick them out with tweezers – do that now, she laughs, and I'd look like an ostrich.

Spinster. Bachelor girl. Female eunuch. The first impression others have of you, Alexander tells her, is how competent you are. It never sounded a compliment. Who wants to be competent when they might be beautiful? Not tall enough, toes too turned out, legs more like bananas than anything else. Brooding about what can't be changed is so much waste of energy. Incompetence is no good to anyone either. She has worked for Rio Tinto Zinc, and spent a year in the Istanbul headquarters of Borax, and been an account manager at J. Walter Thompson. Private life occupied the sliver of space left between a professional career and the spider's web woven out in Italy by Dina. Perhaps she got off to a bad start with Nico, she sometimes wonders; love, to her, is still redolent of damp towels. In her experience, men have been far too enamoured of themselves to be able to share any of the feeling with someone else. For instance, Eddy Fitzpatrick, Etonian, winner of the Craven Prize in Oxford days, and willing to condone Alexander as some sort of a genius 'in his own way'. Eddy had persuaded her to enter the City, he'd make a bond-dealer of her, they'd work together. He still flaunted the pink and yellow ties which had slightly put her off him, and sometimes he took her out to lunch to ask advice about yet another woman whom he couldn't make up his mind to marry.

Ursie's flat is on the upper two floors of a terraced house in West London. Below is a man who collects the cards which used to be given away inside packets of cigarettes, and sometimes he cannot contain his excitement at completing some series featuring sportsmen of the past, reptiles, or steam engines, and he buttonholes Ursie on the stairs. A light operates there on a time switch, and if he can, he delays her until they are both left standing in the dark. Her front door opens into a sitting-room, where a pair of squat white sofas are like blocks of sugar on the plum-coloured carpet. On the walls she likes to hang abstract pictures and kelims. And the photograph on the mantelpiece – a testimony of regret – shows her as a child on the terrace at La Grecchiata, not in the arms of Dina but of a Luciana fat and jolly with affection.

This is home base, and for all his entreaties she doesn't want to leave it to move in with Charles, for much the same reason that he won't sell his house, a much grander affair. Property is property, and since the escalating inflation of the early Seventies, an essential asset for anyone with an eye to the future. Charles Bray's first wife ran off with their tax accountant to Santa Barbara, taking little Stella with her. Placing an advertisement in the *Straits Times*, Charles found a Chinese housekeeper, and steered her brilliantly through the minefield of permits and immigration. The woman's invisibility reaches such an extreme, and so deliberately, that Ursie feels herself undermined by it, as though she were being treated as someone whose indelicacy and even aggression are best blotted out. In the spare moments of what passes for a London summer, Charles and Ursie and several friends organise tennis matches on a semi-derelict court which is within view of a hospital, a school and a prison. Then Charles offers everyone dinner in the house, and Ursie spends the night. Also after the theatre: now and again Charles has backed a play, and fancies himself as a mogul, cigar-smoking. On mornings after, the chauffeur calls to drive Charles to his merchant bank, and Ursie to her office. Watching, the housekeeper is hardly more substantial than a shadow, but her eyes declare: I may be the servant, but you are lower than that, a woman for his pleasure.

'I don't know which of them hates me most,' Ursie says, 'your housekeeper or your mother.' To stay with Charles's parents is like being plunged into a refrigeration unit. The mother is a bag of bones, small and taut; the father a retired parliamentary draughtsman. Reading the newspapers, often aloud, they comment on the events of the days as though finally disposing of all opinions except their own. Argument is bad manners. They never refer to Charles's ex-wife or to Stella, displaying no feelings, as though feelings too were bad manners. 'How nice,' they might say at any mention of Dina or her interests, or 'how very interesting,' the equivalent of posting a No-Entry sign on the conversation.

A flight of stairs separates the rooms in which Ursie and Charles are put. The flatness with which Charles's mother says, 'I hope you'll be comfortable' expresses her wish never to have to see Ursie. Sometimes the father makes a point of staying up late reading, his door ajar, on sentry duty. In the end, though, the lights are turned off, and it is possible to tiptoe on the stairs.

Don't let yourself be upset by them, Charles says, any more than you are by Dina. It's not their fault, it's a generation thing. He lists his own virtues, for instance he likes women, he's kind to them, he enjoys their company. 'You could do much worse than marry me,' he says, 'as things stand, you'll already be a geriatric mother. Hurry up.' And he knows a great many people, useful and successful people at that, he travels round the world, he's learning Italian to please her and it's a cinch, something to do in odd moments out of a teach-yourself manual.

121

'You should have a child,' he urges, 'it's biological.'

Determination makes up for Charles's lack of skill at tennis, and at a great many other things too. With no chest to speak of, no biceps, a shambling uncoordinated gait, he looks undeveloped and deprived. He hangs his head, he waves his arms and often spills the drink in his hand or knocks over a bottle on the table. Much of this is the affectation of a man who doesn't want to show how much he resents not having his way, never mind losing. Speech to him is a roundabout apology for coming out on top, full of superfluous tags which qualify and withdraw even as they assert: so to speak, in a sense, I mean to say, oh quite, empirically, pragmatically, and the long-drawn and quiet 'No no no no' in a tone fit for children.

The bridge of his nose has a tiny deflection, a bump over which his skin, otherwise a slightly coarse and middle-aged pink, draws whitening. His glasses habitually work over this bump of gristle, and slide down, so that he has to peck at the frame with his fingers, always right-handed. Because Ursie has made personal remarks, he has become self-conscious about this.

I couldn't marry an intellectual, she tells him. You couldn't marry anyone else, he replies.

On a Friday when she is going to Maydeswell, he can play hurt, especially in the car heading for the City. You should be shot of that whole situation, he tells her, at your age it's a trap, they're imprisoning you, brother and mother alike. It's emotionally crippling.

Can't be helped.

On this particular day, the wind and rain are thrashing against the glass walls of the office, in a spell which gives the lie to what is called the greenhouse effect. Like being inside a dishwasher churning through its cycle. On her fourth-floor passage is the communications centre, where wire-service machines and telexes chatter out prices and news. She passes it with Pavlovian apprehension because Avvocato Bellini uses the telex as a shortcut to her, and then the secretary disdainfully deposits a coil of paper in front of her. So the latest crisis in the villa, or some immediate leap in Dina's mood, reaches her, to nag at her conscience about being an ungrateful and irresponsible daughter. Eddy Fitzpatrick in his office likes to lean back in his chair with his feet on the desk, rolling his eyes at whoever passes down the passage. Her colleague, Berndt, from Bremen, speaks better English than she does. Young Mr Beeby is self-important, especially if he happens to be hurrying upstairs in response to a summons from his father.

The computer terminal whips up sets of figures in quivering lime-green rows. Norwegian 7.75% State Oil, City of Barcelona 8.175%, the Ecu, interest rates and their impact on bond prices: money is like the weather, with its highs and lows which have to be plotted, and acted on accordingly. She's got a definite feel for money, they say of her in the office, and it's true. At her desk she is at the controls, with Extel cards, the specialist press, company statements, the analyses that pour in such conflicting variety out of banks and economic departments. What have you got for me? is the question that fund managers ask, and there has to be an answer. Backing her instincts induces well-being, as though she toned herself up in a gymnasium, to become fit. If you don't look after your own interests, she tells herself, no one is going to do it for you.

It's a bone of contention with Charles, who teases her about being tight-fisted. When she studies her own portfolio, she doesn't see spending power or the possibility of satisfying some want, but independence. This is her achievement, and it's going to keep her in old age. Nothing will be owed to Dina or to Alexander. A calculation has to be made about how much is enough, in these days, when money is steadily eroded by the almost unbelievable incompetence of public administration: it's as though our elders and betters were deliberately planning to prevent her being her own master, and her defence lies in the papers on her desk and those lime-green figures on the terminal. Office conferences are like pauses for re-grouping. She enjoys the atmosphere, the exchanges of ideas, the often unexpected consequences and odd swings between camaraderie and hostility among those with whom she does business and has lunch. We think the world of you, old Mr Beeby says, putting a hand on her arm or her shoulder, but not as an Italian might, without any suggestion in it.

Aren't you longing to be in California, Berndt wants to know. When you look at the kind of summer we're having.

She is hoping to persuade her old friend Val to accompany her on this freebie to California, where there are clients to see, among them Shearson Lehman's, and Mr Ishiwara who takes her out to lunch at the Savoy when he's over. A man of impenetrable silence, he is known in the office as Ish, the richest Ish of all. For the moment Val can't make up her mind. I wish I'd been infertile, Val complains. If she's absent for as long as a week, she fears she'll come home to find her husband has deserted her, and the children will be in the hands of the police.

Through the tense evening crowd, Ursie pressed to the station. The countryside was stained silver. To be returning to Maydeswell was to raise expectations which could only be dissipated. Nothing was quite as memory insisted that it should be. The branch line no longer existed. Where the train stopped now was more than twenty miles from the house. Puddles glistened on the platform and across the uneven surface of the car park. Wet, Alexander's hair straggled in rat's tails down his neck, exposing a baldness which can no longer be hidden, like a little inverted saucer. Like Dina's, his eyes had pouched with fatigue. With a sweep, he cleared off the front seat of his car a layer of books and papers, a road map, cassette tapes, a wire coat-hanger. The bypass in the Maydeswell direction dispensed with a network of lanes whose high hedges had made it impossible to see what might be coming, and too narrow to allow another car easily to pass. As usual, half the coloured light-bulbs draped round the sign of the Fox and Goose had blown.

Before selling up and disappearing into tax exile, Michael Crane-Dytton had obtained planning permission on his land. A man with a chain of local garages had developed it. Briefly he had lived in the Abbey, but now it was empty, the ground-floor windows boarded against vandals. New housing lapped almost up to it. Along Ditton Crescent the brick bungalows had garages to the right; on Ditton Prospect and Abbey Drive, the garages were to the left. Between dwarf conifers and shrubs stretched fly-mown grass.

'Liz lives at number twenty-eight,' Alexander said. 'I'm grooming her as my new secretary. You'll find two American girls in the house, by the way. They're quite sweet, they're on their way to India as soon as their Dads send the tickets.'

All his life he has picked up strays of the kind, she thought, and where did he find them? Girls who went barefoot, with frizzy and unkempt hair, likely not to be wearing anything under shapeless T-shirts, with water-marks visible on their necks, and hands like paws, toting rucksacks practically half their size from some uncertain starting point to an even more doubtful destination, materialising in the kitchen around mealtimes, good eaters but not cooks. Some of them had drifted like thistledown into the house, to drift out again almost at once; others had lingered, and proposed a life of caring and sharing, maybe a commune with friends like themselves. One or two had tried to prove their skills and adaptability by growing vegetables organically in some corner of the garden, organising a concert in the village or a protest against nuclear energy or the American air base in the next-door county. The one called Pet had tried to secure him through laying siege, invading Ursie in her flat and crying until all hours. Most of them had been champion weepers, but then they had had something to weep about. One with red hair had evidently loved him and might have made a go of it, but she ran smack into his refusal to consider having a child.

As though following her train of thought, Alexander

said, 'We met in Evesham, when I was looking at the canals. You'll like them, you wait.'

Beeches staked and guarded in old days were now grown trees. Victim of a storm, a sycamore lay where it had long since fallen close to the house, brambles encroaching, with the opening of a hole like a mineshaft at its roots. Grass grew in tufts as high as molehills. What had been the garden looked a wilderness.

Walking up the path, she concentrated on the paving bricks, their shape and fit, under her eyes like the reel of an old film, with everything in its rightful and well-known place. Inside the entrance, blocking it so that she had to edge round, was a Spitfire propeller, painted and varnished for presentation, as if it had been a commemorative oar or a cricket bat. 607 Squadron, she saw, and then the pilots' names in gilt capitals. I mustn't notice that the windows haven't been cleaned, she told herself, I mustn't look at the sills for the dead flies, and I really can afford to go shopping for these two American girls, I mustn't take it out on them.

The dining-room had become his office, with a computer and word-processor rising out of the wrack of papers, reports, bulletins, books open face downwards.

'Business is okay,' Alexander said. 'I'm in the process of buying a third barge. Here's an article, from last May, about how much you save on conventional transport costs, and I rate a mention. The chap came to interview me.'

Was there anything he hadn't worked at? Barges were at least as sound a prospect as his ventures into travel promotion, a record company, textile design, films for television, a couple of years at a polytechnic studying architecture.

In her City suit, she confronted Esther-Anne and Jeanie, who scrambled to their feet as though caught out in some misdemeanour by a headmistress. Five tea-chests stood in the drawing-room, and their contents were spread out over the floor: brown manila envelopes, folders, bundles tied with string, correspondences com-

126

plete with carbon copies and replies, with references and date stamps.

'The factory rang me up out of the blue,' Alexander said, 'they were clearing out a warehouse and found these things in store, private property, to be returned to Mr Lumel. That propeller too.'

'In college I did a course in librarianship,' Jeanie said, 'we're at the preliminary sorting stage. Then we'll know what we're dealing with.'

'Beaverbrook,' said Esther-Anne, 'that's a funny name.'

Sopwith, Ursie read, Sir Thomas Inskip. Robert Vansittart. Panhard, Bristol Aero-Engines, R.J. Mitchell. The side of their father's life that they knew nothing about; the work, important to him, which he'd always felt they were too ignorant to be taught. Randomly picking up a technical paper on the performance of the Spitfire engine, she recognised her father's handwritten comments on it.

The sofa on which Dina used to sit upright with a history book in her hands had been a light brown, with a slightly darker thread in it, like the skin of a healthy animal. This upholstery was coming apart at the seams, and through the holes on the arms grey stuffing protruded. Alexander had placed a wide-screen television set on the table at which Andrew had liked to sit and write, perhaps where he had studied this report on fighter engines. Long-burnt-out ash was heaped in the fireplace.

Upstairs was the debris of Alexander's life, in the form of suitcases without handles, dog-eared magazines devoted to fads that were over, some abandoned girl's handbag, three-legged chairs. The floorboards squeaked in the same places, to the same sounds. Conical and spindly, the fire extinguisher had not been touched since first installed on the staircase. Certain inanimate objects, stopcocks and taps, for instance, the bathroom pipes that curved as heavily as cables, a glazed vase that nobody had moved from Dina's room, Alexander's dusty lead soldiers and childhood books with her name written on the endpapers in juvenile capitals – these were what brought her irresistibly back, while also perplexing her. How come that there was an element of reproach? That things stayed faithfully in the same place, but people managed to betray?

What's for supper? she had asked, resigned to the fact that she was going to have to prepare it. Minestrone, and against all prediction Esther-Anne had made a decent imitation of it. Vegetarians, of course. On their way to an ashram somewhere near Madras, full of swamis, with half-digested notions of harmony and mysticism which owed more to industrial Michigan than anything Hindu or Indian.

'And what does the name Iris Warren mean to you?' Alexander asked.

The paper was a deep, almost royal, blue. Around the edges ran an engraved band, and in the top corner was the initial I, in the shape of a Doric pillar entwined with foliage.

A pile of love letters. My darling, darling heart, treasure mine, I wish I was with you. That evening. Perhaps I shouldn't have suggested the new Coward, he does seem to have gone off rather lately. And Ursie read aloud from one of the sheets, 'I suppose I can't offer you anything so fabulous as this villa sounds, but patience is a virtue I do have. And, darling, we can always travel.' His mistress, then.

The paper was compact in the hand, like an enlarged pack of playing cards. Why was it that whenever they were together, the subject of conversation was their parents? Did nothing else bind them together? It should have been possible to let this go, never to unpack the crates but request that the factory burn the whole lot.

'It doesn't ring a bell.'

'I'm going to have to teach myself Dutch. He kept letters from his mother too, they're here. We'll be able to learn about his origins, and whether there's any truth in the story of his illegitimacy.'

When she grimaced, he went on, 'I've got the material here for a book about them, and the whole background. If running the barges allows me time, I'll settle down to write it. What his contribution to winning the war really amounted to. All I really know about the factory is that I'm still receiving dividends from Vickers, and Lionel advises me never to dispose of the holding.'

Ursie said, 'If she was to get to hear of it, she'd think it was some gigantic Proof. She'd demand that you hand over everything, and fill another room of the villa with it. Why not first ask Lionel if he knows who Iris Warren was?'

'Why shouldn't I ask her myself?'

It was their chance for a breakthrough, he thought. By the look of it, the parents had bought the villa to keep their marriage going. The Proofs and Unite the Impossible were some way of mythologising unhappiness. Dina was the loser staying on in this country, perhaps Andrew had lived with Iris Warren. Dina might have been mourning for him since the time well before his death, that's why she had been recreating him and his apparitions visual or audible, in a manner she could control. 'That's it,' he said, 'and I shall get a great book out of it.'

The chaos of paper spread over the carpet as Jeanie and Esther-Anne unpacked the chests. And such a book, Ursie was thinking, it wouldn't help, you couldn't really clarify or even record behaviour like Dina's, and certainly not by trailing through its murky antecedents. He and these two, like witches, were really after dirt, of which they were exponents, more likely, than critics. Was he sleeping with the freckle-faced minestrone-maker, or the older ex-librarian with this delight in making herself useful, or both at the same time, three in a bed? Nobody should know about other people's sex lives, specially not about their parents'. They did it, and one was born: that's fact enough. What underlay these conversations with Alexander was an instinct that they had turned out the way they had because there had been no choice about it, and the parents were to blame. But it couldn't be true that parents were the equivalent of a grim historical determination. She had a job, she was good at it, saved money, didn't have a house falling down around her, nor, come to that, Vickers dividends to pay for fantasies.

Iris Warren. Mrs Ackroyd would know. She couldn't

129

help wondering what such a well-placed witness would say; she would be drawn there after breakfast next day, with an undeniable longing to pry into the past in spite of herself. The walk used to be out at the back of the kitchen garden, and into woods. Straight ahead was the way to the Abbey, to have tea with the Crane-Dyttons, who even in the days of rationing had milk that was almost cream, from the Jersey herd in the park. Across the stream wobbled the three planks of a bridge with a rickety handrail. In spring, wild garlic grew there, and Andrew had rubbed some on the children's hands to prove how lasting the smell was, and to watch Elsie Crane-Dytton wrinkling her nose to detect where it was coming from. Sometimes the labradors from the Abbey would come bounding to meet them, and, lean as lions, imprint muddy paws on their tidy clothes. Michael Crane-Dytton used to shout at these dogs in a voice which brought an almost human response from them. A whole room was lined with cabinets containing silver, huge bowls and candelabra, which looked too heavy for one person to lift; it was like stepping into Aladdin's cave. The woods might not have been the huge expanse that she remembered, as mysterious as a cathedral, the light hardly filtering down from high above on to the fallen beechnuts and leaves which formed an underfelt. Nothing of it remained. Turning away from the Abbey into Ditton Crescent, she hoped that deep and damp under these houses the stream must still run, eventually to ruin them.

Mrs Ackroyd's cottage is in the old village. Since she gave up bicycling, she no longer comes to help in the house unless Alexander fetches her. I can't manage it any more, she apologises. The work-worn hands look red and swollen, but she swears they don't hurt, and she's got nothing to complain of. She cooks for herself. They'll have to carry her out feet first, she says.

'Course I knew that Iris Warren,' Mrs Ackroyd said, 'a lady, she was. Once she gave me a five-pound note. One of those white ones we had in those days. Proper money that was.'

'Did she stay often?'

'I couldn't tell now,' Mrs Ackroyd answered. 'But one thing you can be sure of, that those American girls he has with him won't be leaving five pounds, not even one pound. You'd have thought he'd have learnt by now. I tell him to his face, you find yourself a decent woman. And now it's barges.'

'The thing is,' Ursie said, 'the factory telephoned the other day. They delivered some papers of my father's, and among them were letters from this Iris Warren. From the sound of it, they must have been having an affair.'

'Good gracious, I couldn't tell,' Mrs Ackroyd repeated, 'and if I could, I wouldn't.' But she also added, 'If you knew the things I've seen, my dear girl, I'm the one who ought to be writing a book. But I shan't tell, my lips is sealed.'

'So she was his mistress, but you don't like to say so?'

'One thing I will say, and that's that your mother ought to be living here where she belongs. Not in Italy on her own like that. It's not right. No wonder she gets queer ideas. And what little money he's got left, he has to go and be wasting on barges.'

'You never did think they ought to have bought that house in Italy, did you?'

That weekend Alexander drafted a letter to Dina, and he read it to Ursie and the American girls.

Dearest Mother,

Fear of offending you has kept me in check until now, as well as the inhibition natural in relationships with parents. But what I have to tell you is long overdue, and I blame myself for not having spoken up much earlier. I want to discuss with you the religious ideas which have taken over your life and its purposes, and which are bound to have a dramatic effect on those who love you.

Much of what you advocate is true in a more or less general sense. With a proper training in philosophy or theology, you could well have done first-class work. Unite the Impossible, I take it, is your way of stating that human beings are self-evidently equal. I value what you are doing in this respect because you are sticking out your neck as few are willing to do. In addition, it seems to me valuable – more than that, absolutely amazing – that someone of your background with its rather exclusively secular and social dimensions, should develop these concerns. It's not a literature I'm familiar with, but your Flowers of Meditation, as selected in the Newsletter you once sent me, convey insights of a felt and personal kind.

Pushed and Blocked, and what you call Proofs of your Spiritual Realities, raise rather different questions. These concepts endow you and Father with a responsibility for world events, of a kind that saints and prophets would hesitate to claim for themselves. Your claim rests upon your hearing Father's voice on various regular wavelengths of the radio. Somewhere inside you is surely another voice insisting that the physical laws of the universe cannot be suspended. Nothing can be true unless it is empirically verifiable. Quite literally, he cannot be speaking to you in this manner.

You may answer that churches believe in miracles, that it is not your business to submit your experience to empirical verification and that churchmen of the highest rank pay tribute to you. Their motives can hardly be considered objective, and may even be self-interested. Some may positively wish to take advantage of you.

Beyond that, have you considered the role in which you have cast Father? A scientist by training, he had no bent that I know for the metaphysical. On the other hand, I feel that I hardly knew him. His calendar was always crammed, his work had an absolute priority. Now it happens that the factory has delivered to me a number of packing cases of papers which he kept in store there. My immediate reaction is that I am going to use this opportunity to learn about him, to recover the missing past through writing a book around him, by means of these quite extensive papers. A cursory glance already tells me that I have more than an adequate base for research here. There are letters, and I think, diaries, from his mother, which ought to clear up what we know of his origins. If really he was an orphan when he arrived in this country, then his career is all the more of a credit to him.

Correspondence about the factory and indeed the whole aero-nautical industry has an importance beyond dispute. There is also a handful of letters of a personal kind, from someone by the name of Iris Warren. Others may turn up, the papers have not been exhaustively catalogued.

It is of course not my intention to quiz you about what is none of my business. I am proposing that we read these letters together, and you can steer me towards the truth (that resolutely pagan goddess). My book, I suppose in the manner of all books, will be primarily a self-discovery, and not a revelation of intimacies concerning you and Father, which should remain private. I am only too aware of how my life has been a strategy of rejecting moral commitment, which explains why it has been without conventional achievements, though still in a conventional sense, productive and enjoyable. This book will enable us to communicate as we have unfortunately been prevented from doing, and it is my hope that by this process we may reach the emotional centre of Unite the Imposs-ible. Moral commitment of course includes my impulse to unburden to you, in what has been already far too long a letter.

You prig, said Ursie, you pompous prig. Might have done first-class work if she'd had a proper training in philosophy – which just happens quite by accident to be what they gave you. And what's that crap about 'still in a conventional sense, productive and enjoyable' and empir-ical and verifiable and the rest of it. Charles spouts like that, you bloody Oxford graduates are all the same, anything human in you all squeezed into verbiage.

I see, Alexander said, you're afraid this'll put the cat

among the pigeons, and then she's bound to leave the villa to the Church. We'll be disinherited. Well, I couldn't care less.

No, she said, as she took the quarrel to a deeper level. You're getting at her because she's a soft target, and you haven't got what it takes to settle the score with the one who really matters to you, and that's Lionel. Still dreaming about him?

There was one certain consolation, she told herself, that the letter was something to be got out of his system, and he would never send it. Not him, a coward if ever there was.

TEN

Checking out of the hotel in downtown San Francisco, Ursie had noticed someone in the lobby making a fuss about a telephone call: shoulder-length hair, a bosom with a deep sunburnt cleft, exposed legs. But why such a loud voice, and why was it so deep? The penny dropped slowly. The vengeful image of this transvestite pursued her throughout the day. Somehow she was at fault. Those she was supposed to see were late for their appointments. The man who rented her a car spoke incomprehensibly out of the side of his mouth. On the freeway system the green signs were overbearing, the abbreviations misleading, not corresponding to the small-scale map on her knees. Litter and novelty were almost indistinguishable. U-Haul, she read, Bar-B-Q. It fascinated as it frightened, this scrapyard the size of a continent.

Immense, the sinking sun caught and inflamed streaks of thin high cloud. The heat was constant. Big Sur, she had assumed, was a proper place, somewhere to spend the night, with associations of Henry Miller, Anaïs Nin, Lawrence Durrell: not thrown for a moment, *they* would have turned that transvestite to some imaginative purpose. Why couldn't she? What's the difference between timidity and being ladylike? Alexander might have picked the transvestite up. By association, she thought of Dina with her Proofs and Andrew broadcasting to her. Never knowing whether to laugh or cry about it was more than exhausting, it wore through inner reserves, to the bone.

At sea level, a track led to some dunes. Nobody was on the beach, a desolate stretch where rocks pockmarked the vista of sand. Down there, the breakers could be seen for what they were, towering cliffs of water which from the distance crashed and roared through to the shore. What finally seeped in was an icy spit, matted with seaweed. Circling back, she walked alongside her own soggy footprints, to give the impression that more than one person had passed that way. In London, it would be mid-morning, and Val was probably wild-eyed over her children's latest outrage, cursing herself for missing this chance to see the Pacific coast.

As in Italy, night fell with a swoop, as if impatient for the change. The ocean turned leaden, the pines a satiny pitch-black. Over the horizon lay Japan – she had an appointment in Los Angeles with Mr Ishiwara. Climbing and descending again in one switchback after another, the road south twisted between belts of forest on either side. No lights anywhere broke the darkness. Beyond the silhouette of a headland, the ocean sometimes gleamed under a rising moon. On the map no place-names were marked. Perhaps there were no settlements, no motels, none of the glitter which it had been so easy to despise earlier.

The entrance which she reached was lit by lamps arching overhead on a wishbone standard of concrete, to reveal a lodge and a closed iron gate topped with spikes. A wire perimeter fence stretched out of sight. The young man who eventually emerged from the lodge spoke to her through the bars of the gate. There was nowhere around for miles, he said, and people did come here, and yes, sometimes they put them up for the night, why not? Right now it might be a problem, as they were having a gathering of the Project, and the Chief himself was here.

The Project. Part of the contemporary scene, like an outdated pop group whose name swam somewhere in the memory without one being able to say quite why. Either they were childish, or scandalous. Were they the ones who advocated free love, copulating randomly out here on the edge of the Pacific? In any case it was a sect, upmarket Moonies or Scientologists, guaranteeing happiness out of bits and pieces of this, that or the other. Why do these things happen to me, she complained to herself. It's

136

creepy. Why do I have to live with Unite the Impossible, and run into transvestites and kooks?

'In you go,' the young man said, as he pressed the button to open the fortified gates. He meant to sound encouraging when he called out, 'It'll cost only a few dollars.' Fear of the unknown was the American experience above all others.

The building proved to be low, a ranch house with a flat roof, its glass façade allowing a view into an open-plan hall. On the wall behind the reception desk were huge blown-up photographs of Presidents Ford and Carter, and standing against them was the Stars and Stripes, as well as a blue flag at whose centre was a capstan, in white, evidently the logo. A rack contained a number of books and pamphlets whose shiny comic-strip presentation was enough to put her off.

The woman who arrived to register her might have temporarily left a formal dinner party. Wearing a skirt to the ground, and peep-toe shoes of gilded leather, she made sure to smile, that fixed uptwist of the face supposed to put strangers at ease. Ursie filled in her name, address and occupation. Mr Langridge himself is here, this receptionist said, and if he can, he likes to meet with our guests particularly when they're British, 'he just loves the British'.

She handed Ursie a brochure, and showed her to her room. 'Sure we'll find you something to eat,' she said, 'but you'll be alone in the canteen, Mr Langridge's lecture is about to start.'

Over cold food, Ursie read the brochure. The Project was an experience in understanding yourself and the meaning of your life, and no project could possibly be more worthwhile than that: hence the name. Dropping out and failing were luxuries nobody could afford. Civilisations and religions one and all had taught harmony and balance, and this was the way to curing those with difficulties in adjusting to today's realities, the alienated, the inadequate, the unsuccessful. Biosthenics was the means to harmony and balance. As devised by the wisdom of Evan Langridge, it offered a synthesis of civilisation and religion. Nobody need feel excluded. Biosthenics crossed all divides, it was fellowship, a way of life for whoever enrolled and committed himself to it. Quotations were provided from what were clearly intended to be celebrities – doctors, actors, professors – to the effect that the Project and Biosthenics had made them what they were. And all of them unknown to me, she thought, marvelling that there could be such promotion and activity around nothing at all. To judge by the place and its trappings, though, there had to be money in it.

In her room was a single bed, a table and chair, the bare walls of a cell, extremely clean. Opening the window, she saw that this part of the house was cantilevered over a shelf of rock. The beach below flattened away to the sea. And somewhere in the grounds out of sight, a rhythmic shouting began, audible in bursts, as though a response to a cheerleader.

When there was a knock on the door, she had not gone to bed. Evan Langridge did not look as she had imagined. An inch or two shorter than her, he peered across the room, as if shy. Broad-shouldered and bulky, though; heart-attack material. The head was too large for that body. Cheeks and nose were grained with tiny veins. Those were the sad shifting eyes of an animal sensing a trap and not quite sure where to turn. She thought: elephant's eyes, too small in proportion to the rest of the face. In grey flannels and a blazer with the capstan emblem on its breast pocket, he was not so much the Chief as someone hired, an attendant in uniform, a team member.

'Still hot, isn't it?' he said, and then flatly, 'You're familiar with our work.'

She shook her head.

Someone was hovering behind him in the corridor. Also in the uniform of flannels and blue blazer, and obviously in a hurry to be getting on, accustomed to act the policeman.

'Meet Wally,' Evan Langridge said. 'Princeton man. We couldn't do without him and his brains.'

The unplaceable accent was not American, not quite English either. He moved to the open window. 'Looking out to sea? I've always wanted to bring a boat up here, but it can't be done. No anchorage.'

'What's that shouting?'

'Here in our work we find that people best get in touch that way. Saying things together is a stronger bind than doing things together. These are some of our most experienced staff. Pillars of the Project.'

There was something clammy about him, but Wally, edging in and stopping, was more impersonal, the *éminence grise*. He held out to her two paperbacks, saying, 'For special guests, a special welcome.'

'You should enrol in the morning after reading them,' said Evan Langridge.

Light Years by Walter J. Willson had a red and yellow laminated cover, and 'America's Bestseller' was blazoned within an exploding star that might have been drawn for a cartoon. What Biosthenics were, and how he had come to elaborate them, was the theme. Five minutes of glancing through it was enough. Evan Langridge's *The Living I* was an autobiography. She learnt that he had been born in Western Australia. His father had been a soldier, but a man with a grudge. A forebear had emigrated because he had been the victim of injustice. The House of Lords, it appeared, had denied this forebear his rightful claim to a peerage which had gone into abeyance. She skipped to a passage describing how the thirteen-year-old Evan had flown with his father in what had been one of the first light aircraft in that part of the country. The engine had failed. What he best remembered, he had written, was how his father's last words had been violent cursing. He himself had been unharmed in the crash, though it had been three days before they had found him in the outback. Turning the pages, she picked up that he had been a prospector for mineral deposits, a sailor, a writer of science fiction.

Anything unbelievable is boring. Men who claim extinct peerages are cranks by definition, if not worse. Nor do boys step out of crashed planes and wait to be rescued.

Surely nobody could hand out such stuff to passing strangers, and expect to be taken seriously. In the atmosphere of Unite the Impossible, the story of the aircraft might be considered a Proof. Religion like Dina's was based on drawing connections where none existed other than chance. She wished that she could lock the door to the room. What a pair, in their blazers. That elephant's eye and its oblique gaze was mournful enough to set the imagination racing. Writers of science fiction thought up things like Biosthenics, and in response people stayed up late to shout in the dark of a Californian night. And what did they do after that? In the corridor outside there was silence. Against the door handle, she jammed the table and chair. It was not much of a barrier.

When she left early in the morning, it never crossed her mind to take the two paperbacks. The thing to do was to get away, to pay at the reception and skip breakfast in the hope that she could last out until a stop, which might be as far as San Simeon or even San Luis Obispo. At least Mr Beeby wouldn't be querying the night's expenses. It was another cloudless day. Sprinklers were revolving on the grass in front of the house. Biosthenics and its practitioners belonged to the night, were over and done with.

In San Luis Obispo, the post office was in a mock Spanish style, with in front of it a row of spindly trees whose flowers were an incandescent purple, stiff like paper cutouts. Parked outside, buses were heating up in the sun. From the ceiling was suspended a huge fan, to slice through the dusty calm. An operator put her through, and she heard Eddy Fitzpatrick's voice as though he were in the next cabin. A slight change of schedule, he said, she should now call on Wells Fargo, and he gave her a name in the Los Angeles office. 'Bad news at home, I'm afraid, though,' he said, 'they're bombarding you with telexes. I haven't read them, actually, but I gather your mother's unwell.'

On the wall in front of her, someone had carefully written in capital letters, 'Lurlene loves her work. Give her a ring any time of night or day.' Italy, said the telephone operator, which state would that be in? Nobody could ever have called Sant' Ambrogio from this sweltering spot.

'*Pronto.*' It was Adela. 'No, I'm afraid you can't speak to her. She's in bed, and I doubt if she would talk on the phone if she was down here. No, it's nothing physical, well, not primarily. Mind you, she's making herself ill. It's that she's had a letter from Alexander.'

ELEVEN

You should have been here when Madame read the letter, Chantal is to say. *Quelle comédie, alors.* Not that we laughed at the time, I can assure you. We were far too frightened for that.

I took in the post as usual, Adela says. I recognised Alexander's handwriting, and I remember thinking, Oh good, that'll give her pleasure, she'll be in a good mood for the rest of the day. She so rarely hears from him. And the postman was hanging about, he had spotted that the stamp was a new issue, and he was after it. She's always very understanding about letting him have whichever ones he wants.

We were all rather late that morning, Chantal says. She didn't come down till just before lunch, and then there were lots of newspapers with special three-asterisk articles which had to be clipped and filed.

So she didn't read the letter till she was back upstairs on her bed, preparing for a siesta.

Sometimes I take the afternoon off myself for a bit of a rest, Chantal continues, but it was really lucky that I happened to have some washing to do. I heard the screams. An accident, was my first thought. She must have tried to open the window, and it's broken and she's been cut badly. Or a snake. I've got an absolute horror of them, and Armando's always telling me about vipers in the olive orchard. Ugh.

Luciana and Ubaldo also heard her. Read this, the *baronessa* was shouting at me, Luciana remembers. She was shaking. Waving the letter in my face. Go on, read it, but of course I couldn't, it was in English, and Chiarella couldn't read it either.

We were all up there, Adela tells Ursie, standing in a line along the bed. It's all very well for you to laugh now and tell us that it must have been like a Rossini opera, no it wasn't a joke, not one bit. The curtains were closed for her siesta, but she'd got the bedsight light on, and you could see that she had changed colour. All livid and black. Corpse-like. He's trying to murder me, she was shrieking, look what he's written. Here. Read it. But I couldn't, I didn't have the courage to translate a single sentence for the others. What a fool you are, I thought to myself, for tearing off the stamp and not checking the contents. If I'd been quicker on the uptake, I could have prevented the whole thing. Shows you it doesn't pay to be discreet.

The *baronessa*'s eyes were specially alarming to Luciana, seeming to pop out, right out, with rage. Pools of black bile. I remember thinking we'd have to tie her down, we'd need a straitjacket. It was insanity. Really it was.

She wouldn't eat, you know, she wouldn't dress. She lay there raving about murder; and about blackmail. That book was his method of having himself bought off. He must have run through everything, sold his Vickers shares and maybe Maydeswell as well. A curse had fallen on her for being too lenient with her son, she'd spoiled him rotten. Look at everything she'd done for him, and now here he was slandering the Church and its priests, that's what it had come in. How dare he bring Iris Warren into it? What did he know about it?

None of us had ever heard that name before, Adela says, how were we expected to deal with the situation? Luciana nudged me with her elbow, as much as to give me a warning, but she saw it, she doesn't miss much. And there she was off again, about how we must all be in this together, and didn't we know that this letter was being hatched, and it was a plot against her. *You all want to kill me*, I can see her now, pressed back against her pillows, in her petticoat, and letting go as loud as she could.

Crumpled Dr Melegnani took his time about arriving. He doesn't care to be called out from midday onwards, especially not into the country. Emergencies don't suit him.

You'd have thought she'd died, the way they were all standing at the bedside, Dr Melegnani says. First thing was to take her blood pressure. It was too high. With a history like hers, caution is to be recommended. I decided to give her tranquillisers, and keep her under observation for a couple of days. When I saw that the pacemaker was all right, and that she was indulging herself, I had my good idea. There's nothing like a bit of unorthodox medicine with patients of that type.

The tranquillisers worked like a charm. She slept well, but not too well to miss Andrew. Towards dawn, she was tuning in to a programme on French Radio about the Khmer Rouge and the aims of Pol Pot, when he interrupted. 'May, my darling,' he said, 'now you're to do the right thing. The boy has shown you how it is. Old Silvers is your man. Leave the villa to Silvestri. He'll make it over to the nuns, and they can safeguard our Spiritual Realities.'

That morning when I came in, Chantal likes to repeat, I was dreading it, frankly. I was scared at what I might find. After one of her storms, she might seem to have blown herself out, but you have to watch your step, oh ever so carefully, or she's off again. There she lay as good as gold. Furious in the evening, all golden in the morning. How is one to guess? And all because Monsieur had told her what was to be done.

Dr Melegnani waited a few days before starting his treatment. *Sanguesuge*: the word was new to her, and she showed little interest in it, let alone disgust.

I had the good fortune to study under the great Professor Krumecki at Pittsburgh, the doctor explains, he was the first to incorporate unorthodoxies into Western medicine. Nobel Prizes go to geniuses like that. Yes, leeches. I've had a word with Vierchowod at Ogni Santi, and he approves. Or doesn't disapprove. Without being technical, leeches reduce the blood supply but also discharge into the system exactly what's required for bringing down the pressure. Much better our little squirmy friends than anything chemical.

'I already have leeches on my back in the shape of my children.'

'One moment now, I've known them for as long as I've known you.'

The leeches travelled in the glove compartment of his car, in a jam jar. Over in the spa of Montecatini there was a man who bred them. Slug-like, they slithered together. It felt like intrusion to have leeches applied in her room, Dina said, and so Chantal helped her into a dressing-gown and led her next door, to lie face down on Ursie's bed, with a towel over the lower part of her body. With the kind of spatula that he would have used to inspect a sore throat, Dr Melegnani levered the leeches out of the jar, and they wriggled clumsily as he dropped them on to her back. Spaced out, they looked like a tuft of hair, or blemishes. Where they bit and sucked, they left a mark in the shape of a star. Sated, swollen in size, they were returned to the bottom of the jar, no longer crawling but inert.

Do they hurt? Chantal wanted to know, or is it more of a tickling than a pain? They're not very nice to look at, these little friends of yours.

To Ursie, Chantal was to say that she used to feel quite sick at the sight. Nothing in her nursing experience had been like that. But what can one say? Strange as it was, the leeches have done her some good, the doctor must know what he is doing.

Avvocato Bellini prefers his clients to make appointments and visit him in the drafty confines of his studio with its quattrocento vaulting. I make an exception for the *baronessa*, he admits. That big top-heavy frame sways with the impact of the politeness which he wishes to convey. Smiling presents a difficulty for him, as if he had had a stroke and was attempting to relearn which muscles to use, in order to pull his face apart into the appropriate expression.

It has been a how-shall-I-say *delicate* discourse, in his words. Very sensitive. She summoned me, because I was to draw up the deed of donation whereby Monsignor Silvestri was to acquire the villa, and turn it over to nuns. They were going to discuss later exactly what role these nuns would have, but undoubtedly their chief duty was intended to be the maintenance and propagation of the Proofs. They'd be living witnesses of Unite the Impossible.

These developments took place in July, at a season when children and grandchildren are beginning to return to Tremaldi and the surrounding mountains and valleys for their holidays, swarming into villas and converted farmhouses otherwise shuttered for months on end. Rich foreigners with a taste for the romantic pay exorbitant rents for such houses as are available to them. Leonora Pigri invited Dina to one of her parties for the summer crowd. My little friends tire me out, Dina said, I have hardly the strength to get off my bed, what with the lawyer and the doctor.

In Kashmir, communal rioting was escalating, and Indira Gandhi appeared to have manoeuvred herself into a dead end. The Frankfurt stock market was performing with a strength which gave another perspective on the Deutschmark. In a last flicker of violence from the Tupamaros in Uruguay, a senior policeman in Montevideo had been shot dead. A school of whales had been stranded near Anchorage.

And now Andrew cut into a report of the preparation for the trial of the self-styled Emperor Bokassa, rumoured to keep human flesh in his refrigerator.

'My poor little girl,' she caught Andrew saying with utmost jauntiness, 'we are having a thin time of it, aren't we? The one who really ought to have this villa is Bishop Harold. Stick to your own.'

Out loud she said, 'But only the other day you told me it ought to be Silvestri.' Instead of an answer, she heard from the radio about the diamonds which the Emperor Bokassa had presented to President Giscard d'Estaing.

146

That was truly Chiarella's lucky afternoon, Luciana is to say. You don't need three guesses about where she'd spent her time. That woman can't have enough of it. The *baronessa* rang the bell, but Chiarella didn't come. It had never happened before, she dressed herself and went to look for her. What a disaster there might have been. As she made her way downstairs, the front door opened and there was Chiarella. Where have you been? the *baronessa* asked. Without hesitating a second, Chiarella said that she'd been out with Armando helping him to prune the olives, and it had been hot work, so she was coming back in. Have you ever heard anything like it?

So I had to return to the villa to take these latest instructions, Avvocato Bellini says.

And you still didn't point out the craziness of these ideas? Ursie asks him. I mean, the contradictions. How could you possibly allow her to draw up in the same week two different deeds of donations, one to Catholics, the other to Protestants? Doesn't it speak for itself? She couldn't have been in her right mind.

Offended, he insists that it is none of his business to instruct clients on the consequences of their actions. He deals with people who know their own minds, and are accustomed to act on it. Besides, she hadn't actually signed either. A choice lay ahead.

Pushed and Blocked would settle it naturally. Don't you worry your pretty head about it, Andrew said on a Spanish-language wavelength which she'd accidently caught. Remember what I've always told you about Pushed and Blocked.

The only person to discover the detailed contents of Alexander's letter was Don Alvise, for she read it to him, sentence by sentence, translating as she went.

'I want you to know what my son is like,' she said, 'what I have to put up with in my state of health.'

'What is there to say?' Don Alvise spread wide his hands, as priests do. 'We have higher guidance. We have Proofs.' His voice was shrunken.

Inspiration seems to have come to her then and there.

'Fetch my handbag,' she ordered. 'And a pen from the writing table.'

While she wrote out the cheque, he remained standing, immobile, his thoughts apparently far away. As though coming out of this trance, he said, retreating, 'No, no, you have already done more than enough for us with the *campo*.' Then, surprised, 'You haven't filled in the amount.'

'That's for you to decide.'

Undoing buttons down his scuffed soutane, he fetched out a brown wallet, its corners becoming unstitched, and folded the cheque into it. Without a word.

TWELVE

The day of the outing to Corubbio was fresh with a summer breeze. Light so strong had almost a crackle to it. Driving with dark glasses on, Ubaldo also complained about the number of tourists recklessly overtaking on these back roads. Square and high, the Armstrong-Siddeley never cornered well. The countryside out there is speckled with farms, ancestral groups of brick buildings each on their hump or hill, with here and there a castle or villa occupying a height. Vineyards climb in serrated lines.

Along one of the rare flat stretches is a shop built in some modern composite material, white blocks which give it the look of a displaced bathroom, a look underlined by the way that up to a level of about six foot the blocks have been picked out in black. Everyone shudders about the eyesore, but they go and buy there just the same. The shop sells the product of a pottery kiln about a hundred yards from it. High netting encloses the ground between, on which are displayed terracotta vases, flowerpots, ornaments in the shape of pineapples or acorns, statues of Venus and of Pinocchio, dwarfs, heraldic creatures designed for gateposts, a job lot collection which catches the eye. Beyond this open-air showground, the road passes a wayside restaurant where four or five little tables cluster under a striped awning. There the flat ground turns back on itself in the most complete and steep of curves, the first of a long series towards Corubbio.

As Ubaldo changed gear to negotiate this descent, there was a harsh grinding noise. Then a thud. Lurching, the car slithered away to its right, hitting against one of a line of posts strung out at intervals between the road and a drop of hundreds of feet down the steep and rock-bound incline of the mountain. Ubaldo shouted out. Dina was thrown across the back seat. Swivelling under its weight, the rear of the car broke another of the retaining posts. A crump, a sudden stop, and the car tilted, one wheel hanging out over the drop.

A shaken Ubaldo climbed out. In spite of the dramatic appearance, the car in fact had come to rest in little or no danger of rolling over into the valley below. Other cars pulled over. The restaurant owner and his family and customers soon stood round to listen to the over-excited Ubaldo explaining how the steering wheel had gone dead in his hands, and what a lucky escape it had been. Other people heaved Dina out, and escorted her back to the restaurant. There she sat on a wicker-seated chair under the striped awning, with a view up to the stricken car and the gathering bystanders.

It wasn't his fault, Ubaldo repeated, something must have given, snapped, he had had no control, they'd been so lucky that it was a miracle. A miracle. Nothing less. A car like that was built of best-quality steel, not like the alloys they use today. Think of the weight that must have hit those posts, no wonder they had been knocked somewhere far down the slope. And the *baronessa* had a pacemaker, she might have died of shock alone.

Tom, Lady Una's son-in-law, arrived to fetch her, and he said, 'You've certainly come up smiling. That could have been nasty.'

Skeletal metal was revealed beneath the blue paint-work, where the side of the car had been caved in. This was the car in which she and Andrew had first driven to Corubbio, to Mugniomaggio, to the villa itself. It repre-sented almost a lifetime.

'Aren't you wonderful?' Lady Una said, 'not even late for lunch either.' And with hardly a pause, 'Lambkins, you're not to do that, get off, do you hear?'

A trestle table had been laid out of doors. What courage, what aplomb, her friends said, congratulating her on being unharmed. According to Jacques Lemasle, 'Every-one has a sense of when their time has come. Like soldiers in war.' Didn't she agree, and wasn't this the basis of courage?

That was also the day when Yasser Arafat had offered to mediate over the release of American embassy officials held hostage in Teheran. 'Is that going to lead to anything?' Leonora Pigri wanted to know.

'I'd rather been wondering about taking my profits from gold,' Roberto Canavese said, 'but from what you're telling us, we'd be premature to do that. Wait till the Republicans get elected in November.'

'You're under special protection,' said Anna Karcz.

Of course we all knew about the letter she'd recently received from that bad boy Alexander, Anna Karcz is to say, and how it made her ill. Was that the right moment to mention it? It was her first day out since the whole upset, and now this had to happen as well. Dear Dr Melegnani, he can't resist a bit of gossip, he's gone about telling us all. To say nothing but the truth, we were longing to ask her about these leeches, and we would have done if it hadn't been for the crash. He swears by his treatment, but I wouldn't care for it. Rather horrible.

I accompanied her home after that lunch, Anna Karcz adds, none of us thought it would be right if she were to have any sense of being abandoned after a crash like that.

At the scene of the accident they stopped. Ubaldo and Tullio had already organised the removal of the wreckage. Only a tyre smudge in a broad grey wake across the road revealed where the car had smacked into the posts.

'That car was Andrew's pride and joy,' Dina said. 'I wonder what I ought to do.'

The big end had broken and a new part would have to be specially made, which might cost as much as a new car. The model was long obsolete. Besides, the chassis had now been pushed out of alignment. Shall we tell them to dispose of it as scrap, Ubaldo wanted to know.

'The *barone* will give insructions,' Dina answered.

I didn't know where to put myself when I heard that, Ubaldo is to say, I mean how are you supposed to answer to such a thing? It's no good pointing out that the poor man

151

had been dead these many years. I didn't want to be sacked, and I would have been if I'd spoken out. There is no choice, you and I and everyone has to humour her. Even the Marchesa Piccolomini does, and she's one to speak her mind.

And Andrew did give instructions, interrupting a Moscow English-language broadcast which was accusing the United States of using the Teheran hostage crisis to stir up an imperialist war. 'The journey of our car,' Andrew said, 'is also the journey of Unite the Impossible. Bury it decently, make it a monument which tells our story so that others can benefit. Silvestri will know what it is to be done.'

There was no time to be lost. Adela was due to leave for a holiday in Rimini. The conference season had begun. She summoned Don Alvise to track down Monsignor Silvestri, who happened to be at the Pope's summer residence at Castelgandolfo. Don Alvise himself was due to take a party of boy scouts camping in Umbria. Avvocato Bellini was about to leave for the grouse moors. That they could gather together was itself a tribute to the powers of Unite the Impossible.

Even in the cool of the *salone*, Monsignor Silvestri unfolded a handkerchief to wipe his handsome forehead, and then flapped it like a fan. He had insisted on bringing in Don Alvise. Luciana served home-made water ices.

'You intend to make an attraction of it?' he wanted to know. 'Something that people will visit – a museum? With an entrance charge? We might wait until we can incorporate it here with your other Proofs, when we've decided what's to be done about them and their future.'

The Andrew and Edwina Lumel Ecumenical Centre, he suggested, with a permanent exhibition. Some part of the villa might be devoted to the Proofs in showcases; rooms might be reserved for scholars researching into her diaries and notes and Flowers of Meditation. Nuns would be the right caretakers.

Montetremaldi was the avvocato's idea. The last farmer to have lived there was a relation of the neighbour who persisted in breaking the villa's drains discharging under his field. The place was now abandoned; he had himself put in some work on its future on behalf of the Church, and was sure that the ecclesiastical authorities would prove amenable.

Since first Andrew and Dina had been there, the approach to Montetremaldi has changed, almost beyond recognition. At the bottom of the hill, a packaging plant has been erected, and alongside it a sawmill. Timber lies in untidy and jagged stacks. For trucks, an open space has been cleared in what used to be unspoilt woodland, and this parking lot has an air of a battlefield, scarred, cluttered with battered oil drums or tar barrels, refuse, worn-out tyres, discarded fittings like rusted boilers or holed baths. From down there, the track still runs up to the church, but it has been levelled with stones and smashed tiles.

Anxious about his car, the avvocato stopped short of the summit, so they walked the final stretch in the dappled light under branches of overhanging chestnuts. On the path, almost underfoot, lay the slim amber and pearly quill of a porcupine.

'You are all witnesses to another Proof,' Dina exulted. 'The first time we were here, Andrew picked one up just about on the spot where we're standing and he wanted it to be a pen.'

'I'd imagined them as faraway creatures,' Chantal said, 'in Africa or somewhere. I didn't know we had them here.'

The quill was passed from hand to hand: an unquestioned Proof.

Above rose the shaft of the bell-tower. The church and its door, the farmhouse and its windows, were barricaded now behind metal shutters, bent and dented where attempts had been made to force them open. The abandoned seed-drill still stood in one of the barns, and at first Monsignor Silvestri proposed that this might be the car's location. So to speak, in a pavilion of its own.

To Dina, the car and the church went together, under one roof. If the church had been deconsecrated, then why not inside it? Otherwise she preferred the main room of the

153

casa canonica, with its rustic walls. Cement would have to be laid for it, and the door enlarged so that the car could be hoisted into position, and then a pair of inner doors installed to close on it.

Sardinian shepherds are supposed to tend flocks higher up in the mountains: what if they or their sheep were to break in and to shelter in the interior, fouling it? Passersby might also abuse the monument, sleep there, who knows what, now that nothing is sacred? There must be no means of access.

There the Armstrong-Siddeley is to remain for centuries, for ever, a monument that faith did survive into our age, to be as representative in the future as the bell-tower has been in the past. Inspired by Unite the Impossible, people from all over the world would one day be assembling at the villa and here at Montetremaldi too, where they will want to inspect for themselves this eternal Proof. When the outer walls are finally closed off, apertures will have to be provided, with glass, through which these visitors can look at the immobilised object within. An explanation, a statement of intent, exhibits such as photographs or specially mounted Flowers of Meditation, will have to be prepared, and much consideration will have to be given on how best to present them.

You know I have prepared a deed of gift for the villa? Dina asked the monsignor. He had heard, he nodded. The avvocato had informed him.

After we have held a service of dedication here, Dina said, I shall sign that deed.

THIRTEEN

What a way to spend one's holiday, Ursie thought – for there, in the half-light of the room was her mother, prostrate and face down on the bed. Under a slipping towel, vulnerable and fatty flesh was exposed, with shapes creeping and arching on her back like so many monstrous eyebrows.

'How can you do it to her?' she asked Dr Melegnani. 'In this day and age it's not possible to believe that leeches are of any value.'

'Come to my office and I'll show you the literature,' he answered. 'They use them in plenty of leading hospitals. Natural remedies are far preferable to surgery.'

A madhouse. They came at her from all directions, and there was nothing for it except to pretend that this was normality and to rein her reactions in behind a stiff and shameful smile. Like a sprain, the hypocrisy wouldn't go away. She could hardly wait to meet Charles in Porto Ercole, joining friends to sail from there to Elba. Berndt, her German colleague, was staying with his parents on the island in what was reported to be a house with a private beach.

Even the cypresses along the drive were shrivelling to a copper colour with some disease. To arrive there had involved a train and an expensive taxi. Ubaldo sat all day on the sofa in the kitchen, interrupting his crosswords only to describe once more what a lucky escape he had had, or what sort of new car they ought to buy now as a replacement.

Tears have always come easily to Luciana, bright as they roll down, while nose, cheeks, wart, chin, motherly bosom, wobble with emotion. Where will it all end? Giulia is threatening to put out the eyes of Chiarella. *Tutto sbottonato*, Armando stands there openly at the bottom of the stairs, laughing, and she laughs back. The nurse is honest at least, but the others are robbing the *baronessa* blind. Whole trays of flowers, and boxes of apricots and vegetables, simply disappear. They sell them off and pocket the cash.

And so what if they do? Ursie asks herself. There have to be some compensations for the madness. Wouldn't we all be doing the same in their position? It's not as if one single old lady could use all that stuff herself, it would otherwise go to waste.

Besides, there is no evidence of any such enterprise. In the garden are the desiccated roses only to be expected in August. The old storerooms round the back contain the usual litter, apparently complete down to the cobwebs. Wouldn't it be profitable to sell the historic lathe and tools instead of a few flowers?

And this was where the hairy-legged Chantal was said to be having her affair. The place looked abandoned. Unable to stop herself, Ursie tried the door of the *camera del Tedesco*, and peered in while her eyes adjusted to the dark. In this house where a dead man supposedly speaks at any hour over the radio, the lovemaking may be another figment, imagined by people without enough to occupy their minds.

Giulia's front room has always been a masterpiece of cleanliness and polishing. Ageless, high-cheeked, hair pulled back, she does have Red Indian looks, as Ubaldo likes to say, though he does not mean it as a compliment. We see everything that goes on in the villa, she tells Ursie, we aren't deceived. You know how Ubaldo fakes the household expenses, he puts down twice as much in the books as ever had been bought. Go and ask the butcher in Sant' Ambrogio, or the shop on the piazza. Everyone will tell the same story, because these are the facts. How else, she'd like to know, have they been able to buy themselves a brand-new house in Civitale?

And the villagers are saying something else too, which

she ought to know about. The news is that Don Alvise has got his hands on the *baronessa*'s fortune. The English bishop and his wife may think that they are going to grab everything, well no, it's too late. It's all been given to Don Alvise. He may not look so shrewd, but he is, he's a deep one. Now there's also this Tonio who's living with him. A boy like that, who ties his shirt-tails into a knot around his stomach, and nobody quite knows where he's from. Don Alvise was supposed to be off camping with scouts in Umbria, but – the face sets into a glare of implication – he returned early.

There's no avoiding the Satterthwaites, who appear to have colonised the villa for the summer. Like cuckoos, they are noisy with claims. As though to make a point, they leave open the door of the spare room, to reveal suitcases spilling out clothes, their books, the bishop's work. Whether they are up there, or down in the *salone*, or reading through the collection of newspaper files in the library, the loud and intelligent pitch of their conversation is enough to track their progress.

The Flowers of Meditation remind me of Saint Catherine of Siena, the bishop says. Or one of the great mystics like Meister Eckhart, perhaps. How privileged we are. And so refreshing to have access to a writer with the moral directness of Don Alvise.

In the evening, they like to sit out on the terrace as the heat slackens, to take their books to the iron bench round the well, and stroll among the roses. Looking at Armando out watering with a hose which coils for yards behind him, they praise his diligence. Isn't it just perfect here? It must have looked like this two hundred years ago, nothing has changed. Quite certain to be overheard, they bat such phrases between them with a liveliness which makes Ursie think of ping-pong.

Crabbed, stooping, the bishop rarely meets her eye, and then usually with a kind of lunging leer.

'Splendid little church, that place up the hill,' the bishop said. 'Pity they let it go so badly. Still, it'll have a new life now.'

Cath cut him off. 'What else could they have done? It's the same with us. People have moved away into the big cities, and that's where they need new plant nowadays.'

With an expression which signifies Other Times, Other Customs, the bishop purses his lips.

'It's so exciting,' Cath said, 'we've been up there with your mother. It's going to be a whole business to put the car in place. They're planning on cranes at the moment. It'll be lovely once it's inaugurated and so moving.'

'Alexander wonders whether the car shouldn't be put back on the road for her. You know how he loves old things like that, he's got a Spitfire propeller at home.'

'*Poor* Alexander,' but exactly why he was to be called poor, Cath did not say.

She wouldn't talk like that, Ursie thinks, and the bishop wouldn't be squinting at me with such trouble, unless they possessed all the facts. They've read the letter evidently, and they aren't about to challenge the application of the leeches.

Caligula and Justinian both immortalised their horses, the bishop reminds her, and hadn't Napoleon too, building a memorial to the charger on which he'd ridden during his most spectacular victories? And what about Lord Uxbridge after Waterloo, with a monument to the leg he'd had shot away? The Armstrong-Siddeley could be seen in that light.

'Most certainly not,' Cath said indignantly. 'It has spiritual associations going far beyond mere commemoration. People need such things. Really, Harold. It's a Proof of her spiritual realities.'

'We like Monsignor Silvestri so much,' the bishop said. 'Wonderful chap, indeed he is. A few years ago, and a thing like this would have been out of the question. The Catholics have come a long way towards realising Unite the Impossible. He's very willing to tolerate an Anglican presence in a historic spot like that. Your mother has been truly prophetic in her ecumenism.'

No longer ping-pong, Ursie tells herself, but a duel to the death. She looks at the flowery cotton which folds over Cath's concave chest, and at his grubby linen jacket and pipe, and she imagines this pair as the future owners of the villa. Only a few more years of plotting, and they must have managed to retire here, levering themselves into comfort by means of the Proofs. Is it possible for them to be sincere about the Armstrong-Siddeley as an ecumenical symbol? Aren't they really testing to find out what she knows or doesn't know about Silvestri? From what they tell her they are also in touch with Avvocato Bellini. It's a standoff. Because Dina has the whip hand. She's the arbiter, she'll decide who has won. One party has only to rush off to her with firm evidence of the other party's insincerity, and that'll be that. The moment he's back from Scotland, the avvocato will be called out, and she'll put her signature to the deed.

Like in old days, Nico Piccolomini fetched her, for an afternoon at the pool at Mugniomaggio. And what about Charles, he asks, when are you going to marry him? Next time round, he promises he's not going to let her slip through his fingers so lightly. He's made it up with his wife, he sighs, but she's no more faithful than he is.

'Nico's always saying he should have married you,' Sandra Piccolomini told her, 'he's worse than your brother Alessandro. What's the matter with these boys who had every advantage handed them on a plate, and don't know what to do next?'

Old lovers are like dreams, leaving an impression but no substance. Ursie can't remember what she once saw in this fussy businessman, rake-thin with spindly legs, vain and a mild hypochondriac with a worry that the water's chlorine content might induce allergies or worse. Sandra crops her white hair short. A determined swimmer, she wears the same black costume that she has always worn. Sunbathing has given her arms and thighs a crinkly look of cured meat.

'That letter should never have been posted. We all think that,' Sandra said. 'It made her ill.'

Isn't it a question of love? Ursie wants to know. Of love, and the shadow of loneliness which is its Siamese twin? 'Sometimes,' she said, 'I promise myself that I'm going to

159

break through. I'm going to find the courage to go into her room and wrap my arms round her and give her the comfort she needs so much.'

While she's speaking, an inner voice is also warning, Dreams, romance, pure sentimentality. That's a mother too frightening ever to be a friend as well. Let Alexander take the flak. Besides, has Dina ever wanted to be wrapped in her child's arms, and wouldn't she be more likely to complain of the way her shirt was being crumpled up?

'Even the weather is supposed to be governed by him,' she said. 'Hearing voices is generally considered a symptom of schizophrenia.'

Sandra said drily, 'She often tells me how proud she is of you. You've done so well in the City. You've got a brain like hers.'

But I can't think about Uniting the Impossible, I can't even make up my mind to say yes to a man who loves me. Because he pushes his specs up his nose as if he'd got a nervous tic. Because I'm always making selfish and unlovable excuses when all that's required is to say yes to Charles and yes to Dina.

'We Italians have one great virtue, we never wait until it's too late.'

Not love or its absence, Sandra thought, but fear of death was the motivation. The secret wish to buy a seat in the Members Enclosure in Heaven. Let's hope it's going to be like a superior Jockey Club up there. Wouldn't it be too awful if we were to find ourselves totally indistinguishable from the billions of others who have ever lived? No culture, no background, no allowance for education or sensibilities. Savages on all sides. Selectivity's no bad thing wherever you are.

'My father was very strong and self-sufficient. I can remember that. Now he's like a good little boy, he speaks only when he's spoken to.'

Whatever would he have said, Ursie wants to know, about what's going on in the villa, and about the Proofs and the rest of it? 'What she likes to call Andrew's voice seems rather obviously to be only what she wants to hear.'

An arthritis sufferer now, Pippo sits in a deck-chair, elegant in a white straw hat the shape of a trilby. He said, 'He was very good at canasta. No talent for languages, though, unlike Dina. *Bisogna begonia*, that kind of thing.'

Sandra said, 'I believe in his voice. Whether she hears him out loud or whether it's just in her head makes no difference. For her, it's real.'

'But every lunatic who thinks he's Jesus Christ hears voices which are real to him. Our English bishop has even begun to talk about how Napoleon built a memorial to his horse. If my mother hadn't been able to afford her whims, she'd have been locked up by now.'

Pippo winced. That wasn't fair. Everyone respected and admired her, they could testify to her exceptional political and financial acumen. Neither he nor anyone else could suppose for a moment that she wasn't in full possession of her faculties.

'My mother paid for the building for a church in Libya,' he said, 'at Benghazi. And it was bombed to the ground in the war. Quite to the flat. And she subscribed to the roof of the church at Fatima, an absolute horror. It almost ruined my poor father. I don't see that you have much to complain about.'

'That bishop may not know our laws,' Sandra said, 'but I've told you a hundred times that in this country parents are obliged legally to leave the bulk of their property to their children. There's no need to be so hard on Napoleon, he codified the laws under which you and Alexander are obliged to inherit. My friend the monsignor wants to do her a good turn, that's all, he says that she has patrons in high places and he must cultivate her. The walling-up of the Armstrong-Siddeley is rather delightful. In the best tradition of those English eccentrics who built obelisks and pyramids in their parks, and which today tourists pay to visit. He thinks Montetremaldi will be an attraction.'

And what about Iris Warren? Ursie asked. Neither of them knew the name, or had heard anything about Andrew having had a mistress. Sandra said, 'There's never been a man who didn't have a mistress. I'm sure she wouldn't mind telling you. Ask her. See for yourself.'

Dropped home in the evening, Ursie pushed open the front door under whose varnish the outline of the hammer and sickle from years ago could just be detected. At that hour, the sun at the back of the villa projected rainbow spots of light here and there through the dark interior, on the furniture and flagstones. Dust could be seen floating in its rays. Then she heard the slap of sandals on the stairs, which could only mean Chantal.

'Your mother wants to see you.'

A summons to her room. In the dreadful hour before dinner, who could guess what storm might blow up? What accusations or gibberish? She might be expected to listen for Andrew's voice, and if she then said that she had heard nothing, the hopeful face opposite would diminish into a scowl. In a moment, the quiet of the villa was transformed into the heartbeat of panic.

Dina was sitting as usual in her armchair, newspapers and books piled on the floor within reach. High and low, the two bells of Sant' Ambrogio began.

'You've been talking to Sandra and Pippo,' Dina began, 'I had a telephone call from her. It seems you have things you want to ask. Ask me whatever you like.'

Had Alexander's letter been transformed behind her back into safe ground?

'I am blessed,' Dina said, anticipating her, 'I am looked after, I should have realised it. In any crisis, he tells me what to do. I have only to trust my radio. Poor boy, poor old man, I should say, seeing how Alexander has turned out. What are we to do to give him a sense of purpose? His life's so empty. It's beyond him to understand the richness of mine.'

The sharp nose wrinkled and twitched, but with amusement and humour. In conversation like this, there would be none of the evasion of that Ha h'm. The radio lay on the bed. Otherwise the photographs, the Flowers of Meditation, her battery of pens, were as tidy as in a barracks.

'Well, what are you waiting for? Ask away.'

162

She still hesitated before she could bring out, 'We had wondered about Iris Warren.'

'Her? If I have a good look, I think I can find you a photograph of her. When last I heard, she was in Vancouver or somewhere. Probably she's been dead for years, she disappeared from our lives. She was a bit of a gypsy, she belonged to rather a fast set. I liked her very much, but I don't think your father did in the end.'

The church bells stopped. Ursie drew back the curtains which were kept drawn against the day, and the room brightened with evening brilliance.

'And what are you hearing about the Federal Reserve's policy?' Dina asked. 'That sort of monetarism isn't going to work, is it?'

'Now you're the one to be asking questions.'

When she wants, Ursie thought, she can be more charming and winning than anyone. There's something almost coquettish about the grey curl over her forehead, something feminine which undermines and even contradicts the hard and self-sufficient personality.

She's hardly ever been like that, Ursie is to say afterwards, marvelling. I felt I'd been such a bad daughter, it's awful to have laughed at Unite the Impossible, and I had to make amends and this was my chance. Do you think she was deliberately making me feel guilty? Maybe it had something to do with the way the room was laid out, so you could see the pitiful little radio, and that notebook of hers and feel yourself in touch with all her obsessions. And staring you in the face was that horrible portrait of her own mother, as blank as an icon in a Greek church, there's nothing to be learnt from it. That's quite likely the root of the whole trouble, she never had an example, there was nobody to teach her the simplest facts about being a mother or a wife. Like a waif.

At any rate I hugged her, Ursie says, she who's always so disliked being touched. And I thought, how you torment yourself with that bloody little radio and those damned leeches, and somewhere deep down you know very well what you're doing and are testing out everyone's reactions, who's friend and who's foe. Let's go down, the Satterthwaites must be getting impatient on their own, I said, and she laughed and said, never mind, they can wait, they're used to that. I'm so glad we had that moment, it was the closest either of us have been in years. And in the morning, guess what, she'd fished out that photo for me. A studio pose, typically Thirties sort of thing, hair bobbed, a single row of pearls, a woman like so many others. She keeps that photograph of Iris Warren in the drawer of her writing table. The power of the past. Think of it. Worse than the leeches, masochism like that.

That morning too, before leaving to join Charles and their friends, she walked through the garden and out into Sant' Ambrogio. In Don Alvise's house there was no sign of Tonio – perhaps that relationship was an invention too. And how's *la mama*? Don Alvise asked. Alexander's letter is a thing of the past. The car crash put paid to that. The spirit of Unite the Impossible won through.

Sheets of paper held with clips littered the surfaces available on chairs and the table in his front room. These were chapters from *Francesco and the Birds*, a version of the story of St Francis updated to the southern village of his other books.

'The English bishop is reading your whole series,' she told him. 'He admires your work.'

Palms upwards, he spreads wide his hands.

And Montetremaldi. What would people say about burying the car there? Lots of rumours are spreading. Can the Church really be going to allow it to happen? I thought I'd gone too far, Ursie is to say, the shock of his expression made me stop. While I was talking, I was thinking, good God, it's taken me all these years to realise that I despise this man, with his corpse-like appearance and tombstone teeth. His eyes are smarmy and treacherous, he can't look at you, the bishop's positively straightforward by comparison. All the while he was fumbling with the buttons on his dirty and smelly old habit, and reaching in for his wallet. I had no idea what he might be doing.

The cheque which he fished out to hand her was greeny-grey, drawn on the Swiss bank where Dr Golaz manages the account. Besides the date, only Dina's unmistakable signature was on it.

'The *baronessa* insisted on it,' he said. 'You know how nobody can argue with her. It was for the parish, the *campo*, the poor, whatever I wanted. But of course that was out of the question. People do get to hear of these things, I can never imagine how, and they're already saying that I have been humouring her in order to extract money, and it risks compromising her whole work. They'll see the car as another donation, they'll respect her for what she is. It's the greatest relief to me that you have come this morning, and I can return this cheque to the family. I leave it to your judgement whether or not you tell your mother, or just tear the thing up.'

I'm only too well aware that anyone who looks at me can easily read my thoughts, Ursie says, and I suppose I was as transparent as one of his puerile little books. The eyes give it away. Anyhow what he said was, 'I can tell that you're thinking I must be a good man after all, and I wish you didn't look so surprised.'

FOURTEEN

On the far slopes of the valley a shoot was in progress. Bursts of what sounded like flattened handclaps echoed up to the villa from first light onwards. Shooting is not compatible with Unite the Impossible, and Dina is in the habit of contributing small sums to the pressure groups seeking to have the sport curtailed, the shooting of songbirds especially. It was a bad omen on the morning of the inauguration of the shrine at Montetremaldi. Andrew had given no warning of it. His last intervention had been to dictate another Flower of Meditation: 'Make Souls Shine Out'. The words were to be chiselled on to a tablet, and affixed on the wall next to the car. As she was breakfasting in bed, those subdued volleys sparked small spurts of corresponding outrage in her.

What Andrew had arranged, however, was a fine day; a still and brilliant November afterthought of summer, when the countryside has the clarity of a pane of glass.

That is no surprise; indeed the one aspect of the plan on which she had counted. Organisation for the event has been exhausting, unthinkable without the help of Don Alvise. He's devised a service, he'd been in contact with the cardinal and Monsignor Silvestri, both of whom are eager to attend. It is an honour. Tonio, he has said, is a youth from a highly disturbed background whom he has taken in for a while, and he will supervise the arrival of the guests. Dignity, he assures her, will be the keynote.

The guest list was a matter for her and Adela. Finding somewhere to put these people up has been a strain. So many competing claims. Lionel and Minou have to occupy the spare room. A partner now in Lionel's old firm, Micky is too busy to come, which is lucky in its way. But

166

Una Macleod has had to be pressured into having Bishop Harold and Cath. Anna Karcz can invite nobody to stay in that little rabbit-hutch of hers, and Leonora Pigri pleads that she has a nightmare schedule which will involve racing from Milan at the last moment, and so regrets that her very large house can't be at Dina's disposal. The local hotel will have to do for Isabelle and Albert Golaz, for Holly Strickland, and even worse, for Pater Auhofer and Père Destouches. A couple of kilometres on the far side of Sant' Ambrogio, this place is new, cobbled out of prefabricated concrete strips and plate glass, its interior all orange tiles and rubber plants and posters about sporting events, with tubular plastic-seat chairs designed for stacking. It's embarrassing for her, but there's no alternative.

Nor does she much care for the new car that Ubaldo has insisted upon; it seems small, a bit of a box after the Armstrong-Siddeley, but he swears that it is the best of modern Italian designs. Again, there hasn't been much of an alternative.

Favours can't be asked endlessly of the Piccolominis. Already she's had to borrow from them a spare service of white china, and glasses of several sizes which have to be wrapped in newspaper, and then packed in cartons for safe transit, and knives and forks and serving dishes. In all the years in the villa, there's never been a party like this, and the resources aren't up to it. Lunch for between fifty and sixty. In the new car, Ubaldo has been ferrying the stuff. Luciana and Giulia have coopted friends to prepare and cook a turkey and a ham, to chop tomatoes, and they have made sure that she knows every step they have taken, consulted on the choice between pasta and rice, and which salads are suitable.

Wonderful to be here, Lionel says, we wouldn't have missed your big occasion for worlds. How many years is it since that time you and Andrew stayed with us on your way out here, and I tested that car out? Pre-war quality, post-war engineering. A collector's item. Nothing on the market's so good.

'Ursie's arriving in good time,' he said, 'but what about Alexander? It's a safe bet he won't show. Not until the eleventh hour, in any case.'

Lionel still tries to pull his shoulders back, and stand erect, conscious of the figure he cuts. The gold clip has survived all those years, and he has a roll of hundred thousand lire notes stuffed into it. Somehow the suits don't quite have the same metropolitan smartness, as if he didn't fill them any longer. Not so carnivorous when he laughs, the drawn lips and teeth are more like a promise that there's life in the old dog yet.

You could do a lot with this property, he tells Dina. Out at the back, for instance. Rooms galore, all unused, nothing in them but worm-eaten workbenches, and demijohns. Why not do those rooms up and rent them? People pay fortunes for that sort of place, with a really marketable character. Luciana had shown him into one which already had a bed and basin in it, spinning him some tale about how she'd almost been raped there by the Germans. Any German soldier who raped that woman would have deserved the Iron Cross for bravery.

When he talks like that – when he refers to lead in his pencil, and getting it up – he shows no awareness of any possible displeasure on the part of others. To him, Anna Karcz is a dry old spinster who has never been getting enough of it, and the bishop and Cath typically English in being sexless, and Holly Strickland an arty lesbian. He entertains them with inside stories of Sotheby's and Christie's and the goings-on on the Onassis yacht, and what Princess Caroline really did at the ball whose antics are reported in last week's *Paris-Match*.

There never was much resistance in Minou, and now there's none at all. Physically she's an apology, with a waist hardly more than a digestive tract. A study in neutrality, she is not taking sides, and can be held to no opinion. If Lionel didn't insist on her wearing expensive clothes, she might almost be invisible. Still, she bridges the awkward moments when Lionel can't quite restrain himself. For instance when he asked, 'Which did old

Andrew do best, pushing or blocking?' with a shout of delight at his cleverness in playing with the words. For instance when he said with another roar, 'I know what Unite the Impossible is, the bishop and his wife after lights out.'

You know how he is, Minou murmurs, Lionel can't ever be serious about anything. It's his way. You know how to make allowances, you can explain it to Cath who looks daggers at him.

'My contribution is going to be to film proceedings,' Lionel told Dina. The video camera is protected in a case of aluminium, hard and bright, and he loves to use the equipment of light meters and reflectors, like expensive toys.

To Ursie, he said, 'I have hopes that my old chum Andrew will show up on film. No, really, I have to have a record of this. Nobody will believe it. You and I must have a talk about what's to be done. It's pitiful to see her brought to this. Priests are bad for your health.'

For the ceremony, he and Minou looked as if they were about to attend a fashionable wedding. Dina wore her sable coat, and a black hat. Anna Karcz and her nephew Julian and Don Alvise joined them in a procession, out on the road past the hotel where the others were staying. A crowd had already collected on the parking lot of the sawmill, not only Martin Cammaerts and Jacques Lemasle, the Francks and the Canaveses, but truck-drivers and workmen curious to see what was going on. As arranged, Tonio was in charge. Only Dina was to be allowed to drive up the track, and the cardinal too, when he arrived. Pippo Piccolomini had to raise his voice to Tonio, to insist that someone like him with an arthritic hip was either going to go through in the car or return home.

Straggling out over several hundred yards, everyone else picked their way over the surface of awkwardly levelled stone and rubble, deceptively carpeted now by husks of sweet chestnut off the trees. At the top, what was left of the grass had been cut and stripped by the builders and their van. Clumps of stinging nettle around the buildings stood out stiff, in vivid green. The *casa canonica*, and the area around it, had become a work site with bags of sand, planks, a mixer, heaps of stone where the end wall had been taken down. At the far end of the house, fresh concrete had been spread over the floor of what had probably been an old storeroom. An interior door leading into the rest of the house had been closed off.

The Armstrong-Siddeley is sideways on.

'We had to hire a winch,' the builder explained, 'it couldn't be offloaded in there any other way. Quite a job.'

He and his three labourers were in dusty overalls. We didn't believe we'd get it done in time, the builder said, not a thing as difficult as this, with so much that could go wrong. Also he'd been frightened to leave the car so exposed, he had had to persuade his brother-in-law to come and spend the nights up here as watchman. You never could tell what ideas people might have when they saw a car left here.

The car has been raised on blocks.

'Where are its wheels?' Dina asked.

The builder said, 'They'll be replaced.'

Between the side of the car and the interior wall there is just space to squeeze past. One last time, Dina edged round it. Then she opened a door. 'Hold that pose, will you,' Lionel said, 'while I film you. What's that place where they found those tablets in Mesopotamia? In a thousand years they'll excavate here. Nineveh, do I mean?'

As soon as the ceremony is over, the builder and his men are to replace the stones now heaped outside so loosely, to raise again this missing wall and shut the aperture off, so enclosing the car in its stone coffin. Nobody will then be able to gain access to it, and there it will rest down the centuries, a memorial, Uniting the Impossible. Once more Dina went over her instructions: in the wall two openings are to be constructed, in the form of arrow-slits, not more than ten centimetres wide and of course glassed in, so that visitors may peer through at the car in its eternal home but cannot reach it or climb in, even if they were to break the glass. A recess a few centimetres deep is also to be provided between the two windows, so that in due course she can have a carpenter make a showcase with an explanation of the site and its meaning for posterity. Also the tablet will be attached here, in marble.

The cardinal's car raised dust as it came to a stop. With him were Monsignor Silvestri and his personal assistant, whose scowl expressed as plainly as words that in his opinion the cardinal was too frail and venerable to be gadding about like this at the back of beyond, and ought never to have been inveigled out here. Slow, stooping, the cardinal stood for a while, as though recovering his breath. Altogether he provided a magnificent splash of colour, scarlet, with his gold pectoral cross, and white hair fluffing under his skullcap.

With Monsignor Silvestri supporting him under one arm, and Dina under the other, the cardinal said, 'I grew up in a spot as lovely as this. We were nine at home. I see my mother now bending over the tub washing clothes. Are you like me, unable to remember what it was you heard yesterday but recapturing the past clearly? If you killed a pig, I could still make black sausage for you. You never find it properly prepared these days.'

'I wasn't allowed anywhere near my father's work,' Dina said. 'If he thought I was interfering with his paint or his brushes, he'd push me out.'

'What a misfortune to be an artist,' the cardinal said, 'but how we ordinary mortals are in need of them.'

Under the limpid light of that day, Don Alvise looked all bones and suffering, every inch the El Greco martyr, as he intoned the opening prayers. His voice dwindled with humility when he declared that the purpose of this shrine was perfectly resumed in the *baronessa*'s phrase, Make Souls Shine Out.

'With so many English speakers present,' he said sadly, 'I must apologise for my pronunciation, and hope to make amends with a translation as *Fate Risplendere le Anime*. These words, in both languages, will in due course be recorded on this wall. And this is my prayer, *Domine, dirige nos in viam tuam per hoc vehiculum.*'

In a brief address, in masterful French, Père Destouches then struck a biographical note; he evoked John Napier and his art, his friends like Aldous and Maria Huxley and Iris Origo, the cosmopolitan culture of that background, and its perpetuation at La Grecchiata by Andrew and Edwina Lumel. Their values of excellence came from the spirit. The Armstrong-Siddeley had many associations, he said, *'comme signe, voire signification, dans un monde prêt à la reçevoir, de la pensée si belle et bientôt sans doute répandue d'Unire l'Impossible.'*

While he was speaking, a car scrambled towards them, pulling up at the edge of the assembled guests. Alexander in a leather jacket and jeans, and a girl in one of his shirts much too large for her, its tail hanging out. They were just in time to catch the culmination of the service. The cardinal's assistant was holding out reading glasses and a telegram. This was a message of good wishes from the Holy Office. The cardinal presented it to Dina, and then he pronounced a blessing.

Most of those present think that Bishop Satterthwaite has only himself to blame for what happened next. The cardinal was tired, they say, of course he wanted to go home and rest, and it was only natural for Dina to escort him away, only natural for the other guests to assume that the little ceremony was over. Nobody had warned them that the bishop might have a contribution to make. In any case, he'd been slow enough about it. If he had coordinated the thing as he should have done, then he ought to have been quicker. The fact was that by the time he was ready, had found the place and was reading aloud Psalm Forty-Six, only Leonora Pigri and Alexander and Liz were still paying attention to him. Already the builders had begun to reinstate the wall. If we don't hurry, they said, the Sardinians will strip what they can.

It's a suitable text, the bishop says in his own defence, you know how it goes, about knapping the spear in sunder and burning the chariots in the fire. Was it really too much to have something English and Anglican for Dina's sake? That was pretty flowery French for most of us, never mind the dog-Latin. They might have waited as a matter of courtesy, surely that's not asking a great deal. Not just turned their backs on me.

That's what he tells people at the party afterwards, airing his grievance. Had there been something about the little ceremony which generated bad temper?

'How could you?' Sandra Piccolomini wanted an explanation from Alexander. 'Like a tramp, and with a girl like that. Who is she anyhow?'

Liz, my secretary, he said, and a neighbour too. She's never been abroad, so I took her on as helper and co-driver. We had a breakdown, we couldn't help that. If we'd gone first to the villa, and stopped to change, then we'd never have made it.

Lionel went about saying, Typical Alexander. At the Day of Judgement he'll be late. No sense of what's due.

On the subject of feathers from the Archangel Gabriel's wing, Jacques Lemasle quarrelled with Père Destouches. I've seen them with my own eyes in a monastery in Portugal, Jacques Lemasle said. But these things aren't to be interpreted literally, according to the priest. 'And what about the Armstrong-Siddeley, then, how does a lump of metal become a symbol, *voire signification*?'

Several people thought that the car must have been maltreated by the builders to have acquired so many scratches and bumps. The wheels must have been stolen. If you'd lifted the bonnet, you might find that the engine had vanished too.

The back door was opened, so that the party could spill out onto the terrace, and enjoy the view. In the valley, the crackle of shooting had shifted, and soon it would die away into the afternoon.

At which point, Bishop Satterthwaite went upstairs. As he tells the story, this was absent-mindedness, pure and simple. He had quite forgotten that he wasn't staying in the house. Out of habit, he'd made his way to the spare room to fetch some tobacco. During the performance of religious duties, he makes sure never to have any on him, because it creates a distraction, and one of which he feels ashamed; he finds himself patting his pocket and thinking of a smoke when his mind ought to be on higher things. Picture his discomfiture when he had found Lionel and Minou's things up there. Beating a fast retreat, what should he have seen at the end of the corridor but Monsignor Silvestri slipping into Andrew's room. He'd therefore set after him to have a word. Quite frankly, he had thought it opportune to raise with him the way they'd spoiled the reading of the psalm.

Certainly, the monsignor allows, he had noticed that the bishop had slipped away, and he couldn't help wondering why. He'd assumed that the bishop would have gone into Andrew's room, and there had to be some purpose behind it. What? The man had been acting strangely towards him for quite some time. Look at the spoiled and childish way he'd just behaved at the service. Avvocato Bellini had warned him that something might lie behind it – no, he wasn't going to be more specific than that. There he had been, standing in the room, when the Anglican bishop had crept up on him.

What absolute nonsense, the bishop contests it hotly. The monsignor had been snooping. Estimating the value of the property more like. He wasn't a fool, he kept his ear to the ground. The monsignor intended to lay his hands on the villa in return for the burial of the car at Monte-tremaldi on church property. Nuns were due to be moved into the villa, he'd had that on good authority. How can the monsignor deny it? It just goes to show the type of slippery people you have to deal with. That was one reason why he'd wanted to recite that psalm, for the moral text it provided.

When I caught sight of his face coming towards me, the monsignor draws himself up and glowers, I understood that he wanted revenge. He felt slighted. He hasn't any understanding of the ecumenical spirit. His accusations are contemptible.

What had actually occurred depends on who is

describing events. As Alexander likes to point out, it's hard to believe that the bantam bishop deliberately went to pick a fight with the bruiser monsignor. In the left-hand corner a chinless wonder, in the right-hand corner a heavy puncher. Look at the bishop's hunched shoulders compared to what the monsignor can pack. The bishop is the tiresome boy in the class whom everyone, including the master, likes to bully, but the monsignor is the master.

'I had turned my back to him, on purpose,' the monsignor says, 'when suddenly I was assaulted, grappled, thrown down.'

'It seemed to me that I could appeal to him in the name of Unite the Impossible,' the bishop says, 'so I was going up to him as a man of the cloth to plead for reconciliation, when the next thing I know is that he's barged into me, winded me, and he's half on top of me, wrestling.'

Those who have tried to reconstruct the incident have concluded that one or other of the two must have lost his footing, either by tripping over Andrew's monogrammed velvet slippers, or else by treading on the carpet in such a way that it rucked up under them both and slid across the shiny tiles, hurtling the one into the other. There was no undercarpet. The slippers had been scattered into different corners, the carpet had shot under the bed.

'Popish bugger!' The monsignor is quite certain that he heard these words, and his English is perfectly adequate, thank you, to understand that.

'*Testa di cazzo! Frocio!*' The bishop claims that these insults were bellowed deafeningly into his ear, and that wasn't the sort of Italian he had learnt as a young theologian at Cuddesdon.

Una Macleod and Sandra and Pippo are sure it was an accident. Aggressors don't begin by swearing at each other, that's a reaction to events. First you lash out, then you curse. Retrieving the slippers and the carpet, Anna Karcz was the first to work out how they must have fallen into each other. Lionel grins. His regret is that he wasn't in time to film the scene.

In the collision, someone's foot had kicked the easel supporting the portrait by Golovin. Its frame smashed, one corner has been badly torn. Also the easel must have landed on the monsignor's hairless head, and blood poured from a jagged gash. Half the buttons had been ripped off his soutane. As for the bishop, he was writhing on his side. His full weight, and the monsignor's, had come down on the pipe in his pocket. He was almost in tears as he removed the broken pieces of bowl and stem, repeating that he had lost his best friend.

Pictures and easels can be repaired, and Holly Strickland has promised to see to everything. Chantal fetched antiseptic and sticking plaster. Rather than go home and so abandon Dina, many guests stayed to reassure her that of course it was an accident. Pushed and Blocked, like the shooting at last coming to a halt as the day drew in.

FIFTEEN

A conference. Lionel proposed to meet them wherever it suited, he would invite them out to dinner afterwards. Enough was enough. This joke had run its course. Until he'd witnessed it with his own eyes, he hadn't realised that things had reached a point when priests were fighting to the death over the spoils. Something had to be done to scupper them. You can't let your mother go on drifting to disaster, he said, and I can't sit by either. That's a valuable property.

Minou and I stayed on, he says, which was extremely inconvenient, it meant we had to cancel plans to stay with the Ruggieris, he's the pharmaceuticals man. We felt that her whole world was collapsing, and she couldn't be abandoned. That was probably wrong. She has amazing powers of recuperation, she just seems to be able to shut out anything that doesn't fit the scheme she's invented. That circle of friends she has there is very supportive, they all rallied round as well. Perhaps they flatter her. Were you still in the villa when some of them returned that day because she was going to add that Vatican telegram to the other Proofs? You'd already gone? I suppose she timed it so you wouldn't be there. The trouble with this Pushed and Blocked business is that she can use it to justify anything. It's an all-purpose explanation. Whatever happens is all right, and whatever doesn't happen is all right too.

One look at him as he sat in Ursie's sitting-room was enough to sense how uncomfortable he was; that he had no experience of climbing stairs where time switches might leave him in the dark, or being within walls on which kelims and abstract pictures were hanging. It was as if he couldn't bring himself to believe that there was no ice to put in his Scotch, and that Alexander hadn't even considered cutting his hair or wearing a tie for the occasion. When he glanced at his watch, it was with a lawyer's gesture of setting a time limit to his patience.

'Item for the prosecution,' he said, handing them an envelope.

Inside was a photocopy, pocket-sized, of Dina's Flowers of Meditation.

'As from last month, it's bang up to date. She had some premonition that the original might be lost, and posterity would be deprived of these pearls of wisdom.'

The most recent entries were: 'Make Souls Shine Out', and 'In my humility is cause for pride in you, O Lord.' And finally, 'Humiliation in God's cause is reason for pride in mankind.'

'Not bad,' Alexander said, 'not a bad response at all to the war of the priests. You can't help admiring the old girl's turn of phrase.'

'On the fly-leaf,' Lionel said, 'see where she's written her instructions.'

Sure enough, in ink, in capitals, and underlined, 'To be published after my death.'

Had she always been like this? they asked Lionel. What sort of a woman had she been when first he'd met her?

If really you're intending to write that book, Lionel said to Alexander, you'll have your work cut out trying to interpret it all. For the likes of me, it's beyond understanding. She's always been secretive, too deep, one of those people too clever for their own good.

And what had she and Andrew seen in each other?

Andrew was a man for his work primarily, for him the success of the factory was what mattered most. My friendship dates from before the war when he wasn't married, Lionel said. I specialised in patents at the time, and someone had stolen one of his inventions, RBQ 113, I can still remember the registration. To do with petrol feed. It gave aircraft a much longer flight time. I was closeted with him for months when that case came to court.

I admired him, Lionel continued, I was away when they got married, it was in the middle of the war. I can't imagine he wasted much time on courtship, but then he wasn't that kind of man. He wanted to have a family, a son who could take on the factory.

Was he religious? Had there been anything like a mystic streak before?

Good Lord no, Lionel said. If Andrew knew half the things that were being done in his name, he wouldn't be able to stop laughing.

And what about Iris Warren, whose photograph Dina has in her bedroom in the villa, and is now prepared to show?

The name rang a bell. It came to him. Once, while passing through Varendy, Andrew had mentioned her. Somehow the woman had influenced the decision to buy the villa and move to Italy. It can't have been serious. A fling, at most. Andrew wasn't someone to have an affair which might break up his marriage. And he winked at Alexander. 'Not like us, eh? We prefer to taste all the dishes on the menu.'

Part male model, part hunter stalking prey, Lionel has retained a habit of rising to his feet when he's pleased with himself, and circling round before resuming his seat. There seems to be a lot of white to his rolling eyes. More than before, though, he likes a second Scotch, and a third.

'So what steps are we going to take to stop daylight robbery?' he began.

'The danger may be over,' Ursie said. Their war must have ruled out the priests' chances. And she told the story of Don Alvise's return of the blank cheque that he had been given.

'What did you do with it?' was Lionel's immediate question.

'I tore it into small bits, and stuffed them into the rubbish.'

Who'd ever have thought that the funny little scarecrow might be honest? Of course there might be a sinister implication. He could have returned the cheque because

179

he'd set his sights on the villa. Why accept a part when you might collar the whole?

I've consulted Bellini, Lionel explained, as one professional man to another. From what I understood, she has drawn up separate deeds of donation, and was in the process of making up her mind which team was to win the jackpot, the Romans or the Protestants. It was Andrew's job to make the final decision for her. Can any of us put his hand on his heart and promise that something isn't going to blow up which risks bringing one or the other of them back into favour? No, right. Let's create an alternative structure. Ownership of the villa could be transferred to the trust set up for Maydeswell, but in that case some way would have to be found to compensate Ursie. A Lichtenstein trust, maybe, in the joint names of you both, or under nominees, whereby the villa was out of her name but she'd retain a life interest. I could present that as tax-efficient, saving you whatever penalties you'll incur from the Italian state on her death.

His voice had become thicker. 'Shall we go for that? Shall we? I might be able to find a way to link it with publication of this notebook. A very limited edition indeed, I'd imagine. Like that Newsletter we used to hear about.'

'Leave it to me,' he said, 'that's all right then. Trust me.'

SIXTEEN

'We met in California,' this voice on the telephone said. 'You haven't forgotten? You stayed with us.'

The conversation continued at cross-purposes, while Ursie thought, But I didn't stay with anyone.

A prospective client, possibly. 'You gave us this address when you signed in at the reception. I particularly asked about your work, I already had this trip in mind.'

The American flag at the desk, and the blown-up photographs of retired presidents, were a memory that returned with a sinking of the stomach, as if she had been caught out in some misdemeanour. You go somewhere, you make a chance contact, and the next thing is that this contact arrives to haunt you. 'I was rather scared there.' The words had come out involuntarily.

'Why would that have been?' He sounded surprised. 'What was there to be frightened of?'

He wasn't going to take no for an answer. She must have heard about developments, hadn't she? It had to be dinner, he wasn't prepared to discuss money matters over the telephone.

The hotel in which Evan Langridge was staying is one of the most discreet in central London, Edwardian in character, with mahogany panelling throughout the ground floor, and a dining room famous for its food. The senior managers wear morning clothes at all hours.

An elephant she had thought him, but that was to make him out larger and wilder than he was. He stood still as though not knowing quite where to turn. His colour was suffused to the point of bruising. The weak and watery eyes forced her into exceptional politeness, and he responded, saying, 'How pretty you look. I mightn't have recognised you.'

As before he was in a blue blazer with the capstan emblem on its pocket. Mrs Langridge was in a belted brown dress. Taller than he was, she spoke as if wanting to get herself across before anyone prevented her. She didn't drink, she said, and she couldn't bear anyone to smoke in her presence. London was a pokey city, nothing in it worked. If Evan hadn't wanted her to accompany him, she'd have much preferred to stay in California.

'Wally you already know,' Evan Langridge said, 'he's completing the foursome.' He too wore a Project blazer. He shook hands as if to inflict a calculated degree of pain. Dressed so identically, the two men looked like elderly coaches of some team.

The meal had been ordered in advance. In deference to Mrs Langridge, water alone was served. It was hoped that everyone had a sweet tooth, because the chef was preparing for them his speciality, a soufflé with ice and fresh fruit at its centre, and a raspberry *coulis* on top. It was worth crossing the Atlantic just for the sensation in the mouth of hot and cold at the same time.

Biosthenics was spreading, Evan Langridge said, and at a pace which he could never have imagined. So many unhappy and alienated people were searching for some understanding of what it meant to lead a happy life. They could be shown the opportunity. Europe was ready for it, they might expand into several countries. They were leasing a house within range of London, and if the launch went right, then they proposed to buy the property. The funds were there, and for the time being they wanted to place them in an account with the accent on income.

'Interest rates being what they are,' Wally said.

What sort of sum did they have in mind?

What they'd like is to have specimen portfolios drawn up in bands from a quarter of a million to one million, so that they could study and judge for themselves. The final cost of Ingersham was under negotiation.

'Ingersham,' Ursie said, 'the place they converted into a

182

school but it didn't take off? It's on one of the roads you take to London from Maydeswell. You see it standing on a hill. Before that, it was a monastery.'

'And what's Maydeswell?'

'Where my brother lives.'

He's a businessman, she explained, always with a new idea, for the time being he's reviving barges and canal transport in the Midlands. Otherwise he's writing a family history.

Then they must meet, they had so much in common. He too had started out as a writer, in his case of science fiction, that's what had attracted him to California. They had the best magazines there. Only when he'd realised what a contribution Biosthenics was had he changed direction.

Mrs Langridge said, 'Evan's always hankered after a boat. It's his dream that one day he'll just sail away from his responsibilities and live on a tropical island. That's what sci-fi does to you.'

'Boats and writing,' Evan Langridge said, 'you must tell me how to contact him.'

The famous dessert arrived. The headwaiter lifted a silver-plated lid but something quite different was under it, more like a cake. With a gesture of anger, Mr Langridge sent it away, and asked for the chef.

The message came back that unfortunately the chef was too busy with his work that minute. Many pairs of eyes in the dining-room followed Mr Langridge as he rose clumsily to his feet, and strode between tables towards the service door, which swung and banged as he went through into the kitchen. They stared again when he emerged, his fists tightly balled, his stumpy frame swollen with anger. They'd get what they had ordered if they had to wait all night.

It was unspeakable – as Ursie is to describe the scene – the four of us sitting there, and nothing to drink. We had to pretend that everything was normal, while the whole restaurant was eyeing us and obviously fascinated by the row. You could feel them wondering what had got into

him to make him storm into the kitchen. Who's the funny
little fellow? I couldn't think of what to say, I kept wanting
to giggle, it was worse than being with the dreaded Mr
Ishiwara. It seemed hours before the chef arrived with what
had actually been ordered.

'And can you have any confidence in this pair?' Mr Beeby
was to ask, listening next morning to her account.

Confidence for Mr Beeby means the prints on his walls,
the sofa where he likes to stretch out for forty winks in the
afternoon, his son in an adjoining office, and staff like Ursie
on the other side of the desk.

'Of course not,' she said, 'the worst of it was that I
couldn't help feeling rather sorry for him. But clients are
clients. He's speaking of a lot of money.'

'Commission for you,' said Mr Beeby drily. Before there
could be any dealings, they would have to have the money
in hand, and references from the bank. Respectable banks
at that. No waiting for telexes which failed to arrive from
the Cayman Islands and Curaçao. Consult the library, he
said, check out this Project, there must be articles in the
press about it. If they pass muster, let's have them to lunch.

The expense-account lunch is his forum of expertise. In
order to make a favourable first impression, he adopts a
tone of superiority, jocose to the point of mild sarcasm.
Take it or leave it, is the implication, which Mr Beeby
believes is also what he learnt from those who years ago
taught him the skills of management. 'Good for you,' he
says to Ursie, and 'How's it going? Setting things up?'

The day of the lunch had a yellow haze to it, of low and
impenetrable cloud. Mr Langridge and Wally arrived in a
chauffeur-driven car. The raincoats of both men had
elaborate buckles on the shoulders, and belts whose ends
hung down: always the uniform.

And were there any areas in which the Project wouldn't
want to be invested, Eddy Fitzpatrick asked.

'What does that mean?'

A man with few social graces, Mr Langridge is deliberate,
he orders a small meal and inspects what is on his plate as if
he had never seen such food before.

'Some clients don't want involvement in South Africa, or open-cast mining or timber-logging. I don't really know what your ethical position is.'

'The only investments we don't want,' Wally Willson said, 'are the ones which go down.'

The need for bank references was understood. No problem there. First they would study the prospective portfolios, and then come back to them with a decision.

The City's not the place it was, Mr Beeby explained, it's so regulated now that you have to have permission to go to the bathroom. The schoolmasters are in charge.

'I'm due at the College of Heralds,' Mr Langridge said, 'to see what the latest is about my claim.'

'Let me come with you,' Ursie proposed.

I thought I'd cornered him, she says. Charles and I were going to the theatre that evening, and he'd arranged to pass by and pick me up at the office. So I was going to work late anyhow. I said to him, it's a ten-minute walk from here, we can go along together. And Wally, that ball of fire, was whisked off in the chauffeur-driven car. That dirty old man's mac he was wearing, with useless loops and flaps, like a flasher's. He looked sort of small and dwarfy, weighed down by his fantasies. It was a bit like when he'd sent back the pudding, I couldn't help feeling sorry for him.

As they walked, the street fell away before them, with a view of the river, as remote as a moonscape, with factories and a cold-storage on the far side. Insect-like, a few drops of rain fluttered on them as they reached the College of Heralds and its iron railings.

The interior of that building pays homage to a masculine shaping of the world: portraits of men in uniforms conscientiously preserved from the past, devices and shields and the echo of obsolete weaponry and trophies.

The Pembroke Herald wore a three-piece suit, with a watch-chain. On his bloodless face, veins at the temple showed a sickly hospital blue. Tall, the man stooped with a certain scholarly elegance. On a table in his room were

185

spread out the Langridge papers. In the eighteenth century, it appeared, the name had alternative spellings; and a House of Lords decision not to grant the title to a female claimant in 1823 had been reached on incomplete evidence. That claimant had married Mr Langridge's great-grandfather. The Pembroke Herald thought that there was a chance of substantiating this claim, but it was a slow and tedious process to wade through parish records and wills. He needed some time.

'It's familiar to you,' Mr Langridge said to her, 'it's all in my book.'

'I didn't read the details that closely, I must admit.'

That evening, while she was waiting for Charles, a parcel was delivered to her office. Another copy of *The Living I*, with a compliments slip inside.

SEVENTEEN

Later, when Alexander was able to take some distance from what had happened, he said that Evan Langridge had introduced himself as a customer. He'd heard about the barges, he was planning to buy a boat but needed advice. And wasn't Ursie to blame for mentioning Maydeswell to him in the first place, so that he'd only had to look it up in the local directory? Not much detective work there. He'd rung up and invited himself over from Ingersham.

That was the December when Evan Langridge took advantage of chance remarks. In that heavy raincoat of his, he was prepared for the worst of the countryside. A pork-pie felt hat completed the appearance. Over the lank wet grass, past the fallen sycamore, he and Alexander went on a conducted tour of the place, through what was left of the kitchen garden and out towards the housing of Ditton Crescent.

Unpredictable chap, isn't he? Alexander is to say. He liked that new housing. Progress, and all that. When we were back indoors, he took off his shoes, in case the damp had got through the soles and he'd catch cold. One good reason for living on a boat, it seems, is that you are in a relatively germ-free atmosphere. Now I think about it, there's a hypochondriac element to Biosthenics. At the time, I noticed how narrow his feet were. More like trotters. You have the impression that he's always on the point of losing his balance, and maybe that's why you feel the need to look after him, to get between him and what must be an accident.

'What are all these papers, then?' Evan Langridge asked. 'I've been told you were a businessman.'

Late in the afternoon, over cups of tea, Alexander spoke

of Andrew and Dina, and he explained about Unite the Impossible, and the tragicomedy of the priests as they fought for possession of the villa. He selected for him the Beaverbrook file and the Iris Warren letters. There was a book in it all right. Understanding them, he would understand himself.

'Before the Project, I was a writer myself,' Evan Langridge said. 'And though I say so myself, a bloody good one. Ever heard of *Jupiter's Hawk*? I used to write a whole journal once, with pseudonyms. P.K. Donald, that was the most famous one. I borrowed the name from the husband of my ancestor, the woman who couldn't get her claim to a title allowed, so they migrated.'

The villa is a bit like science fiction, Alexander said. My poor mother's evidently been off her head since her heart went wrong, but everyone's in a conspiracy to humour her. I tried to break through, I wrote her a truthful letter. I expect she'll cut me out now. She certainly would have done if there hadn't been that punch-up between the priests. It was all due to be settled with the lawyers.

'She can make it over to the Project, then. We intend branching out in Europe.'

Could Evan Langridge really have said that, Alexander is to ask himself, when he reflects on the matter. It seems too brazen to be true. But that big, slightly hangdog face comes back to him, and the mournful brown eyes, the vulnerable stockinged feet, and he has to believe his memory. I took it as a bit of a joke against himself, Alexander concludes, I mean, nobody would say a thing like that if they'd had a real intention of starting out on a course to cheat you. He has a loser's charm, that's his secret.

Maybe the Project would be of interest to you, Evan Langridge said. You never can tell who's going to be helped by it. All sorts volunteer, those with careers and those without, the successes and the failures, bohemians and businessmen, though not so far anyone with the right yacht for sale. It's a commission. Find me something old-fashioned, pre-war, four cabins at least, because I've got a wife and child and we'll have Wally aboard too.

'And what is this word, Biosthenics?' Alexander asked.

Conflict in life arises from failures of perception. Anyone who knows himself properly understands his capacities, and his limitations, and can convert them into advantages. Essentially we believe in harmony and happiness as attainable. You might want to be very rich and yet have the satisfaction of giving everything to the poor. You might want to live in peace, but happen to be in an age when your country's politics force you to go to war. You might want to write a good book, but not have the talents for it. You might love a girl who doesn't love you. Contradictions of that kind are part of the human condition. Accept them. How to do so is what Biosthenics teaches. Basically, it's a set of exercises in reconciliation. A technique.

A lot of things came together as I listened, Alexander says. To be honest, the barges were a failure, there turned out to be no money in them. You can't put the clock back so simply, people aren't going to switch freight to water transport when they've got roads, and they don't actually give a damn about ecological benefits and all that stuff. So there was another failure to be chalked up. And then that yacht. With one part of myself I hoped, sort of, that he actually meant it. And then there was my Ph.D. Perfectibility is a wonderful subject. When I've done my book about the parents, I really ought to get back to that, and finish it. Curiosity certainly came into it. I was intrigued. I thought I'd like to see what Biosthenics were, I was a sucker, or at least in the mood to be one.

The worst of it, he adds, is that he did explain the aims of the Project. I heard him say that it became a way of life to those involved, so much so that voluntarily they make over to it their money and anything else they possess. Like a monastic order. I suppose I was deceiving myself, I just didn't want to understand that the yacht he proposed to buy was really paid for out of other people's money. I've only myself to blame.

That was the December when Alexander visited Ingersham. The house looms up in one of the few remaining

189

bits of countryside between Maydeswell and London, a landmark on the journey. A Gothic-style monstrosity, its stone is liver-coloured, and its ogive windows fit for a church. Victorian whimsy is evident in the silhouette of angled roofs, pepperpots, bell-towers. For years it had been a school, and the fields around the house still contained goalposts.

The Project: a white capstan had been painted on the blue background of a board at the entrance. A security guard waved him in. The house was dank. On the staircase hung boards recording athletic feats; once a school always a school.

I had this interview with our Wally Willson, Alexander says, he's the man with the brains behind it. Evan had the idea, the way a broken-down science-fiction writer might, but Wally has the organising capacities. Princeton, by the way, just happens to be the place where he was born, he lets it drop as though he'd taught there. I paid for a course, and had to come back at the weekend.

The rooms were on the top floor. There was no curtain; little light either, because a parapet rose immediately outside the window. The window couldn't be opened, a receptionist explained, because they must have wanted to stop the boys exploring on the roof when it was still a school. The bed had sheets laundered to the scratchiness of straw, and a grey blanket. Along the corridor was a bathroom, with double rows of basins, and a smell of damp rising from the duckboards of the showers.

The place had only just got going at the time, Alexander says, and there weren't more than a dozen of us. They'd heard about it by word of mouth, mostly, and we were all shy, not knowing quite what to expect. One of them had had some experience of it in America, and there was a married couple who held hands, and a man who said he was a film-processor. I thought of him as a rapist, he had frightful grudges against women, and couldn't talk of anything except that. How they claimed equality while practising superiority. He took against Milly from the start. I quite liked the one who was a designer. And there

190

was the diminutive black man, from Ghana, who hardly dared raise his voice.

The room in which they were introduced to Biosthenics had been the gymnasium and was still equipped with wall bars.

I've never been on a jury, Alexander says, but I imagine it must be rather like what we were put through, to begin with anyhow. I was selected as the foreman. A question of education, probably, and my Oxford accent, the way it always is in this country. The instructor was American, a blond footballing type in track suit and trainers, poised on the balls of his feet, ready to swivel this way and that. Wally or Evan Langridge may have preset the programme, for all I know, anyhow he picked on me. I had to tell everyone who I was, who I thought I was, and why, and how. An autobiography. He was experienced at it. A good cross-questioner. Out it all came, I think because he'd got me interested in the process and I wanted to see where it was leading. I told him about Lionel and how I dreamed of using one of his own whips to kill him. Then I couldn't stop myself, something went click in my head. It was as if I was on a road leading out of sight, and if I went on over the horizon, I'd find what I was looking for. That click was a real sensation. Remember those two American girls I picked up? Jeanie and Esther-Anne, who are in India. They didn't know it, but they were going to carry a suitcase of rupees out of India for a friend of mine caught in the exchange control regulations they have there. Once before I did him a favour. There's no real risk, and nowadays twenty per cent in it for me. By the time I was confessing that I was putting the girls in this position because I needed the money, the instructor had his face a few inches off mine, and he was shouting. Liar, criminal, parasite, bastard, I don't know what, and he was making the others shout too. I thought, they're right, I'm in their debt, they're doing me a favour.

That was the December when Alexander was brainwashed.

191

At night, in his room under the roof, he felt overpowered by the truths that he had learnt about himself, and what seemed to be the beauty of the discovery. It was like the life-cycle of some grub, out of which finally a butterfly is born. The American instructor really cared, he had the strength to be cruel in order to cure. How the group must have despised what they had heard. Disconnected memories surfaced, of Professor Austin congratulating him on his First – but that had been a charade where this was a revelation. Of the sad lemony face of the Egyptian who had owned the bicycle shop in Luxor where he had idled for a year. Of Bruce Chatwin on a pack horse in the Pamirs. Of Don Alvise, with a blue-white pallor more the consistency of bone china than flesh, intoning *dirige nos in viam tuam per hoc vehiculum*. And who was he to reproach others? It was the moment to make amends. Don Alvise should receive another cheque, with the amount inserted in order to oblige him to cash it without hesitation. It was a wonderful release that he could make Maydeswell and the Vickers shares over to Evan Langridge and Wally, and so dedicate himself to the Project. Freedom. Perfectibility was possible. And what would Bruce Chatwin say now if he was to ring up out of the blue after all these years and propose that they ride once more in Afghanistan, or wouldn't the *mujaheddin* and the Russians now allow it? And he would throw himself in humility at Lionel's feet, begging forgiveness for failing to understand what had been well-intentioned corrective methods of education, aimed to fill the gap in his upbringing created by his own father's preoccupation with the factory. To hit the conceited boy that he must have been, to knock him to the ground, had been acts of love. Hadn't Lionel arranged the formative evening with the pair of plump and carefree Lebanese tarts? Wasn't that the gift of the sexual archetype?

That was also the December when Milly walked into his life. She opened the door to his room. He turned on the light, and recognised a silent member of the Biosthenics group.

'I had to come and find you,' she said, 'even if they catch me. It's terrible what they did to you. Let's leave now, while we can. Take me away.'

She was shivering. She was barefoot. About his age, with grey-blue eyes in a broad face, and a lower lip with a scar, criss-cross, suggesting a car accident.

That was the December when an unknown woman in a nylon dressing-gown sat on his bed, and all they did was argue.

EIGHTEEN

As you may well know [Evan Langridge wrote to Dina], I am founder and leader of the Project, already a worldwide movement of human rescue and rehabilitation. It has been among my many privileges in this connection to have come to meet your children in recent times. In their different spheres, they are now associated with my work.

On the technical side, Ursie has been instrumental in financial administration in preparation for our fine new premises in Britain, at Ingersham, a setting of great beauty near your family home. Alexander is a gifted and valuable follower of Biosthenics, the course we advise for whoever takes up the Project, and dedicates himself or herself to it. If he chooses to pursue it, as I have every reason to hope and believe he will, he will surely have a great future with us. He informs me that he is currently planning a book to put our philosophy into a popular form which will be accessible to those without his formidable intellectual capacities. We are truly proud to have with us someone of his calibre.

Alexander has passed me a copy of your Newsletter, and I can see where his powers of expression come from. We have discussed your work. Your profound insight matches my own perceptions of current problems and predicaments, and the steps mankind has to take for assuring the future. Any individual properly aware of himself or herself also realises the divinity within that self. It so happens that I may be in your region of Italy, as we are planning a branch of the Project there, in accordance with our European expansion. If so, then I would enjoy the opportunity to discuss with you in more detail Unite the Impossible, and the common ground we have.

Hard-hitting, Evan Langridge thought, a letter to convince. And he didn't post it until he was sure that Alexander had already informed the old lady that he might turn up. Private contacts like these are best, in his experience, when one person passes you on to another. You never can tell. A difficult assignment, though. From what he'd heard, from the picture projected by the son and the daughter, she had to be off the planet. He liked to know where he was; that was how to avoid mistakes. Still, he'd got a letter back, typed by a secretary evidently, to say that he was welcome whenever he liked.

The villa astonished him, so imposing, with steps leading up to the door, and a coat of arms overhead that dwarfed everything else. He was never quite to get over that first impression that this was a place where hundreds could be housed. The secretary introduced herself, and then the nurse. Adela and Chantal: he was never very good at retaining names. Walking ahead up the staircase, the French nurse showed him to his room; he'd never slept before in a four-poster. Finger on her lips, the nurse pointed to Dina's room, and bent her head in imitation of someone sleeping.

The person who used this room, who had papers stored in it, he discovered, was called Holly Strickland. The drawings were meaningless to him. Not his line. Standing at the window, he gazed out at the box hedges of the garden, surrounding a wellhead with a seat. On the sill lay a butterfly, its wings closed, and he wanted to throw it out. Immediately below were the villa's barn and outhouses, ideal for conversion into cells for the Project. As he looked, someone hurried along under cover of an archway; the good-looking French nurse. Beyond, the colours of the valley were receding into a mist.

In his honour, the fire had been lit in the *salone*. The logs flared up and shifted, and the figures of the Quarretti ceiling appeared to respond, sometimes rosy, sometimes grey, emerging and receding. Electric light in that room was too feeble to resist the shadows and chill of winter. For a long time before Dina appeared, he could hear her on the stairs, evidently negotiating them step by step, talking French and Italian to whoever was accompanying her.

By the time I arrived, Anna Karcz is to tell Alexander and Ursie, the two of them were getting on well. I think she'd been nervous about him, that's why she wanted Una and I to be there for dinner. Several times she apologised to him that he was the only man, but it couldn't be helped, there were so few spare men around. Maybe she hadn't been well, it was my impression that she had a jaundiced look to her. She took to him, and I must say I did too. He was doing his best. Madame, he called her, with an attempt at foreign manners, which was rather charming. Food livened him up. Then he entertained us with stories. About his service in the merchant navy, that's when he became so attached to the sea and sailing. As far as I remember, he's written it all up in an autobiography which he promised to send me.

That is not how Una Macleod remembers the evening. Darling Anna is so generous, she says, far too generous, seeing in others only her own good qualities. Not me. Common. That ghastly blue blazer with the thing on its breast pocket, it gave the game away. Have you ever noticed his hands? More like flippers. Lambkins didn't like him either, he was obviously frightened of dogs. I can't bear cowards. Stuff and nonsense about his war too, as I listened I thought to myself, that's a man who's never even been to sea, I don't suppose he's ever had a deck under his feet, he'd probably be seasick. At one point he also said how he'd stayed in Georgia with President Carter. I tried to snub him by saying, that brother of his, Billy, isn't it, must have been a friend. And he took it literally and answered, yes, Billy had been there, and how he'd always been able to telephone him afterwards if he needed something.

To me, Una Macleod says, it was obvious that the man wanted only one thing. He's heard about the priests, and he was manipulating his way into favour. Cunning but nasty. Alexander deserved what was coming, I can't help it, that's the truth. Oh, and his peerage, I mean to say! Don't you go and give me another tall tale about the Pembroke Herald or whatever you like to call him, you just pay those chaps and they'll run you up a genealogy to Adam and Eve.

Anna Karcz still thinks that there must have been factors which we don't know, and never will. For instance, there's that bizarre little mannerism Dina has of resorting to a Ha h'm, whenever she feels there's something to hide, and she was doing a lot of that with Evan Langridge. And he flattered her, she liked the attention, she was pleased to hear from him that Ursie was truly professional, and how Alexander had tidied himself up and ordered new clothes for the first time in years. Because we're proud of him in the Project, Evan had said, he's become proud of himself. I heard her repeating that, and I can promise you she's not an unnatural mother, whatever anyone tells you.

During the course of that weekend, Dina unlocked the safe, removing the green morocco box of Proofs of Spiritual Realities as Experienced by Andrew and Edwina Lumel. One by one, she examined with him the smaller interior boxes and their contents: the rosebud, semi-precious stones, diaries and bit of postcard, porcupine quills, each with its accompanying description, to record how this particular Proof supported the doctrine of Unite the Impossible. So much writing, such a labour.

Then she read aloud to him from the Flowers of Meditation. 'Not knowing what to believe only makes me believe more than ever.'

You are a Christian, aren't you? she asked him. The Project Unites the Impossible the way we do here. In that case, he would appreciate a recent Flower written as though by God himself. 'I created them diverse – religions, colours, nations – to prove that only through love of Me can all be united.'

Together the two walked through the garden, and into the village, for an introduction to Don Alvise. Having no language in common, Evan and he lengthily clasped hands. Receiving a copy of *Graziella and a Friend in*

197

Trouble, Evan Langridge promised to put in the post *The Living I*. In the *campo*, they watched Tonio organising a five-a-side game of football.

To visit the greatest Proof of all involved an expedition, with Evan Langridge in the front seat next to Ubaldo, and obliged to swivel round to talk to Dina and Chantal in the back. The woods at Montetremaldi were reported to be full of wild boar at that season. The ground was hard, at night frozen. The car slithered to the top, where broken bags of cement, remnants of carpentry, a holed bucket, had still not been cleared away by the builders.

In the exact centre of the newly rendered wall was a showcase in hardwood, already varnished to a shiny brown, and in it were displayed three items: a copy of the Newsletter, a photograph of Dina and Andrew standing beside the car in its prime, and a handwritten announcement that those interested in learning more about this shrine and its founders should contact Don Alvise, in Sant' Ambrogio. On either side of the showcase were white marble tablets, on which was lettering two inches high, incised black. 'Through love of Me can all be United,' were the words on one, and the other had 'Make Souls Shine Out', with Don Alvise's Italian translation below. At the outer edges of the wall were the two peepholes, duly glassed, and it was possible to crane against them for a sight of the Armstrong-Siddeley, a dim outline within.

'What do you think?' Dina asked.

Inspired, he answered, 'You should write something at greater length. To involve people who come.'

That was already her intention, she told him. If only she had the time, she would put down the whole story, her vision, the guidance she received. The world would be astonished by it, the world was waiting for just such a thing. Look at the general disturbance of it, so much violence to be soothed, so many victims in search of peace. A day would come, she prophesied, when the masses would make their way to this hilltop, now so deserted and damp in the afternoon.

'Now you know everything we do here,' she said.

198

No doubt she liked him, Chantal is to say, because he was pleasant. A good listener. Quiet. We get letters from all over the world from readers of the Newsletter, and she's always encouraged by those who write in to her. And it's my impression that she really wanted to learn about the Project, and what it was that had attracted Alexander to it. That had been a lonely Christmas, when he hadn't come out because he was still in the first flush of his enthusiasm for the Project. Feeling unloved, she's always more awkward to handle. The picture in Monsieur's room hadn't been repaired, and she was spending quite a bit of time in there, it was as if she expected to find it back on the easel as it was before the war of the priests. What a business.

For Christmas, Dina had given Andrew a poinsettia, and it stood on the dressing table in his room. 'For my darling,' she had written, 'in grateful thanks for your loving daily care' – bought in Ponte a Maiano, the card depicted, of all things, an English stagecoach rattling through an olde worlde town, the postilion blowing his horn.

I'd put her to bed, Chantal explained, and seen that she was all right with her medicines and the radio. It was a habit of mine to leave my door open in case she called for me in the night. So I'd hear her coming out. She used to turn on the light and walk down the corridor, I couldn't have slept through all that anyhow. Then she'd make sure that she shut the door to Monsieur's room. I used to be frightened she'd catch cold in there, in just a dressing-gown. Sometimes, I think, she lay on the floor, because the bed showed no signs of being disarranged in the morning. On other occasions, the bedspread had evidently been wrinkled up. She'd talk to him. I'd creep up to the door, and try to eavesdrop, but I couldn't catch it. She might moan, and I used to think she might be weeping. Of course I didn't dare stay there too long, in case she suspected anything and was suddenly to open the door. There's nowhere to hide in the corridor, and it's a good long way back to my room. I didn't want to be caught, but it used to upset me to listen to those muffled sounds on the other side of the door. I felt so sorry for the poor lady. Imagine turning to the dead for love like that.

The poinsettia flourished. Its blooms were magnificent.

When you come to think about it, Chantal says, you can imagine those flowers to be some sort of microphone. Look at the shape of them.

It must have been after the visit to Montetremaldi, she thinks, because Madame had been so buoyed by that.

In the night, she was closeted in Andrew's room. This time, his voice did not emerge over the radio, but whispered at her straight out of the poinsettia.

'Thank you, my bravest girl,' Andrew said, 'you're looking after everything so well. Evan has been sent to you by Alexander and Ursie. It's Pushed and Blocked. They want him to have the villa.'

When I went in in the morning, Chantal says, I could tell that once again something important had happened. She was awake, she was resting on her pillows and humming to herself. Tunelessly. She'd hardly ever done that before, as far as I know music is about the only thing in which she's not interested. In all the years I've been in the villa, I've never heard anyone play on the piano in the *salone*. He spoke through the flower, she said. She looked so very happy. When I hear him on the radio, she said, people think it's interference, or I'm just picking up a snatch from some programme to suit myself. Well, they can't possibly say that when his voice speaks directly to me through my own gift to him. Now they'll have to believe me. Radiant. That's the right word for her.

The flower spoke. Unite the Impossible was proving its truth. Towards midday, she sent for Evan Langridge; he was to be received in her bedroom. Sitting in her armchair, she greeted him like a queen at an audience, granting a favour. You can thank my children, she told him, so my Andrew says. You are to have the villa. Today's Sunday, and Avvocato Bellini is hard to contact on a Monday. The deed of gift will have to wait until Tuesday.

200

I suppose a man like that has knocked about the world a good deal, Chantal says. *The flower spoke*, she repeated. Then he bowed his head, and stood there. *Quel coup de théâtre!* Madame, he said, words fail me, I shall try to live up to your ideals. Where one knew that she was really not at all balanced was in her high spirits. It had to do with the pacemaker, in my opinion, and not that she was off her head.

That Sunday, Anna Karcz brought Italo Calvino to lunch. Nondescript, slightly preoccupied with himself, Calvino at that moment had been writing some lectures which he had been invited to deliver in an American university.

He'd come to collect me, Anna Karcz remembers, he'd been pleading with all his friends for support. He was due to read one of those lectures in the evening at some literary gathering in Rome. It was a practice run, and he was terribly nervous about it. If the lecture isn't a success, Calvino is finished – he used to talk like that about himself, in the third person. I agreed to go with him, naturally. I told you I thought Dina hadn't been too well earlier that weekend, which was one reason why I was glad to bring Calvino to lunch to distract her. I was sure they'd get on, though he could be very self-centred. On the Sunday, she was altogether a different woman. So much younger, and prettier. You could almost decipher her state of mind from her appearance. Whether she combed her hair with curls in it, you know, flirtatious little touches like that. Calvino wanted to hear all about the Project, and the two of them were soon talking about physics, I think, or was it chemistry? Anyhow theories. They were getting on very well. Calvino liked eccentric types, and he told me afterwards that it had been rewarding. We learnt that Evan Langridge was some sort of writer himself. It was only afterwards that I heard from Chantal about the flower. That was the first time she'd heard Andrew talking directly. But you'd never have guessed that anything of that kind was going on, all through that lunch she seemed so normal. She had a way of keeping things in separate compartments. What a secretive personality.

After the departure of Anna Karcz and Calvino, Dina as usual went for her siesta. On his own, Evan Langridge let himself out at the back, on to the terrace.

Innocent explanations of his behaviour are possible. He may have wanted to inspect what was about to become his property, and to have a close look at the buildings which he had observed from his window. That winter's sacks of olives were propped there, one against the other, dead-weights, distended like balloons. Next to the old olive press were wicker-covered demijohns. The protective laurel hedge and the brick arches do indeed invite exploration.

At any rate, he opened the door of the *camera del Tedesco*.

Adjusting to the semi-darkness, he took a step or two, and banged against the sharp corner of the washbasin. Losing his balance, he fell forward, and caught hold of something indefinable as he stumbled.

'*Finocchio!*' came a yell. '*Va fanculo!*'

According to Armando, the *professore americano* had known exactly what he was doing. Only the day before, Chiarella had laughed with him about the way the elderly *professore* had tried to look up her skirts on the staircase as she'd been showing him to his room. That puffy red face had the look of a pervert. Probably he'd been hanging out of his room trying to figure out Chiarella's movements. No, he never could be sure in advance if she was going to come. Sometimes yes, but often she was too busy, especially when there were guests like that day. The *baronessa* didn't lose anything, he'd always worked from sunrise to sunset all round the year. No holidays either. Nobody could accuse him of failing to look after the garden. He used to come in the afternoons, and take off his clothes, all except his socks and his vest, which he kept on in winter in that room. Then he'd lie there on his back, anticipating her arrival, how she might slip in and fling off everything, and so of course he got excited. Instead, in blundered the

202

professore americano, and grabbed him down there, a red-hot pain as if he had been trying to twist it right off.

In reaction Armando lashed out, and it was his foot which had caught Evan Langridge full in the face, and gave him the monstrous black eye which immediately started to swell. Thrown backwards, Evan Langridge landed hard on the floorboards, and cracked the back of his head, either on the side of the bed or against the washstand. Blood spurted down the collar of his shirt. In the collision, the Project blazer was ripped at the seams. As he rushed out, Armando had to jump over him.

Nothing was broken. Evan Langridge could stand. Light entered the room where Armando had left the door open behind him. He made his way back to the house.

When eventually Chantal came to give her side of the story to Alexander, she told him that she had been in her room, when she heard shouting. Nobody dared to raise voices in that house, and above all not during the hours of siesta. So it had to be a crisis. Sure enough, there was *ce monsieur*, a shocking sight, with dirt and splashes of blood all over his white shirt. He was sitting in a daze just inside the back door. Already his right eye had closed completely, he couldn't see out of it. The bruising was raw.

I got him to stretch out on the ground, she says, in case he was concussed. He made a bit of a mess on the flagstones, and of course the site wasn't so well chosen, right there in front of the safe with all the Proofs inside. He was what you might call an anti-Proof. I got some cotton wool and antiseptic and bathed his eye. It was a bad cut on his scalp, really it would have been best to have the doctor put some stitches in where he was. After the trouble we'd had with the priests, though, I didn't think Madame could bear the strain of it, I wanted to spare her that.

'Now I understand what was going on,' Evan Langridge said. 'I saw you slipping out there the afternoon I arrived.'

She said, as she applied the plaster to his head, 'I have nothing to hide.'

'Nor do I,' he answered, 'I shall tell the truth. I wasn't to know you were having an affair in that shed.'

'And you think she doesn't know? Giulia and Luciana tell her every week. I'm a good nurse, and that's all that matters to her. If you believe she's stupid, you'd be very wrong.

'One look at you in that condition, and she'll have nothing more to do with you.'

I packed his grip for him, Chantal says, that was no trouble, and I telephoned for a taxi. And where am I going, he asked. To the hotel the other side of Sant' Ambrogio, I told him, we put the priests up there, it's modern and a bit bleak because the famous Italian sense of design doesn't seem to be what it used to be. And I arranged for Dr Melegnani to call there to put in the stitches. In the end, he needed seven. Quite a performance. And what if I don't go, he threatened me. You will, I said, because otherwise I'm going to call Armando in, and he'll finish what he's begun, he'll give you the thrashing of your life. You know what Italians are. He'll kill you, most likely. You will have offended his pride. I'm standing between you and him.

And another thing, I told him, there's no point you thinking that you can obtain this villa. Legally, it's impossible. She can hear whatever she likes coming out of that flower, but she's still not able to disinherit her children. That's the law here.

Chantal is to say to Alexander that she saved the villa for him. Things worked out for the best, definitely. I put him in the taxi, and accompanied him to the hotel. You have to laugh sometimes.

For myself, I don't ask anything, I'm not that kind of person, Chantal says. My work is reward enough. She's exceptional in every way, Madame is, and I wouldn't have missed the job here for anything. I do believe I saved you the villa, though. When I got back, they were all four of them in the kitchen, going at it like cats and dogs. What a row. I had to listen to it all, and how I was a *putana* and a *figlia di putana*, and they were going to do this, and they were going to do that. How they'd been made the laughingstock of Sant' Ambrogio. Giulia I could have understood, but the strange thing was that Luciana was the really angry one. Now why was that? Could that great big mountain of lard have wanted Armando for herself? While she was coming right up to me and shrieking, I couldn't help thinking, it wasn't German soldiers who took her into that room, but Armando, of course, what an idiot I am.

They were going to the *baronessa*, they shouted, they were going to tell her what really went on in this madhouse, now was the moment to clear the air, and all the rest of it, until I suddenly noticed what the time was, and that nobody was paying attention to Madame. So I hurried off, and there she was – at the top of the stairs – she must have heard every word. She never referred to it. All she said was, I was really beginning to wonder where you are. Monsieur Langridge has had to leave, I explained, for his health. She may have thought that I was the one he'd tried to assault sexually, but she didn't want to know, she never questioned me. That's a clever old lady, and you'll never be able to persuade me otherwise.

I was actually quite pleased to be free from Armando, you know how it is after a while, it's boring, you've had enough. You have to laugh sometimes. You know, when I said goodbye to the gentleman at the hotel, it just came to me, I've been with Madame so long that I've come to think the way she does, and I said, You'll be sure to understand, it's Pushed and Blocked, *quoi*.

NINETEEN

The poinsettia spoke only that once. Whether the winter temperature had been unsuitable for it or not, it soon started to wither. Intended for immortality, the plant could hardly even be preserved as a Proof. The photographer from Ponte a Maiano was summoned, a man who earned his living from sentimental portraits of little girls in white at their first communion, and then those same girls a few years later, in white once more, at their weddings, by which time they had learnt not to smile with their teeth showing. He could hardly believe the commission, wanting to pose the flower in its pot out in a garden setting, or with ornaments of some kind, to humanise it like his usual sitters. Close-up and just as it is, Dina ordered him, and where it is too. By then the flower consisted of dried-out stalks, tobacco-like.

On the back of the photograph which she finally selected Dina wrote, 'In his own room, on February 15, 1981, Andrew spoke to me by means of this plant. I had given it to him for Christmas, but his gift to me is infinite. Eyes they have, and see. Ears they have, and hear. So we are blessed with the truth.' A copy of the photograph was framed and hung on the wall in Andrew's room, behind the spot where the poinsettia had once stood. Close to it was the Golovin portrait, duly repaired and back on its easel.

'How beautiful,' Don Alvise said, and in return another copy of the photograph was printed for him. He would decide exactly which corner of the church of Sant' Ambrogio was appropriate for it.

In theory, she acknowledged no such thing as disappointment or setback. What might look negative as it happened would later be revealed in all its glorious purpose, much as the sun scatters fog. To keep track of these reversals, the newspapers had to be marked with asterisks, and clipped by Adela for the signs of the times had secrets for one who could interpret them. She read, she studied, she wrote. Sometimes the global picture clarified in sharpest focus, at other times the confusion was evidently history still in the making, not yet to be analysed.

Una Macleod had brought over two guests, both elderly ladies from Edinburgh, on the day that Pope John Paul II was shot. Serving them, Ubaldo asked baldly, 'Have you heard the news?'

In St Peter's Square, where she herself had left her car in order to have her audience with a predecessor. She couldn't eat, she couldn't breathe.

'It's not as if he's anything to us,' one of the Edinburgh ladies said, intending to be helpful. 'I mean, the man who did it must have had very strong feelings. To do a thing like that.'

A Bulgarian, according to reports. But Dina knew better. From the moment she heard, she said that the Soviets had been out to sabotage Unite the Impossible. They might not have actually heard of the doctrine, but it was a form of reconciliation of human ends utterly at variance with theirs. All they see is he's a Polish Pope, she said, but in themselves they know, they know.

She kept on repeating *they know*, Una Macleod says, but quite what it was the Russians were supposed to know she didn't fully explain. The poor darling was like that, wasn't she? If you couldn't follow her, it wasn't her business to help you out of your stupidity, you were to blame and ought to look sharper. But that hit her hard, it demoralised her. If you ask me, it was the beginning of the end. Obviously, it wasn't really much good plotting minutely around the doings of Mugabe and Idi Amin, the likes of them, if in another part of the globe something so brutal and unexpected as the shooting of the Pope happens. She could recognise reality all right. Only she didn't want to. Do you blame her?

In order never to be surprised by another world event of the kind, they needed a television set; the idea was Luciana's. In the evenings, especially at a time when there were no priests and the children inexplicably preferred London, the programmes would be a distraction.

The set was installed in the kitchen. The first time that Dina sat herself down in the saggy leather sofa in what normally was Ubaldo's place, Sonny Liston happened to be on the screen for a title fight. She had never before seen a boxing match, and was gripped by it, applauding the champion. After that, she took to watching wrestling, soon as familiar with the Mammoth of Messina and Chief Running Buffalo (actually a Tunisian on the Italian circuit) as with Brazilian politics or the distressing exile of the Shah of Iran.

From Evan Langridge she heard nothing. Not even a formal note. Bishop Satterthwaite, however, was in Cyprus, from where he wrote that he was attempting to recover some church property in Kyrenia. He and Cath were installed in a house overlooking the sea, they found their health much improved by so much bathing. The friendlier in manner the Turkish authorities were, the more they actually obstructed them. Who ever saw such brilliant friendship as that? He and Cath hoped that they might have a chance to return one of these fine days. And meanwhile he enclosed his bill.

'Item,' Dina read, 'to receiving your instructions in connection with the transfer to the Anglican Church and its holdings of Villa La Grecchiata; to consulting cadastral surveys as to value of the proposed donation, and drafting deeds for the purpose; to initiating enquiries into legal and other implications of said gift . . .'

What actually she thought of the demand was something she also kept to herself. The sheet of paper was to lie on her writing table, neither filed nor thrown away, a reminder of the bishop every time she sat down at her diaries or Flowers of Meditation. Everyone who came into the house was shown it, though, and the bishop's standing was never to recover.

Sandra Piccolomini said she'd feed him to the Mugniomaggio pigs if he dared to show his face again.

'Bloody cheek,' Una Macleod said. 'Imagine sending you that bill. What a hide he must have. A rhino in a cope.'

Père Destouches and Pater Auhofer also defected. The monsignor might have frightened them off, or they have had to attend too many committees and ecumenical congresses to have time to spare for La Grecchiata. There was also a perceptible closing of the ranks after the would-be killer Mehmet Ali Agca had fired his bullets outside the Vatican.

She hadn't really come to terms with the outrage before there was worse, with the assassination at a military parade in Cairo of Anwar Sadat. After his peacemaking, he had been a hero of Unite the Impossible. In grim silence, she watched his funeral on television.

That was a bad year, Luciana says, if it hadn't been for her friends, the *baronessa* might not have been able to hold on then. She wasn't herself any more, not after so many shocks.

A fortnight after the death of Sadat, Albert and Isabelle Golaz were due for another of their quarterly visits. Now that the Armstrong-Siddeley had been laid to rest, they came in their own car. They drove in convoy too, for Lionel followed them down from Geneva. There was to be another business conference, a grand climax. She'd lost her independent judgement. Somebody had to tell her the truth, and he was the only one in a position to do so. It was his responsibility, he told Albert Golaz.

The Shah's downfall had been a shock to him too, he'd done profitable legal work for him in Switzerland. Why, it seemed only yesterday that he and Minou had been guests at Persepolis to commemorate all those thousands of years of the Peacock Throne. What a sumptuous occasion, and soldiers loyally lining the streets for miles. Who'd have thought it could have come to this? For his once-eminent client, he was hoping to arrange the lease of a house made available in Panama City by General Torrijos. And it was funny to think about, but remember how Andrew had turned his back on socialist England? We had Mrs Thatcher now. It was safe to return. In ten years, England would be its old self. You listen to the radio, you're very well informed, Lionel told Dina, but I meet the people themselves.

Lionel has never been someone to waste time. One day

it's a drive to Rome for lunch in the embassy to meet the new ambassador; and another it's an invitation to a castle near Perugia, whose owner, an industrialist, is reputed to bank-roll the Liberals. On the drive, Lionel crunches across the gravel in his haste to be away on his programme, and again as he comes racing home in the evening. Then he pushes his way into Dina's room, to make up for the hours when he was doing something other than putting pressure on her.

'Unite the Impossible is balls,' he said to Albert Golaz, 'absolute cock. You know it. I know it. But how the hell am I to tell her?'

'She's so strong-willed.'

'That's one way of putting it.'

There must be no shock, but there can't be any more talking flowers either. Sometimes his attempts to break through involved most of a morning in her bedroom, she not yet dressed, he champing; sometimes they sat with Albert and Isabelle in the *salone*.

Albert Golaz and Lionel had prepared specialist publications from Swiss banks and from New York financial institutions to prove that stock markets all over the world were due to reach record levels; every index pointed to bullish prospects.

Dina did not agree. She said, 'Now is the time to be liquid. I smell a crash.'

Smell? asked Lionel scornfully, *Smell?* One doesn't smell things like crashes. Thatcherism was working. You've been so long immersed in your private concerns, he told her, that your powers of judging the situation aren't what they used to be.

'I want to be liquid,' Dina insisted, 'and I want US Treasury Bills, we have to safeguard ourselves against currency fluctuations. Albert and I will work out the details.'

Besides, she asked him, did you make as much as I did in the recent gold rush? While you were on a jaunt in Persepolis, I was on the telephone to Geneva.

And what about the house then? This villa. The children weren't to be trusted to be sensible. Alexander now, his latest escapade was with a bunch of crooks who were trying to get their hands on Maydeswell and his money. Face it, he's been a bit of a poor fish all his life, but this business with Langridge beats everything.

'Pushed and Blocked saved the day,' said Dina.

But will it always do so? Alexander has been instructing him actually to make Maydeswell over to this Langridge. Don't you see it's a crisis? Under the terms of the trust whereby Alexander has the house, luckily, this can't be done, or at least it can be dragged out for years until he comes back to his senses. What if he gets his hands on the villa and simply makes it over to the fellow?

'My dear Dina' – Lionel is not without eloquence – 'with my own eyes I saw how the priests fought over the spoils. Now I hear how Langridge treats you and Alexander, and the fiasco that happened here. Another fiasco. It won't do, really it won't. Now what are your plans for the future of the villa?'

It is to be a museum, a shrine to the Spiritual Realities as experienced by Andrew and her. People write to her from all over the world, the postman brings a bag of tributes every day, already, before Unite the Impossible has been placed on a public footing.

Who's to run this museum? He wants to know.

Pushed and Blocked it is. We'll have this museum, and Albert and I will be trustees of it, we'll see that your wishes are carried out. We'll tie it up any way you want, but without any more Langridges coming into it. We'll go to your friend Bellini, and get the paperwork done while I'm still here.

Italian lawyers are slow. Lionel did not understand the language, and called for official translations. The business conference moved to Avvocato Bellini's office.

In the evenings Lionel watched the Mammoth of Messina win a European contest, and in the whole of his life, he said, he'd never watched so much television.

Afterwards, he promised, he would invite her to a long lunch in a restaurant behind Ponte a Maiano, which he had read about in the magazine sent to holders of American Express cards.

So she signed. She signed.

211

TWENTY

Among journalists of his generation, Simon Smith-Dawson has a reputation. To his satisfaction, the world has proved much as he had imagined it to be as an under-graduate. Experience has served to confirm his precon-ceptions. Everywhere the shits are in charge, and it is incumbent on someone like him to say so, never mind that he converts into one of the shits himself. Like all para-doxes, that is only amusing.

The Hotel Continental was the book he published in 1976, and it took its title from the hotel in Saigon where he had lived for three years as a correspondent. In the recrimination which followed the débâcle of the Americans in Vietnam, the book achieved some status. Everyone was to blame, according to its thesis, the French, Ho Chi Minh, General Westmoreland, one American president after another, but above all the journalists who misrepresented events, depicting the Tet offensive as a defeat rather than the victory it was, a body of reporters too lazy and too ignorant to do more than print what they told each other.

In search of folly, Simon has written about South Africa and Eastern Europe, and he loves to mock the young of both sexes who wear rings in their ears and noses, and are stupefied with pills and the din they call music. At a dinner party once, the critic Kenneth Tynan threatened to hit him over what had been at the time a notorious piece, in which Simon declared that the Beatles were without talent of any discernible kind. For a while after that, the satirical magazine *Private Eye* pestered him with invita-tions to contribute, until he answered that they were mistaking their pretensions for humour.

Physically Simon has too much expense-account flesh on too small a frame, as though softening in spite of himself. His own laugh is more of a yap, in recognising some information or detail which once more fits into the general pattern of absurdity. No more coloured waistcoats; but he still has an exaggerated taste for bright shirts, and suits made in the Far East. As with many would-be dandies, the impression of a deliberate childishness works against him.

Accident or curiosity took him to Ingersham. The Project's bankruptcy has already been announced. The house was closed. First he had to find the caretaker, and then persuade him to allow a tour inside. That day, the rooms were cold enough for him to be able to see his own breath. His footsteps echoed in the emptiness. And on what had been the noticeboard various sheets were still pinned up, with instructions about conduct and the times of Biosthenics classes that would now not take place. There he read Alexander's name. Lumel: too unusual to be a coincidence.

Faithfulness to the insights he had as an undergraduate is Simon's version of the old-boy network. The purpose of knowing everything and everyone had been for sorting life out, the way the post sorts mail, sending people to the addresses for which they destined themselves. This way the shits, that way he and his friends. The fact that the man with greased hair had actually moved in an almost unhampered line from his college to a well-reputed seat in the Cabinet is the best of jokes because it flatters his own powers of observation. Sometimes when he encounters columnists and television personalities who happily claim acquaintance with him since Oxford days, he can hardly bring himself to be polite; these people have turned out so exactly as predicted that they seem more like emanations of his imagination than real flesh and blood.

And then there is Alexander. The wild card in the pack. Who did everything supremely well, a stocky and self-confident figure who had stamped himself once and for all as the hope of that generation, juggling with ideas and

213

reproducing the arguments of thick books in a few aphoristic sentences, the future Professor Sir Alexander Lumel, OM, FRS, outdistancing Professors Austin and Zaehner whose star pupil he had been.

In an old address book, Simon has the Maydeswell number, and it is unchanged except for the automatic dialling prefix. A little too emphatic, perhaps, otherwise Alexander sounds his usual self. It's been years, he says, far too long, of course I read you so I've got the feeling that we are in touch.

Simon can remember the days when the Abbey was lived in, the woods had not been cut down, and Michael Crane-Dytton had not yet sold famous English silver to the Huntingdon Library. Like a detective, he files that sort of information. As is the way with houses not visited for a long time, Maydeswell seems to have shrunk, and it looks to him in need of maintenance: weeds on the path, the window-frames drab where the paint has weathered away.

Funny you ringing up like that, Alexander says, I'd been thinking about you. I'm engaged in a couple of writing projects, and I'd been looking up that essay I wrote for the Gollancz book you edited.

Sure enough, there's his copy lying on the floor amid the papers he's half-sorted, and whose purpose he explains. He's laying aside a book based on these papers about his family and his own origins, but only for the time being, for another project. Evan Langridge has suggested that he explain Biosthenics for the general reader.

Milly has moved in with him. Of all the women in Alexander's life so far, she is the only one to have gone shopping without asking him for money. No favours, no confessions either. A year or two older than Alexander, she doesn't like to talk about herself.

You're a natural victim, Alexander tells her, you're a muggee, a murderee.

Her father has been on the management of ICI on Tyneside, her mother a physiotherapist up there. 'The man I was married to at the time,' is a phrase of Milly's and it's plain from what she is reporting that human relations for her have been a natural disaster area. A fourteen-year-old daughter is a pyromaniac, now kept at an institution for disturbed children where there's said to be a fifty-fifty chance of a cure. She's allowed controlled experiments with paraffin and matches, Milly says, but I'm not risking her home again. Milly has a house in Hemel Hempstead, and this girl set fire to the curtains; a few minutes more, and that would have been that.

'Even by my standards, to have enrolled in the Project was a terrible mistake,' Milly said.

She has wide-set eyes of the clearest grey, and that slack mouth with the scar on it, like a line of milk.

Alexander and I, she tells Simon, have arguments about it, he's coming round to my point of view, that the Project's dangerous.

Most certainly not, nothing of the kind, is his reply.

To him, Biosthenics is a fit subject of study, and is to be placed in context. He argues from Durkheim, Pareto, Nietzsche, Sorel, in the true Oxford manner. There is a route to perfectibility after all.

Nobody knows quite what has happened to Evan Langridge, and his henchman Wally has also dropped out of view.

They've absconded, Milly says, they took whatever money they could lay their hands on, and ran. One day, Ingersham was closed down, without explanation, and now it's reported that the money has never been paid for its lease. The only bright feature is that Alexander hasn't committed himself to putting down any money for the yacht Evan Langridge wants. Otherwise he'd be bust. In Southampton there's a company with a boat which had belonged to a Kuwaiti banker, and it would have been suitable. Alexander has already given instructions for a report on it.

'I can't understand what the point of philosophy is,' said Simon, 'if you aren't able to see through nonsense like Biosthenics. J.L. Austin gave you a First, didn't he?'

More than a wild card, Alexander is an enigma. The

way he's turned out undermines old loyalties and certainties, and he can't be allowed to get away with it. Someone else always pays, and there's always another woman, a series of meaningless lays, either too young, or like Milly too vulnerable, easy to exploit.

'You do good work, I know,' said Alexander, 'and you'll do more, but you should keep your mind open to what lies outside your experience. Even if it turns out that Evan himself has no idea of how to handle the business side of things, that doesn't mean his thinking is discredited.'

To begin with, Simon thought he felt anger, because Langridge and the Project were so threadbare and blatant that nobody should be taken in by such things. The realisation of disappointment came more slowly. If I could put my finger on it, he told himself, this is a story of decadence and waste, it's symptomatic too, this is what happens in a country going downhill, suspending the intellect in favour of heaven knows what.

'Have you given up hope of Alexander ever doing anything worthwhile?' he was to ask Ursie. 'Of all our contemporaries, he was the one with the chance of doing something serious and original.'

Ursie invited him to dinner in Charles's house: a Chinese meal cooked by the housekeeper. In the course of his travels, Simon has learnt to count from one to ten in Chinese, but not even this little feat can bring a smile to the woman's face. The *premier cru* wine that Charles has brought out for the meal is meant to set the right atmosphere.

And what *is* it about Alexander, what's the explanation? Ursie thinks it may be in the genes, he's inherited something of Dina's Unite the Impossible. Not to forget Lionel, either, who's always exercised a malign influence, with his one-track mind and his snobbery and his insistence that if things aren't done the way he wants, then they shouldn't be done at all.

Simon said that he wanted to write an Aldington-type 'Portrait of a Success, but . . . ' but of course it was to be primarily an investigation of the Project. What had their headquarters been like on the West Coast? There'd been a scandal when a nineteen-year-old heiress had made over a large sum to the Project, and it was possible that this had been the source of the funds handed over to Ursie for investment. And had she read *Jupiter's Hawk*? The man had imagination, as you might have guessed. As far as he could tell, *The Living I* had pretty well no truth in it at all. At thirteen, Langridge hadn't even been in Western Australia, never mind in a plane crash, and the father had died of drink. As a young man, he'd served in the merchant navy, the fantasy about boats derived from that. Perhaps he really could sail, but even that was doubtful. The fellow at the College of Heralds had got to the bottom of the matter, which was that there had really been a judgement against one branch of the family concerning a title, and who knows, a sense of grievance may have sprung from that. The wish to get one's own back is the truest inspiration for conspiracy.

'The money did arrive, at least quite a chunk of it,' Ursie said. 'Eddy Fitzpatrick bet me a bottle of champagne it wouldn't.'

Evidently Langridge and Wally Willson had been opening as many accounts as they could, in order to shuffle a fixed sum of money from one to the other, in search of credit. They'd been borrowing several times over against the same capital. Somebody, somewhere, was stuck with their bad debts.

We've had the Fraud Squad round, Ursie said, and Mr Beeby is far from pleased. We weren't the losers in this game of financial musical chairs, except in expenses and incidentals. We had written instructions to sell and transfer their money to nominees in Lichtenstein. Who knows where the pair have gone to ground? Where are they now?

Of course I've told Alexander, Ursie explains, but he answers that whatever they may or may not have done is no reflection upon their ideas. But he's coming to his senses, he's already decided he's not going to make Maydeswell over to them after all. Another week, a fortnight and it'll recede into history as one of his false starts. If only Milly can stick the course. I like her.

It isn't possible to eat with chopsticks and to write at the same time. Listening, Simon has taken no notes, assuring Ursie that if he needs to, he'll check the details later. The whole story may fizzle out, he says, it depends on what crops up.

TWENTY-ONE

It was spring, and the wisteria over the pergola was already a blaze of mauve, more flashily peroxide than true in colour. Soon there would be a scent of jasmine through Dina's windows. As though to put the blame on a location and not on people, the *camera del Tedesco* had been fitted with a padlock. The key was handed to Avvocato Bellini. In the hours of the early afternoon, Armando was nowhere to be seen, but if he had discovered some new rendezvous, Giulia no longer complained. And nobody could accuse him of an untidy or untended garden.

In thin-soled shoes which did not grip on ground lately ploughed, Avvocato Bellini had made his way awkwardly to the house of Giulia and Armando. Then he sat on the sofa in the kitchen, in conference with Luciana and Ubaldo, at a moment when Tullio and his wife had also been present. As a result, everyone's wages had been increased. Offered a pay rise in her turn, Chantal had refused, on the grounds that she was happy with things as they were.

The avvocato was summoned frequently in connection with the establishment of the museum. His task was to listen while she dictated her intentions to Adela, and take away her typewritten pages so that he could have them translated and put into a legal framework. The proofs would be on permanent show. The sable coat was to have a display case of its own, in which it would be arranged on a dressmaker's dummy, itself to be clothed like Dina. Her characteristic shirts were to be preserved. Published in a suitable format, the Flowers of Meditation would be on sale, and the original notebooks and diaries open to the scrutiny of scholars. The political and ecumenical press cuttings would provide the central research facility for Unite the Impossible, whose truth was bound to become more and more self-evident. This museum would take responsibility for Montetremaldi. Visitors would circulate between the villa and the church with the car in it.

How was this to be institutionalised? the avvocato wanted to know.

A curator was required. A governing body. Funds. The museum was to possess pictures such as the Golovin portrait. There might be accommodation with the Getty Museum over at least some of the Napier collection; she would have to ask Holly Strickland. During Albert Golaz's next visit, they would hold another conference to deal with these aspects of it.

Everything occurs as it must, she reminded him.

The political crisis of the moment began to cut into her time. Self-declared scrap-dealers had mysteriously landed on the island of South Georgia, and soon afterwards Argentinian forces invaded the Falkland Islands. Simultaneously, the Sandinistas in Nicaragua were arresting or driving into exile the Miskito Indians. To accommodate these events, the household routine changed. Dina insisted on being called earlier, to be able to watch the breakfast news on the television set in the kitchen. She tuned in to the news bulletins; and was back in the kitchen for the one o'clock programme on Italian state television. Her conversation centred now upon Daniel Ortega, the Farabundo Marti Liberation Front in El Salvador, the sinking of the *Belgrano*, the battle at Goose Green, the declared or hidden intentions of Mrs Jeane Kirkpatrick.

Martin Cammaerts had a sister living in the Argentine, and had just returned from a six-week visit there.

Your mother was completely involved, Martin Cammaerts is to tell Ursie, you know how she never did anything by half-measures. Because I'd been out there lately, she was always ringing me up and inviting me round. I couldn't refuse her anything, I admired her, it's not too much to say I loved her. Always that indomitable courage. She had her way of seeing things, and she wasn't going to compromise for anyone. Well, we had a series of lunches with a tray on our knees, as far as I could gather the television set had to be in the kitchen, the reception was bad everywhere else. One of the things I remember was her asking me if I could get hold of *La Prensa* for her. She was quite prepared to teach herself to read Spanish. I'm sure she'd have been able to, what's more. Events in South and Central America, she believed, were going to produce some quite different world order.

Luciana gives an account which contradicts him.

It was a war, wasn't it? she says. And war can't be reconciled with Unite the Impossible. She couldn't make up her mind what she thought about Thatcher and Reagan. I had the opportunity to get a good look at her, and she'd gone all grey and deflated, the big eyes burning in her poor little face, and I used to think, I know what's going on in that tormented head of yours, you're waiting for the *barone* to appear on the screen and everything will turn all crimson and gold at the end of the world, and the *barone* will be seen by millions, and we'll go straight to heaven from La Grecchiata.

It was during a programme about the mass emigration from Cuba that she fainted. On the quay at Miami, a reporter was interviewing some of these arrivals, people who had chosen to flee Cuba with nothing, and whose first action in the United States was to curse Castro.

The way a woman does, Chantal says, she judged on looks. She made allowances for Fidel because he's handsome. Like Gaddhafi. Is it so wrong? Don't people's faces tell you a lot about them? She was always very particular about the way I looked, I can promise you, saying there's a spot on your skirt, or you need to do your nails, or whatever it might be. That time she fainted, she spilled a glass of water over herself. Luciana screamed, She's dead!

I couldn't help it, Luciana says, and the water spreading a stain down her front as dark as blood. I know I cry easily, I have done all my life, but when they carried the *baronessa* on a stretcher down the steps into the ambulance, and she waved at us all standing there, my heart went out to her. I can see that wave and her smile today. That's courage.

Back once more in Ogni Santi hospital, Dina had to rely on Chantal and the nuns to provide her with the news. What is Eden Pastora doing in the Contras, she wanted to know, and Roberto d'Aubuisson with his death squads in Salvador?

Professor Vierchowod rang up Ursie to say that he was keeping Dina under observation. The pacemaker might have to be changed, but there was no point rushing ahead with that. He spoke of strain and exhaustion, and mental causes of illness that might be more damaging than anything physical. On the whole he agreed with Luciana that ultimately the Falklands War could not be incorporated into the vision of Unite the Impossible. Out of the need to protect herself from reality, she had fainted.

'The leeches?' Ursie asked. 'Do we have to have them?'

He had laughed. Of course he had been consulted. At best, they were marginal; at worst, a placebo. A personality like hers might feel reassured, at least singled out, by unorthodox treatment.

I'm glad I persuaded you not to fly out, Chantal says, it would only have frightened her unnecessarily. The nuns there are highly professional, and in any case I could do anything extra that had to be done. We rested, we really did. In the ambulance going home, she said to me that this was one journey she hadn't expected to make. And the first thing I had to do when I got her back into her own bed was to bring her the Flowers of Meditation notebook, she'd had another idea for one.

A week's correspondence had accumulated in her absence, and for a while she didn't deal with it. One of the envelopes from England was of the cheapest kind, as used by unknown fans or pen-friends of the Newsletter. The address meant nothing: Flat 23, Waverley Buildings, Tulse Hill. Then she realised that here was a supreme example of Pushed and Blocked. Iris Warren had chosen this particular moment to break silence.

222

Dearest old friend,

You may have a surprise at hearing from me after all this lapse of time, but not an unpleasant surprise, I hope. Of all the friends and acquaintances I used to have, you are the one most likely still to live at the address I have. In that respect – in others too – I feel sure you won't have changed. Whenever I've thought of you, I'd had a picture of that sumptuous place of yours, really I'd do better to write it as palace. I expect you planted up the garden you used to speak about.

Lewis wrote and told me when Andrew died, and I suppose I might have been in touch then, but I was in Canada and I thought bygones might as well be bygones. Our lives had gone their separate ways. You know that Lewis drove out of a minor road and didn't stop at the junction and that was the end of him and his wife. My Toby died five years ago. He'd been in the timber business, and then it emerged that he and his company was stoney broke, and it had been some kind of accounting miracle to have kept it going as long as he did. The house had to be sold. Of all the relationships I've known in my life, having step-children is far and away the most difficult to handle. I had to do what I could for them. I wonder how your two have turned out. Alexander was always precocious.

Canadians are willing to pump your hand and shout cheerfully in your face, but they don't become close friends. I'm glad to be home. But there's another reason. Health. The usual thing. I've had the lumps cut out, and they think they got the lymph glands in time. At my age, you can go on for years, but I have to have chemotherapy. I didn't fancy laying my bones at Bonnerton Bay, and now that I'm poor as a church mouse I'm only too glad to be able to make use of National Health. I couldn't make it to Italy but I'm hoping to catch you here on your next visit. I feel a bit like one of those figures on a desert island whose only possession is a bottle, and they cork it up with a message inside, in the hope that it'll catch a friendly tide.

'You're crying?' Chantal was anxious. 'What's the matter?'

She wouldn't tell me, Chantal is to say, I could only conclude that this letter had moved her. With her, I had the impression of a volcano. Molten lava was steaming deep down and might explode, and there was a conflict between the heat of the emotions, and the outer retaining crust of intelligence. There'll never be anyone quite like her again.

A month was to pass before the journey, a month in which unseasonal stormy rain shook the blooms off the wisteria. News of her relapse and recovery, and now the approach of a holiday, had created a social momentum. Everyone wanted to see her, as if to give her a send-off. It was high time she went away, they said, and why not stay with Leonora Pigri who was putting on an exhibition in Paris, or take a cruise, inviting Ursie for a comfortable fortnight in the Norwegian fjords.

'I shall be catching up with a friend of mine,' Dina said, 'it's as if she has returned from the dead.'

For years now she had stayed at home because travel left too much to chance. She needed to be sure of her timetable and connections. Porters were a thing of the past, but an airport in summer was out of the question; she had seen too many photographs of stranded passengers to be willing to place herself at the mercy of air-traffic control. It would have to be a sleeper on the Rome express. Chantal was the obvious choice to accompany her, but she wanted a break, and deserved it too. If she came to London, then the expenses would be doubled. Instead, Dina paid for Anna Karcz to have the adjoining sleeper. A car was booked to collect them at Victoria Station. Nobody else was to meet them there, or at the hotel.

I shan't see anyone, Dina said, until I've had forty-eight hours in London to myself.

The trunk she took evoked the era of sea journeys. Heavy and rectangular, it had handles on either side, and clasps to hold the lid firm. The same key fitted both locks. Inside was a tray which could be lifted out by means of straps. At the bottom was an accumulation of tissue paper and mothballs.

During the days of packing, this trunk stood in the corridor outside Dina's room. Into it went her favourite shirts with the attached tie, and her plain suits.

'Put the sable coat in,' she ordered.

But it's summer, they objected, you couldn't want anything as warm as that.

In the coat went, though, and then the trunk was carried downstairs by Ubaldo and Armando. There it was left, close to the altar with the Proofs inside. A careful planner, Dina had supervised her packing all in her own good time. Ubaldo thinks the trunk was down on the ground floor for three days, Armando believes that is an understatement: maybe as much as five days. Certainly it remained unlocked, because all sorts of things were put into it right until the last moment. On the day before her own departure, Ubaldo locked the trunk and drove it to the station, where he registered it through to London. From then on, Dina had the key in her handbag.

Whether through coincidence, or because of the acceleration of events almost invariably brought on by an imminent departure, callers at the villa were more numerous than usual. Afterwards it became important to establish exactly who they had been. Avvocato Bellini, to arrange for the wages and expenses in her absence; Dr Melegnani; Una, and Anna Karcz, a good many times.

I came over to say goodbye, Sandra Piccolomini says, I had with me a cousin of mine, she lives near Viterbo and is practically a cripple.

In their old style, without warning, Pater Auhofer and Père Destouches also turned up and invited themselves to lunch. Since they went for a walk in the garden, they too must have passed the trunk. Their parting gift was a new book about the Second Vatican Council, or Vatican Two, that seed-bed in which Unite the Impossible had been potted out.

Recently Don Alvise had taken to wearing a ring on his little finger, a thick gold band with a red stone set lumpily in it. Did the ring have any value, or was it junk? Sometimes he had been observed twiddling it round and round as if it were a set of worry-beads. Whenever he raised his hands in that supplicating priestly gesture of his, this ring acted like a question mark upon his whole personality. On the eve of her departure, he spent an hour alone with Dina in her room.

Then there was also a young man from the British Institute. Pink-faced, embarrassed, he claimed several excuses that were not quite consistent, how he had written but hadn't been answered, how he'd mislaid the telephone number, and anyhow he had been passing and thought Dina would understand if he popped in. The long and short of it was, would she be willing to consider a substantial contribution to an appeal? A new lift was mentioned, an extension to the library, all sorts of worthwhile projects.

As she finally left, in a flurry of last-minute instructions, Dina was in the sunniest of moods. On the steps of the villa, under the cardinal's arms, she embraced everyone. A united group, they waved as the car drove away down the long diagonal of the cypresses. That evening, Ubaldo's last task was to drive Chantal to catch a train to Liège.

In the grandiose forecourt of the station at Rome, gypsy children mobbed Dina. Of course the intention was to snatch her handbag, but she foiled them by the simple expedient of getting in first, and reaching for her purse and handing out the small notes in it.

I was carrying the overnight bag, Anna Karcz says, so I wasn't much use. We weren't going to fall for such an old trick. I know she had the key with her, we checked it.

The journey went without a hitch. I loved her company, Anna continues, especially when she was as cosy and intimate as that. I mentioned that I liked liqueurs and she had the *wagon-lit* man fetch me a glass. He opened the door between the two compartments, we stayed up late gossiping. When I dropped her at the hotel the next morning, I couldn't have imagined there might be any-thing wrong.

It so happened that Dina had chosen to stay in the hotel where Evan Langridge had made his scene about the pudding. Little or nothing disturbs the silence and comfort of the place. Its deep quiet and order are compounded by the carpeting, polished cleanliness, and not least the appetising dining-room. In its way, it is as much of a fortress against the outside world as La Grecchiata.

The trunk was already in her room. On a table, flowers had been delivered in crinkly wrappings, a bunch from Ursie, and another which Ursie had sent in Alexander's name. To these, Dina never attended. Instead she unlocked the trunk. The sable coat should have been folded in the detachable tray on top. It was missing.

Any one of them could have stolen it. Adela, to impress her carabinieri officer; Luciana, who had packed it, Giulia who had helped and watched. Perhaps Ubaldo had wanted it for his wife, or if not for her, then to cast suspicion on Giulia or the nurse, for simple revenge. Armando could have crept in, to get his own back on Chantal, or to spite Luciana who was the most likely to be held responsible.

Could Anna have taken it? Or Una? What about Sandra and the cousin who might not have been a cripple at all, but whisked it unseen into her car? The lawyer and the doctor had had the run of the villa, and must have found themselves often alone as they passed the trunk. Nobody would have noticed Don Alvise if he had loitered there, to seize the opportunity behind her back. The two priests who had so unexpectedly surfaced after a long absence; the shifty youth who had claimed to be fundraising for the British Institute but had shown no evidence of his *bona fides*. Where had Luciana's Tullio been, and for that matter, Don Alvise's friend Tonio?

Then the trunk had been in the hands of the railway people, the officials who had registered it, and the guards in the guard's van, and whoever had been the carrier from Victoria. All they would have had to do, somewhere on the line, was pick the locks, or make a key, and they'd have had all night to go about it unobserved.

When Dina first rang the villa, Adela answered the telephone but failed to recognise the danger signals. Oh, she said, I'm sure it'll turn up, nobody could possibly want to steal a thing like that. You must have mislaid it.

In a series of summary interviews at long distance, Dina spoke to them one by one. Accusing them in turn, she was soon beside herself with rage. Only Chantal was beyond reach, already on holiday in Belgium. So she then rang Avvocato Bellini, with instructions to search the villa, to make an inventory of the nurse's clothes, to take statements and notify the railway authorities and police in three countries.

Cut in a fashion that was years out of date, the fur was beyond renovation, and had no resale value. Is it possible that a loss of that kind tips the balance of life over towards death?

TWENTY-TWO

'Our guests are our first consideration,' the manager gave an apologetic smile. 'We have to act as quickly as we can, to spare everyone's feelings.'

Unfortunately these sad incidents were more frequent than one might have anticipated. It was convenient that the service stairs led to an exit at the back where nobody could observe what was happening. It was all very discreet. People seem to have so little to do, the manager said, they stand and gape at anything like that.

In his striped trousers and morning coat, the manager held himself stiffly, and his head, like a giraffe's, looked too small for the elegant and angular body. His eyebrows had a sharp arch, as though he had been made up for miming and wasn't expecting anything he said to be taken literally.

'Heart failure, the doctor is certifying,' he told Ursie, 'what with the pacemaker, you've no doubt been dreading something like this for a good while?'

From the appearance of the room, Dina might have just stepped outside, and would soon be returning. She had unpacked her overnight bag, and familiar objects were arranged as they would have been at the villa: photographs of Andrew, including the one of him with the car at Varendy, her bedside clock, the radio with its earpiece for listening to his communications. On the pillow, a pink nightdress. Pens waiting to be used, and the Blue Notebook and the Flowers of Meditation. *To be published after my death*. Wherever had the confidence come from? Ursie turned to the last page. For some reason, Dina had reverted to the French she had spoken in childhood, to write, '*La mort, quelle Espoir*.' And the final entry: 'I am shy to write what follows, but cannot hide the simple God-given Truth that I have Proofs.'

The flowers that Ursie had ordered were still in their cellophane. In the centre of the room was the trunk, open, the tray askew and the neat packing disordered.

Your mother, the manager said, had spent much of the time since her arrival on the telephone, apparently keeping the line open to Italy for long stretches. In the evening, the housekeeper knocked, and entered in order to turn down the bed. Thoroughly trustworthy, the housekeeper had worked in the hotel for years. She'd learnt that a fur coat was missing. Distraught as your mother was, the manager said, at no point had she accused anyone in the hotel.

The key was in the right-hand lock. The manager pointed to it. 'She'd had it with her, the lock's not been tampered with, that's clear. The coat must still be in Italy.'

Then he handed her some business papers which he'd taken into safe-keeping.

That was how Ursie discovered that the villa now belonged to Lionel. She read his letters, a series going back for several years, in which he had been warning Dina against the priests, against Langridge, against her children, speaking the language of trusts and tax efficiency and the preservation of family assets. Here were copies of Bellini's drafts for donations and wills, as these suggestions had one by one converted into documents. Now there was to be a museum, apparently, but the details had not been finalised, and meanwhile the villa was Lionel's, to do with as he wished.

To find oneself cheated is like being swept away in a river: there is danger, swirling currents, underwater rocks, yet the banks are visible and on them everything seems to be in its rightful place, and meanwhile a sense of adventure arises. This is actually fascinating, one thinks, do people really behave like this? What kind of a man is it who acts in such a way?

So that's what he's been up to all along, Ursie thought, that's what he'd planned for us, and this is how he did it. The family's oldest friend. Smooth work. Her heart started to beat faster, adrenalin gave her the taste of excitement. It astonished her that what she most felt was the laughable naïvety of never having imagined the likelihood of such a thing. And she a bond-dealer, or rather an ex-bond-dealer, ordered to clear her desk in half an hour on the Monday morning after Mr Beeby had read Simon's article.

So much for competence. She had supposed herself to be more or less in charge of her life, someone responsible. Now it appeared that decisions taken on one's own behalf were so many plunges in the dark, based on faulty evidence. That the priests had wanted to lay greedy hands on the villa had been obvious – but what about Lionel's ambitions? Had it been possible to anticipate that he was capable of taking advantage of Dina's illusions in this way?

She thought, It'll come to nothing. Minou and Micky will never allow such a thing. This is only the crazy dead-end of Unite the Impossible.

And meanwhile they had to be told. She would leave it to Alexander to ring them at Varendy. What would be the expression on Lionel's face when he had to confess how he had persuaded Dina to make the villa over to him?

No villa, no job. Maybe Lionel would argue that he had done the right thing and stepped in just in time. Simon certainly couldn't see that he'd done anything wrong in his article. She'd talked to him on the record, they'd both wanted to put a stop to the Project, and rescue Alexander from an aberration. Mission accomplished. Langridge had closed the place down, and Alexander had come to his senses. If Mr Beeby had been completely unreasonable about reading in the press some unflattering details about a client, that surely wasn't to be blamed on the article? Nobody would publish anything if considerations of that kind applied.

Actually Simon's words had been, 'Now you'll have time to show your mother round, and look after her properly.'

231

When the telephone rang, she assumed it to be Alexander. Instead, someone at the reception desk said that a visitor had arrived for Mrs Lumel, and should she show her up? It had been by appointment. Iris Warren, she said.

'You must be Ursie,' Iris Warren began, 'I wouldn't have recognised you, I haven't seen you since you were in a pram.'

Nothing remains of the woman in the photograph preserved in Dina's bedroom in La Grecchiata. That had shown someone lithe and strong; here she was stooped and ill, as if a weight were pressing on the back of her neck. The armchair in which she sat seemed either too upright or too low for comfort.

'It's very like me to arrive when it's too late,' she said. 'We had fixed this time. Now is it true what I've just heard downstairs?'

Iris Warren's eyes are blank, watering, whether from a weakness or the sudden distress. The face is wrinkled, a study in lack of colour, dead as putty, the skin one shade of white, the hair another. She cuts this hair above her ears and the sole jaunty touch is an old-fashioned French beret pulled on one side. Her jacket and skirt are the same dark blue, and so is the handbag out of which she unfolds a handkerchief to dab at her eyes.

'Now that I've come all this way, I hope you'll give me lunch.'

'Let's wait for Alexander, who ought to be arriving any moment. Then we'll eat here.'

I wouldn't know how far you're in the picture, Ursie explains, but for some years now Dina has been rather strange, to put it mildly. It all began when she had heart failure on a visit to Assisi, and had to have a pacemaker and hasn't ever been right since. She came round from the operation insisting that she had had a vision of Andrew, and after that she was always hearing his voice on the radio and in the end even out of a plant. She decided that he was determining everything that happens, and it became a religious mania. She called it Unite the Imposs-

232

ible, meaning among other things that life and death were to be considered the same thing. Alexander and I had no idea how to deal with it, we felt helpless, and couldn't really even raise the subject with her. Lots of clergymen egged her on, I'm afraid. Part of the problem was that in so many other ways she remained normal and practical. That pacemaker changed the personality through some quite simple physical factor, I believe, it may just have cut the proper supply of blood to the brain.

Ursie handed her the Blue Notebook and the Flowers of Meditation.

'And what might these Proofs be which she mentions?'

'Well when he communicated with her on the radio, she'd try to find corroboration of what he'd just told her, something tangible would pop up which she'd call a Proof. In the villa there's a whole boxful of them. One of them was the fur coat he'd given her, and it has somehow been mislaid on the journey from Italy now. That was too much. The last straw. It's killed her.'

'Interference at long range sounds very like the Andrew I used to know.'

Sitting, Iris Warren hunches herself. The voice is dry, on the edge of a cough, an old smoker's voice.

Nobody ought to delve into their parents' lives: it's enough to accept that once there was a union, from which the child resulted. Yet the curiosity to learn as much as possible about the emotions which went into one's own conception is not to be resisted. Today of all days I can ask, Ursie told herself. What else would Iris Warren and Dina have talked about, if not Andrew and the past?

Not long ago, she said, some papers of my father's were delivered from store, and Alexander's been reading them. I haven't. I don't know if he ever will – because he's so changeable – but he proposes to write a book about our parents and the whole background. Therapy, really. Explaining them, he may explain himself. New beginnings have become rather a speciality of his. Some of the letters are from you to Andrew.

'I doubt if I ever wrote to Andrew in my whole life.'

233

'But you did, on pretty blue paper with an engraved edge and a monogram. They seem like love letters.'

'Whatever makes you think they were addressed to Andrew?'

Aren't you too young to remember him? Iris Warren asks. Since we're on the subject, I may as well tell you that I never thought very highly of him. Terribly full of himself and of his own importance. Perhaps he really was important, I wouldn't be able to judge, but that was no reason to be so selfish. I'm not the least surprised to learn that even after his death he found a way to subdue and tyrannise Dina.

These last years I've lived in Canada, Iris Warren continues, and I've lost touch with everyone here. It's all very different from what it was in our day. Now you can do what you like. We couldn't. Dina was so clever and gifted, not her father's daughter for nothing. But Andrew choked the life out of her. I used to beg her to leave him. You've got to go, I'd say, save yourself while you can, he's a monster and he'll make one out of you if you aren't careful. Did she ever speak to you about the Huxleys, and how when she'd been a teenager Aldous had kissed her? That wasn't quite true, it was Maria. Aldous may have known, mind you, they had a marriage with its own conventions. It used to crop up all the time when I tried to persuade Dina to leave, and come and live with me. I saw myself rescuing her, getting her away from that living death. She should have been true to herself, not his slave. Unite the Impossible, it doesn't sound a bad description of their marriage. The things conscience makes one do. He must have laid his hands on letters I wrote to her. Stolen them, for all we know. Not that there could have been much in them, I was never one to be able to express my emotions, I don't have the gift of the gab. I thought he treated her with unbearable condescension, but she decided she was going to stick with him, and that was that. There was no arguing against will-power like hers. And what could I offer? How could I have competed with someone who could buy her a villa in Italy? I hadn't any

234

money, I never have had. So I married a man who'd been pestering me, his name was Lewis Grindley, and that didn't work out. I married a Canadian second time round, but he's dead. And now Lewis has gone and killed himself in a car smash.

Her lips trembled, she lost control and cried. 'I know I shouldn't be speaking like this in the room in which she's only just died. I had a whole heart-rending speech worked out for her, but you've caught me on the wrong foot. I'm ill, and I'm broke, and there isn't anyone else in the world I can turn to.'

TWENTY-THREE

A car nosed up the drive as if the man at the wheel was afraid of unexpected potholes. So many assorted strangers now seemed to find plausible reasons for calling that the front door of the villa was kept locked all day, something that had not been considered in Dina's day. This particular man introduced himself as a professor. His visiting card declared that he was head of a university department of arboriculture. The *baronessa*, he said, had commissioned him to prepare a plan for saving the cypress avenue. Their disease should be thought of as cancer; dead branches had to be lopped, and each tree injected with a special preparation. The chances of success were reasonable, but he could not pretend that it would be cheap. He made the small grimace of someone who is aware that valuable services cost money.

Alexander kept him waiting while he went to find Armando. It was the first that anyone had heard of the professor and his plan. Yet here he was referring with apparent first-hand knowledge to the *baronessa* and her proposals to cure the cypresses. The height of summer elegance, the professor wore white linen trousers and a blue shirt, the cuffs beautifully turned back, and a cashmere sweater draped across his shoulders. If his estimate for treating the cypresses was no longer required, he said with a passing shrug of resignation, then perhaps they'd be kind enough to tell him if the villa was for sale? Places as perfect as this were few and far between.

This is a country in which nothing need be said, and yet everything is known. It is a country in which there is always something more than meets the eye, and where

236

Unite the Impossible might have been more than a brilliant flash of a motto.

'I want you out by the end of the month,' Lionel had said, 'that ought to be time enough.'

In a meeting after Dina's death, he had taken to speaking in a voice several tones lower than usual, deliberately, an imitation of good manners. 'Your mother's wishes,' he repeated, with the gravity of prayer, 'we must respect them.'

At least they had almost four full weeks, and were to spend them in the villa. Now it was Milly's turn to say, 'What a view, it's breathtaking.' It was without precedent for someone to sleep in Andrew's room. I'll do it on one condition, Charles said, that the frightful portrait is removed. I can't stand that sort of submodernism. With its easel, the Golovin painting was carried down to the *salone*, to be tucked away more or less invisibly behind the piano.

'It's a miracle,' Luciana said, 'if only the *baronessa* was here to see you. Perhaps she knows and is smiling the way she used to.'

Between tears and laughter, Luciana can hardly handle her emotions. It's all been so sudden, and she starts to weep, and to wring her hands and exclaim that there never was anyone like the *baronessa*, so good and kind and generous, such a benefactor, everyone in Sant' Ambrogio loved her. Her pudgy face glows a stained red. And then she switches, to hope that Alessandro is going to marry Milly, and Ursie is going to marry Carlo, and the villa is plenty big enough for them all, only they must hurry and have families. Everyone in Sant' Ambrogio is expecting that, everyone is so delighted that they have the villa, and that the priests have been excluded. By which time, she is laughing.

How is she going to be told the truth? Nobody has the courage to break the news about Lionel. In due course, says Alexander, let's do it tomorrow. She'll have to find out.

Who stole the coat, is the question which has priority. From breakfast on, Luciana and Ubaldo raise this topic, they can't discuss it enough. To them, it is clear that the *baronessa* was bound to have died of grief the moment she

237

unlocked that trunk and saw that the sable wasn't there. Everything had to be in its right place, Luciana says, the *baronessa* was so careful and neat with possessions that mattered to her. Look how she filed the newspaper cuttings and kept her notebooks, and always the same style of dressing.

'I drove it to the station a day early, for the trunk to be registered,' Ubaldo said. 'It was so large I couldn't shut the boot. I couldn't lift it by myself either. At the station I found a porter, and we handed it over together. Too many people were watching for anyone to have been a thief. In any case, the *baronessa* had the key with her.'

On the day of the funeral – mind you, they say, on the very day – Chiarella returned to the villa. Could that have been a coincidence?

'Because I left a message for her at her home in Liège,' says Ursie.

For Luciana and Ubaldo, that means nothing. She had arrived with a friend of hers, an old woman with a face like an unripe melon, and they'd packed up her possessions, the two of them, and then they were off. We stood over them, Luciana says, watching what they were up to but we never had a glimpse of that sable, it certainly wasn't in her room or her luggage. She must have arranged to hide it somewhere. Look at how clever she was.

Even dour Giulia becomes eloquent on the subject. Search my house, she says dramatically, it's wide open, come and see for yourself.

'The fact is,' Ursie tries to reassure them, 'Alexander and I don't care. We don't mind. The rotten old coat had only sentimental value, and only to the *baronessa*.' Search, Giulia orders them, I've nothing to hide. And she goes on, I have my ideas on the matter but I'm not saying, I'm not pointing the finger at anyone, I'm not denouncing.

Armando shakes his head. He doesn't think that taking the coat would be in keeping with the character of Chiarella.

'And what sort of a witness is he?' Luciana sniffs. 'After what happened, he's not about to accuse her.'

What about the priests, the neighbours, doctor and lawyer and the youngster from the British Institute? What about a sneak thief who might have driven up the way everybody seems to be doing nowadays? If Chiarella didn't take it, then the mystery is insoluble, therefore she took it.

Before she left, Chantal had time to write a letter to await arrival. In French – no doubt, says Ursie, so that if the others opened the envelope and read this letter, they couldn't understand. In it, the nurse thanked them for what had been very happy years. She'd never expected to stay so long, she wrote, nor to have become so fond of Madame Lumel. Not always easy, but always exceptional, a combination of vision and intelligence. The quality she'd most cherish was Madame's courage. What a pity that her life had ended as it had, the loss of the coat was troublesome (*bien fâcheuse*, in the original) and must have contributed to her pacemaker's failure. As for herself, she had found employment with American sisters, two ladies who owned a house at Dorigny-Les-Ecluses near her own home, but spent the summer in Massachusetts. That would be a change, and good for her English. One of the ladies was a semi-invalid, and wanted her to begin as soon as possible, hence the hurry to remove her things from the villa. Finally she asked if they could be kind enough to send her a reference, as requested by these ladies.

'Nobody screws gardeners better,' Alexander said.

'If it hadn't been for her, Langridge might have nipped in ahead of Lionel.'

Neither of them believe for a moment that Chantal took the coat. It is unthinkable that anyone in the house should have done so, for why ever wouldn't they have taken it years ago when the fur might have been worth something? This is Pushed and Blocked in action: evidently it had been time for Dina to obey her own laws.

Cupboards and drawers reveal the detritus of a life: so much stuff pushed away out of sight, photographs of unnamed strangers on anonymous occasions, letters held in elastic bands, the correspondence of Père Destouches,

239

long-ago invitations from Elsie Crane-Dytton and to Sally Macleod's wedding, candles in case of a power failure, a silver christening mug presumably hers, endless writings about the books she had devoured or concerning Unite the Impossible. Every item involves decision-making, and the drain of nervous energy is exhausting. Where Dina had succeeded in imposing order, as she saw it, there is only chaos.

There will never be anyone quite like that again, they all say, but the cliché this time is true. It is impossible to sit down and think it through with the care that circumstances demand. For the time being, Ursie has in her head an image which is now superimposed on the whole of the past, and has the strength to carry into the indefinite future as well. Dina will not go away, Dina as perceived at the end. She had found herself in a narrow corridor, artificially lit, which led into the mortuary. Chill, a temperature in which to shiver, and a plinth on which Dina lay at a slope, beams of light directed on the face. No special expression about it, none of the expected rage which had governed her, especially during these last hours as she shrieked into the telephone. Somehow smaller with absence. The nose tilted. Someone had tidied the hair, and it curled as she had liked it above her forehead. Wrinkles. Blemishes never before observed from this angle. Hands corpse-cold to the touch, the fingernails beaky. The image is imprinted with remorse and shame. They should never have allowed her to erect the fantastic structure of Unite the Impossible. They hadn't loved her enough to stop her. Don't wait until it's too late, Sandra Piccolomini had once advised her. Now there remained only lost opportunities, and guilt.

'Why did we collude in the madness?' Ursie asks. 'What's wrong with us? It's as though it's been a gigantic plot involving everyone. Look at the connivance of Sandra and Una, or people like the Canaveses. Martin Cammaerts never fails to tell me that he thinks she had some sort of genius.'

Charles answers that rich people can do as they like, and

that's the whole point of being rich, quite simple when you think about it.

'But she would come out with something outrageous about her latest Proof, and all we'd do was smirk and nod, and look as if we agreed.'

Alexander agrees that it wasn't a question of cowardice, but lack of love. The only people you must tell the truth to are those you love. I can't really tell you I loved her, he says, she made it too hard to do that. 'Protecting ourselves, we reinforced her loneliness. There may be a sense in which we actually were promoters of Unite the Impossible.'

'Come off it,' Charles says, 'you were scared. You couldn't calculate her reaction, and you thought you might be disinherited. Like everyone else, you were after the money. If you see what I mean, you have to pay very dearly for money.'

'Not true,' Alexander says, 'anyone who really wants money can set about earning it, it only takes a little time and trouble. Speaking for myself, Lionel's performance seems a masterpiece of irony.'

Take a look at the villa, he goes on, nobody's touched the plumbing and heating in living memory, the roof is terrible, and the servants' wages could only be paid thanks to Dina's incredible skills with foreign exchange and gold speculation. Lionel is doing them a favour.

Within himself, Alexander actually feels relief to which he doesn't like to admit openly. There is a line which he isn't quite sure where to draw, between comedy and tragedy. Dina's ending in that hotel room of chintz and reproduction furniture was rather pitiful, but hadn't Unite the Impossible been farce? And then Lionel had been predictably true to form, rushing into the undertaker's to cancel all arrangements, only to have them reinstated a few hours later. Lawyers know best, it seems. And at the crematorium, assembling before the dismal service, Lionel had come up to him, put his arm affectionately round his shoulder and said in a stage whisper, 'Something sad to tell you, old boy. Madame Virginie's kicked the bucket. Heart failure all round. Shan't know where to have our slap and tickle now.'

At least it wasn't a repeat of knocking him down, as at Andrew's funeral. Hadn't Lionel always been a figure of fun, Tiglath Pileser with his self-importance and his loudmouth sex and vulgarity, finding his level in a brothel in Toulon? Then he had organised one last conference in his old firm's offices, to hand them a prepared folder with the papers relating to Dina's gift of the villa to him. There was the signature, duly notarised. A month to clear out, he had said in that low voice of false drama, and at that point he became tragic, someone who had brought about his own destruction. Someone who really believed it was a game of *vingt-et-un*, and he had only to scoop all the children's matches. There would never again be occasion to dream about slashing him to death with one of his own whips; he had done it to himself, to linger slowly and consciously in his own moral ruin.

The one thing Alexander wanted from the villa was the photograph of Iris Warren: that would have to be reproduced in the book. Iris's letters had revealed nothing, they were trivial, without a single sentence which could be thought compromising. How did one ask someone like her if she had indeed been his mother's lover, and would she kindly tell him the facts and in the circumstances was it likely to be the truth? Might Sandra know? or Iris Origo? Or Sybille Bedford, in whose two-volume biography of Aldous Huxley he was now absorbed? He knew already the references to the Napier family but had brought with him as much of the literature as he could. It seemed impossible to discover whether Maria Huxley might have seduced the young Dina, and if so, with what consequences. The letters and books which Dina had lent Père Destouches might contain clues, and he wrote peremptorily to ask for their return. Answering from Vatican City, Père Destouches said that it would be a blow to scholarship to part with such material, but he would do so if Alexander insisted. He could not refrain from adding that he did not believe Dina would have wished her heirs to act like this.

242

Alexander asked, 'What is the right sum to settle on one's mother's lesbian lover?' Picking up on his own question, he said it all depended on how much she contributed to his book.

Tidying up like theirs is a matter of lifting things off one surface only to place them down again on another. Besides, it is sultry weather. So they drift out to the terrace, to Milly and Charles sitting there in sunglasses. Milly has been collecting the guidebooks that have piled up in the villa over the years on various shelves, and she is skimming between Edward Hutton, Leonora Grifi, Augustus Hare and Vernon Bartlett. She has just discovered with admiration the book by D.H. Lawrence which opens, 'Comes over one an absolute necessity to move.'

'Isn't that a great sentence?' she says. The others take the hint.

Sightseeing is a way of postponing choices. It feels like childish escapade to be commandeering Dina's car from Ubaldo, and to set off for Assisi, to wonder which of the frescoes Andrew had shimmered out of at the moment when the fantasy began, or when the heart failed, whichever is the right explanation of Dina's behaviour. There's a Roman temple in the centre of the street in Assisi, and they lunched opposite it. Was Unite the Impossible different in its essential aspirations from any other religious faith? I'm beginning to understand why I used to be interested in the perfectibility of man, Alexander said. Between the four of them at that lunch, they drank three bottles of wine, with grappa afterwards.

Mugniomaggio has a look of spectacular folly under the sun, with ivy gleaming on its walls and the many doorways suddenly as obscure as dungeons: a child's idea of a castle. Dropping other guests, Sandra insists on taking Milly on a guided tour, through ground-floor rooms full of uncomfortable and blackened furniture into the vaulted hall with its nineteenth-century frescoes of muscular battle. Here, she explains, we used to play cards when Dina and Andrew had just bought the villa.

With a curiosity as irresistible as Luciana's, Sandra also

longs to worm out whether at last love is in the air. To Ursie, she says that this girl is easily the best Alexander has ever produced, and how she hopes he'll settle down at last. To Alexander, she says that Charles is so clever, for a banker unusually sensitive, and she can't understand what it can be that Ursie is waiting for, she ought to hurry and have children. Who's going to live in the villa otherwise?

Our lawyer, Alexander tells her, Lionel's the owner now, it was made over to him.

What? Impossible. *Figurate! Furbissimo!* Sandra claps her hands for silence, and Alexander has to describe for her and her guests exactly what has happened. Disbelief sweeps over them like a breeze over a cornfield. Surely he's exaggerating. Everybody knows that in Italy you can't disinherit your children. As a lawyer, Lionel knows it too, the whole business is too silly for words.

'It was me who found the villa for the parents,' Sandra says, 'I can see them now with that famous car, very ritzy and glamorous, weren't they, Pippo?'

After the war, she says, everybody was poor but here came an English milord, and it was the first hope we had that things might be normal again.

'A bloody foreigner' in his own eyes, but still . . . that's an aspect of his book, and too complex to be explained to fellow guests in bathing costumes round the pool of a country house like this.

Sandra rings up Avvocato Bellini and hectors him. She makes an appointment. She can't be much less than eighty, Alexander says, but when she wants something, she is as energetic as ever. Her parting shot to Ursie is, 'Your objection to Carlo is too foolish. He doesn't wear glasses in bed, does he?'

In Avvocato Bellini's office, no business ever seems to be transacted. His receptionist has an elongated face more suitable to a sheep, and pallid, as if kept out of the sun for fear of damage. Early in the morning, she is already reading the cheapest of scandal magazines. On the avvocato's desk, the photographs of his wife and children are so many spurs to being conscientious.

The Marchesa Piccolomini is right, he confirms. Dina did nothing illegal in signing that act of donation, but the fact of her death immediately invalidates it. One of two things will now have to happen. Either Signor Lionel must surrender a gift which has no standing in the law, or they must bring an action against him to force him to do so. They are one hundred per cent certain to win. However, he must point out that in the event of an action, skilful lawyers could spin the case out for five years, and the costs might then be several hundred thousand dollars, or more than the value of the villa.

Since you knew this, Alexander asked him, why didn't you explain it to my mother? You had only to tell her what the consequences would be of putting her signature on the deed of gift. Why didn't you?

Unwieldly, with the top-heavy gestures natural in an overweight man, the avvocato stands up to reply. It is a measure of how offended he is. 'The *baronessa*, your mother,' he says, 'was very well respected and admired. Marchesa Piccolomini introduced her to my predecessor. I was certainly never going to presume that she wouldn't know what she was doing. My part is to fulfil my clients' wishes, and that's all. A person is entitled under our law to leave a proportion of the whole estate to individuals or institutions outside the family. How am I to know the complete financial picture? I drew up that deed in good faith. In good faith too, I had drawn up previous documents, in favour of Monsignor Silvestri and the nuns, and I was consulted about the proposals in favour of the English bishop. Instructions are instructions.'

How could you just have listened? Ursie wanted to know. How were you able to sit there and let her have her head? How many clients do you have who hand on instructions transmitted by sound-waves from their dead husbands?

Letters from Lionel, from the Church, from Père Destouches, the bishop, all in folders of apparent order but actually a swamp of greed and intrigue. Who could imagine that madness had this form?

Think of the waste of time and money if they bring the action. It may not be necessary because Minou and Micky will refuse, must refuse, to allow Lionel to take the house over as his, and therefore they need only rely on their good-will. On the other hand, Lionel seems really to believe that he has a claim to the house, and so he must consider them suckers. This is his equivalent of Unite the Impossible.

Not at all, argues Alexander, he's a tragic personality, and the nature of tragedy is that it must work itself through to the very end. We can't step in and save him from himself. He should be handed the villa without any resort to law. The important thing is to stand well away from that power of self-destruction, in case it is contagious. To let the villa go is to be free.

Free? Ursie is sarcastic. Isn't there something called equity? Freedom of that kind is the false peace of appease-ment.

Banker that he is, Charles has a different proposal, which is to initiate legal proceedings as swiftly as possible on the understanding that the law is perfectly clear. In the unlikely event of Lionel fighting the case, then they have only to throw in their hand. There's no point spending as much money as the villa is worth, but think what the publicity would do to him.

The Getty Museum was in a different position. There a sale had occurred. Among the callers at the villa was Holly Strickland and a van to remove the Napier collection. It took the men very little time to carry the boxes of drawings down, stack them in the van and secure the load with cords. Muscle-bound, they looked like professional thieves, accustomed to stripping houses in a quarter of an hour. The sight of the boxes as they departed was unimpressive: a disposal of a certain amount of paper.

Since it was midday, they invited Holly Strickland to stay for a meal. She refused. The only way to be sure that the archive was safe, she said, was to stay with it and escort it to the packers in Rome, to be air-freighted to California.

'If you need to consult it for your book,' she said to Alexander, 'you'll find them very open-minded out there, very willing. My own *catalogue raisonné* is due out next year. That'll help you.'

'You were part of the court circle in this villa,' he said. 'Did she have any knowledge about her father's work, or genuine interest in it? When we're back in London, I must have a lunch and interview you properly.'

Charles asked, 'Does one get a commission for arranging a private sale like this?'

'It's standard practice.' But she had the last word: 'Correct me if I'm wrong, but I think you'll find that Unite the Impossible could never have been financed without that sale.'

Poor Dina. What to her had been faith, art, friendship, literature, was in fact extraction of money, deception and flattery. Communing with the heights, she had not noticed that her feet splashed in dirt. Or had it been an attempt to remodel the world in accord with an ideal, and in its way heroic? In another age, and at another time, Ursie and Alexander sometimes think, she might have been a high priestess, a luminary, and Unite the Impossible might have resulted in a valid appeal for the brotherhood of man.

The one person who never mocked her was Don Alvise. If ever there was a disinterested good deed, it had been the return of the blank cheque. It's Ursie's intention to give him the crucifix once a present from Monsignor Silvestri, and which casts a peculiarly sentimental gloom over the whole space between the safe and the back door. But Don Alvise is nowhere to be found, he's gone away without saying where. His angular house in Sant' Ambrogio is closed, the shutters locked. In the café on the piazza, some say that Don Alvise has been disgraced but others think that on the contrary he has been promoted. One opinion has it that he has made so much money out of his writing that he has retired, to live in his village in the south. The villager whose field is next to the olive orchard and carries under it the *servitu* of the villa's drainpipe which he likes to break, has heard a more sinister rumour. According to him, he has a friend whose family are from Reggio Calabria, like Don Alvise, Well, this friend says that there has been a gruesome murder in that region, and the victim's picture was shown on television, and it was recognisable as the young Tonio. Nor is that the end of it. It appears that on the scene of the crime they found a ring with a red stone set in it, and everyone who hears this man tell the story can confirm that Don Alvise had taken to wearing just such a ring. But in that case, why haven't the police started an investigation in Sant' Ambrogio? Ah – he lays his finger along the side of his nose, and looks cunning – who knows in these days of computers and Interpol how they investigate? You'll see, you'll learn.

The others can stay in the villa as long as they like, but Charles must leave this weekend, to return to his office. 'Comes over one an absolute necessity to move,' he quotes the line from Milly's reading. But before the end of his holiday, he wants to visit Montetremaldi. Why not make another expedition of it, and see if they can't drink a bottle of wine each and more grappa at the nearby Badia.

Traffic is evidently using the track up to the deserted church a good deal more than before. The surface is deteriorating again. Cans and old paper and plastic bags everywhere are a speckled harvest of rubbish. The grass patch at the top is spotted with blackened circles where bonfires have been lit.

On the *casa canonica*, the shutters have been taken down, and the windows are open. A wheelbarrow is upended at the edge of a plot of garden newly scratched out of the stony soil, and already set with poles wigwam-shaped. The young man who emerges at the sound of the car and the unaccustomed voices is wearing blue dungarees but no shirt; and the exposed hair on his chest is patchy and as thin as if some of it had been pulled out. The stick arms show no biceps.

'Tomatoes,' he says. 'Planted by me.' The syllables come out cracked, as if he had trouble stringing them together. Not quite right in the head, perhaps.

Above them, the sun falls directly on the slim bell-tower, and the pillars in the dwarf windows are dazzling white.

'I only made it for the ceremony here in the nick of time,'

Alexander tells Milly, 'almost the only man not in a dog-collar too.'

A narrow strip, with the remains of the builders' sand underfoot, has been trodden down in front of the end wall of the house. As they round the corner they come to face the broken fastenings of what had been Dina's hardwood showcase, so vandalised that nothing else remains of it. No sign of any of the contents, such as the Newsletter. Although not prised off, the marble tablets have been defaced. 'Through love of Me can all be United' and its companion, 'Make Souls Shine Out' with Don Alvise's accompanying rendering as '*Fate Risplendere le Anime*' have been all but obliterated by the words *Bologna merda* painted in purple in obsessively shaped capital letters. Other hands have scribbled with a marker dozens of names and dates. A party of Germans have added the rather limited swear-words of their language. Someone with red paint has daubed *Juve* everywhere. Right across the wall, also in a bellowing red, is 'Francesca ti amo' with half a dozen extra o's on the last word, extending in size so that the final one is as large as a target.

The glass of the slit windows has also been smashed. The opening is not wide enough to allow much access, but people have stood there and flicked paint in at the car, red and black and purple, so that daubs and streaks all over the bodywork have a sort of fireworks effect: 'pointilliste', Charles says. Otherwise dust is accumulating, and what appears to be a dead swallow is crumped on the bonnet.

'In Los Angeles or Hamburg,' Charles says, 'we could get a million dollars for a work of art like this.'

It's the motorbike gangs, the young man explains, and he's been appointed watchman to see that they don't do anything worse. At night during the weekend, they come roaring up here, they swarm in from all over, and they bring their girls and their drugs. Look around on the ground, you'll see syringes and he doesn't like to pick them up, in case, you never can be sure. You have to know how to talk to people like that, and sometimes he feels a bit frightened but they haven't harmed him yet. When the church administrators saw what damage was being done to the fabric, they appointed him, they pay him too but not much. All his life, he says, he's been brought up in a church orphanage, and it was strict. If he was to tell them the truth, sometimes when the motorbikes race up the path he's pleased, it breaks the silence and the loneliness. They light fires, and they cook sometimes and invite him, and then for a few days he doesn't have to haul groceries uphill from the village.

Bologna merda: a cry from the heart of our civilisation.

That night Ursie found it difficult to sleep. Thinking of Charles, and what life would be like if she were never to find a job again but had to stay at home and listen to his ironic intelligence, and how intolerable it is to evade reality through flippancy. Thinking of the symmetry whereby Charles has a daughter in Santa Barbara, and Milly has a daughter in an institution – Pushed and Blocked was at work there. And how right Alexander is and how he might never have made his peace with Lionel if it hadn't been for the brainwashing. All she could recapture of him was the smile which exposed the full bite of his jaws, and she could catch his deep voice saying, I deserve it, don't I, because you never loved her, you weren't able to, you don't have it in you to love. Who ought really to live in the villa, if there was justice in the world, is Iris Warren, alone with cancer in Tulse Hill. *Bologna merda* indeed.

The rooster began somewhere in the direction of Sant' Ambrogio, tentatively, as though experimenting with the call. A rival issued a confident answer. As the sun broke over the horizon to gild the landscape, Ursie dressed. It was instinctive to walk down that staircase without making a noise, for fear of disturbing Dina and so ruining the day to come. From what had been Adela's desk, she took the key to the safe. Then she lifted out of it the green box marked 'Proofs of Spiritual Realities as Experienced by Andrew and Edwina Lumel'.

On the terrace, the table and chairs were as they had left them the previous evening, with books and the disordered newspapers in four languages which still arrived on Dina's subscriptions, glasses, plates on which they'd eaten homemade ice. They'd gone to bed too late to have cleared up. It didn't matter. There was no dew. Breakfast would be here too, amid the newspapers. She walked to the well, stood on the iron seat encircling it, and leaned over to tip the contents of the green box through the grille. Down fell the accumulation of stones and postcards and quills and dried flowers, the odds and ends of Unite the Impossible, and with them envelopes marked 'Most Precious' and 'Letter attached to explain this Proof's Significance'. Some of these envelopes momentarily scraped against the brick-work of the well, and then made no further noise on the descent into whatever depth there might be. Left lying on one of the cross-straps of the grille was the 'Happy New Year, Darling' in Andrew's handwriting which had sur-vived in the pocket of the sable coat. When she flicked at it, it too was lost with a quick moth-like flutter.

Then she returned indoors for the cuttings which were supposed to have documented the steady progress of mankind on the goal to Uniting the Impossible. Adela had kept the files immaculately. Down they went too, bundle after bundle. Finishing, she caught sight of the silver chain with the medallion given by Pope Paul VI. As she chucked this in it slithered over the grille. There remained the Flowers of Meditation. *To be published after my death*. Some of the aphorisms might have something to them. The impetus to be rid of this whole business ebbed.

'I thought I heard something going on,' said Alexander. He was still in his dressing-gown. 'I didn't sleep too well in the night.'

Picking up the empty box of Proofs, he runs a finger lightly over the outline left on its lid by the original misprinting of the name.

I've chucked it all out, Ursie tells him, I couldn't stand it any longer and the Proofs are now at the bottom of the old well. Those horrible brutes felt free to hold her up to ridicule with that car at Montetremaldi, and it tipped the scales for me. What do they know? It would have been a similar carry-on here if they'd preserved the Proofs and her papers. And it would be even more humiliating if we were

251

never to hear again from Silvestri or the bishop. In another age, she might have been believed, founded an order, converted the heathen, for all I know become a saint. Religion everywhere is built upon symbols and myths every bit as transparent as Unite the Impossible. I have a sense sometimes that really it's us who weren't up to it, Ursie says, we didn't have what it takes.

Alexander doesn't agree. They couldn't have done anything other than what they did. Mind you, he says, we'll be arguing ourselves round in circles for the rest of our lives wondering about it. At least I've learnt enough to feel sorry for Lionel, he's the one who's going to have to dream about me now.

Is it all to be put down to Iris Warren? Fear of scandal, sexual unwillingness, emotional and financial dependence on Andrew, repression. I'll find out, Alexander thinks, and you'll read about it in my book. He adds, as though it were a truth always and everywhere valid, 'You love only when what you love no longer has power to hurt.'

Beyond them, Armando is out watering the grass and the rosebeds. In the distance, Giulia has hung laundry out to dry on a washing-line stretched between olive trees in front of her house, and it looks like a row of small flags in the freshness of the morning light. Luciana is to be heard indoors placing coffee cups on a tray for them. Whether the villa belongs to a one-time *squadrista*, a rabbit-breeder, the Lumels or Lionel, is only of nominal interest to them, the real inhabitants of the place, going unconcerned about their daily business.

While they are still having breakfast on the terrace, the front-door bell rings. Yet another unexpected caller, surprised to find Alexander still in his dressing-gown. This one is American, and he introduces himself as Verlin Willson, saying that his father is a friend of theirs. They're passing through on the way from Ponte a Maiano and Mr Langridge has asked him to deliver this book: yet another copy of *The Living I*. On the flyleaf Mr Langridge has written, 'Sorry to have heard about your great loss,' and underneath, 'God bless you.'

252